THE LANGUAGE
OF BIRDS

THE LANGUAGE
OF BIRDS

A NOVEL

ANITA BARROWS

SHE WRITES PRESS

Published 2022
Printed in the United States of America
Print ISBN: 978-1-64742-357-5
E-ISBN: 978-1-64742-358-2
Library of Congress Control Number: 2021921553

For information, address:
She Writes Press
1569 Solano Ave #546
Berkeley, CA 94707

She Writes Press is a division of SparkPoint Studio, LLC.

. . . alles Fleisch es ist wie Gras

Ein deutches Requiem—Johannes Brahms

For Ciel

PROLOGUE

Someone told me the story of a chimpanzee named Bibi. Bibi was involved in a study at some university, in the course of which she was taught sign language. She was a quick learner and unusually creative; after a while she was making up original signs to convey to the researchers increasing levels of emotional and intellectual complexity. Bibi's desire to share what she experienced possessed her completely: the researchers learned more from Bibi about the inner life of chimpanzees than they ever expected to.

After some years, the grant that funded the study was exhausted, and Bibi and the other chimps were dispersed to different facilities. Bibi found herself confined to a cage, unable to relate to humans and other chimpanzees as she had been free to do in the laboratory she had come from. No one signed to her.

With no possibility of communicating, Bibi languished. Occasionally her caretakers observed her moving her fingers in what looked like some inner monologue; but after a while her passion to connect with others, her passion to articulate her thoughts, diminished, meeting no response.

Then one day, after Bibi had been in that place for thirteen years, a man who had been on the original research team happened to visit. Bibi recognized him at once—he was on his way down the corridor to a meeting—and she went into a frenzy, jumping up and down in her cage, rattling the bars with all her might, desperately signing over and over, "Me Bibi! Me Bibi! Me Bibi!"

CHAPTER 1

2017

The fluorescent-lit room is small and chilly. My sister, holding a bird wrapped in a towel, bends to turn on an electric heater, draws the injured bird even closer to her body, switches on a brighter light directly over the metal table where, once the room has warmed, she will begin doing what needs to be done.

She doesn't speak to me, but I don't expect her to. She goes about her work as she has done everything since childhood, or at least since a certain point in her childhood: methodically, deliberately, with little notice of anyone around her. This time I'm the only one around. There's been an emergency and there's no one else to assist her. The phone, ringing in the middle of the night, woke me after a long day teaching, a long evening grading papers. "Gracie," my sister said, "can you meet me at the Rescue Center? I need you."

She hands me the bird. "Keep her warm," is all she says. She opens a cabinet, a drawer full of instruments. She takes some of them out, lays them at one end of the metal table. Carefully, deliberately, considering each one and what she might do with it.

I look into the bird's eyes. They seem shocked, absent. The feathers

3

on her breast, though, still move up and down. The wing that is broken hangs limply out of the towel. There's blood on the towel, too, from the places the bird was attacked.

"Do you think she'll make it, Jannie?" I ask.

Jannie shrugs her shoulders. "We have to try," is all she says.

She pours some iodine from a small bottle into a vial of distilled water, mixes it with a Q-tip. The water turns rust-colored. I watch my sister's hands: quick, deft, small-boned. When she was a child, she would flap her arms; her hands looked like wingtips. I used to think Jannie was part bird.

"I think it's okay now," she tells me. *Warm enough,* she means. *I'm ready,* she means.

I'm still translating for my sister.

"We have to clean her wounds right away," Jannie says. "I'd wait a day or two usually if it was just the wing. But I don't want to stress her and then stress her all over again."

Jannie pulls the towel away from the bird's head, looks into her eyes.

"She's still shocked," she says.

"What is she, just some kind of gull?" I ask.

"*Larus occidentalis,*" Jannie says, not looking at me. "Western gull. Probably not more than a year old."

"Does she look as bad as I think she does?"

Jannie shrugs again. Sighs. "She doesn't look good." She holds her arms out, and I roll the bird into them. Very gently my sister lays the bird on the table, unwraps the towel.

"You hold her still," she tells me. "But be careful."

"That cat—or whatever it was—really got her," I say, looking at the bird.

"Probably a large cat. The man who called from the houseboat said he heard it. Heard the gull screaming. Saw something run away when he went out onto the dock. He said probably a feral cat."

"Hungry," I say to her.

"Maybe."

"Nice of him to go out in the middle of the night and bring the bird here."

"He cares about birds," Jannie says. "He's brought others in. And it wasn't really the middle of the night. It was only eleven."

Jannie wets a cloth with the iodine solution and softly dabs at the bird's wounds. My sister has a tenderness for birds that I've never seen in her for people. Even when our little half-brother Justin was an infant, she could find no sweetness in her for him. Everything good Jannie has is for birds.

My sister pushes my hand away from the gull and delicately fingers the broken wing. She examines the damage. "Flight feathers gone," she says, as much to herself as to me. "Pretty bad break. Probably more than one broken bone."

"Will she be able to fly?" I ask.

"Not anytime soon. Maybe never. But we have to try," she says again.

Before she wraps the wing, Jannie puts antibiotic ointment on the gull's wounds and tapes little squares of gauze over them. She keeps a running line of encouragement going as she works: "Good girl, good bird, this may hurt a little, it's really clean now, good . . ."

She checks the wing to make sure it's held securely in place against the bird's body. Then she presses the two ends of the tape together.

"That's all," she says, looking at the bird.

My sister and I walk to the parking lot of the Bird Rescue Center together. We're parked next to each other. I help her put the bird in the crate she keeps in her back seat. I don't think Jannie has ever driven a single human around in her car, but she drives birds all over the place.

"Bye, Gracie," she says to me. "I think it must be kind of late." That's as close to *thanks* as Jannie will get.

It's after two. We're each standing outside our car, holding our keys. "That's okay, Jannie. I hope she does all right."

"Maybe she will," my sister says.

"Could you—will you let me know?"

"If she dies?"

I nod. "Like every day. Give me an update."

"Like the news," Jannie smiles. "News of the Gull."

"News of the Gull," I say, and hug my sister good-bye.

I text Jannie when I get home the following afternoon, and she texts back: *Walking and eating.*

I'm surprised at how relieved I am that the bird is alive. I realize how infrequently Jannie calls me for help, how little I actually do for my sister; at twenty-five, she has aged out of all the supports the county makes available to people on the autism spectrum, except for some kind of independent living skills instructor who comes over once a week and makes sure there's food in Jannie's fridge and her bills are paid. The first time the ILS woman came over, all Jannie had in the house to eat was were two flats of canned pea soup from the Dollar Store, a gallon of orange juice, and a million different kinds of bird seed. Now she has lists on her kitchen cabinets of all the things she's supposed to buy, but I suspect she throws away much of what she actually brings home. Jannie would never forget to feed a bird exactly the right thing and the right amount, but feeding herself is another matter.

I remember I am supposed to meet Kate, my stepmother, at the Mexican restaurant on Shattuck Avenue. She waves to me from the back as I walk in to join her. I tell Kate about the gull, about Jannie's incredible skill. This is the first year she's actually been put on the payroll at the Bird Rescue Center; before that, even when she was in high school, she volunteered. Everything she can do with birds she either taught herself or learned from watching others. She still thinks she'd like to be a vet tech for birds, but she's intimidated by the idea of a real college program. Still, she's come a long way: living in her apartment a few blocks from the house we grew up in. Having dinner with Dad and Kate and Justin three or four times a week has been a big enough step for her.

"It's so good to see Jannie doing what she really loves," I tell Kate, "and being so good at it."

Kate takes a bite of her quesadilla. "What about you, Gracie?"

I don't know how to answer her for a minute. "I'm okay. We're doing Toni Morrison in my eighth-grade classes, and *To Kill a Mockingbird* in seventh. The kids seem to get it, and I'm trying to connect it to what's happening now . . ."

"Gracie," Kate looks at me with that intense look of hers. When I was a teenager, I hated when she did that.

"We were talking about Jannie doing something she loves. I mean, what about your writing? Are you writing, Gracie?"

I take a deep breath. "It's hard, with class prep and grading and everything. Even when I was working for my credential, I seemed to find time at least to write poetry; but now when I'm done for the day I'm too tired to do anything really creative. I don't know. . . ."

"What about that workshop you took?"

"You mean last month? That weekend prose-writing thing? Yeah, I did some writing there, some prompts they gave us. One of them I thought was okay. And they had us figure out what we needed to write about. That was the key word: *needed*. Not just *wanted*."

"And. . .?"

"It was cool, and I think I kind of did figure it out, and I even wrote a sort of beginning of a chapter . . . but then I got caught up in Harper Lee and Toni Morrison, and I kind of let it go."

"So what did you find out you needed to write about?"

"It didn't really surprise me," I tell her. "But I kind of know that until I write about it, I'll probably never write about anything else."

"What is it?"

"Oh God, Kate. You can probably figure it out. It's about that whole time after my mom died. How I dealt with it, how Jannie was then. And you, you coming into our lives . . . and everything that was happening for me in high school . . ."

"So what's keeping you from doing it, Gracie? Being busy with work can't be the whole story."

I take a deep breath, push the plate with my half-finished veggie burrito away from me, and start to get up. "I'm sorry, Kate. I can't talk now. I need to go home and finish grading my papers."

* * *

There's something comforting about rain beating against the roof of the little cottage I rent behind a house in North Berkeley. Here I am, my sister not far from me, taking care of her birds as she always has, though now they include wild birds. Her world has expanded from the cockatiels and conures and parakeets she raised, to all the birds of the Bay Area. Kate's world has expanded to include a son, Justin, who's now in fifth grade. Kate who, when she met my dad, had no idea whether she'd ever have a kid of her own.

And my world? My world is the middle school where I teach English, a few good close friends. An on-again, off-again boyfriend who's a poet and who has a year-long teaching gig at a college in northern Washington. And my dog, Carson.

I lie down on my sofa, watch rain streaming down the windows. What's stopping me, Kate asked. I take my notebook from my desk, find what I wrote in the workshop. *I want to tell the truth about my life, the way I began doing toward the end of that time,* I'd written. *But what if it hurts the people I love? If I write truthfully, it may well hurt them. If I write truthfully about my mother, it might make people judge her. But she's dead; does that make it matter less? More? The same with Dad, even Kate: can I write truthfully about them and know they'll probably read it?*

And if I don't write the truth, what's the point?

I end up falling asleep. When I open my eyes, it's three in the morning: the lights on, the notebook open on my chest, the rain still raining. Carson has climbed up onto the couch and stretched herself next to me.

I check my phone. Jannie has texted me again: *Still walking and eating.* It takes me a moment to remember she's talking about the bird.

Then a second text, dated almost an hour later: *Could you tell me something about Emmi?*

Emmi was the name we called our mother.

Just like Jannie. Out of the blue. Who knows why she asked or what she wants to know? But for some reason it's enough to make me resolve to start writing, whatever the cost.

CHAPTER 2

2002

U ntil I met Gina, I had never told anyone the truth about my life. If I'd told the people at school, I figured (a) they would never believe it and (b) they would avoid me even more than they avoided me already. I knew something about how people saw me: I was the blond girl who sat in the back of the room and never said anything to anyone but sometimes raised her hand in class and usually got straight *A*s. I was the girl whose mother had a fancy job in Germany and hadn't been back to see us in years. I was the girl whose sister was some kind of bird genius.

All that was what I had wanted people to believe. Once I met Gina, everything started to change; but I didn't really notice some of the changes, the way you don't notice grass growing until one day you look outside where there was only dirt and see a faint cover of green.

Before I met Gina, my only real friend was a boy named Martin. Martin lived down the road from my grandmother's house in Badlein, Germany, where my mother had grown up. When I was twelve and Jannie four, Emmi brought us to Oma's (that's German for "Grandma") at the end of the insane trip she took us on, a trip that had no itinerary and no sense. Emmi had basically kidnapped me from school one afternoon and, without telling Dad what was happening, gotten me and Jannie onto a plane to Rome. From there, every couple of days she would take out a train schedule and drag us all over Europe until finally she bought an old Renault and drove us to Badlein.

In Badlein things began to seem normal for a while until they became nothing like normal; but during the normal time, I made friends with Martin, and he was the best thing that happened to me in all those months. Martin's mother was British, and, like me, he spoke both English and German. He was the only one who knew that my mother and Jannie lived upstairs at Oma's like two hidden people; to everyone else at the little school down the road in the small German village, I would say that I had been sent by my mother to live there because she had such a demanding job that she didn't have time to take care of me.

It was at that school that my lying began, and I got so good at lying that I kept doing it long after my father brought Jannie and me home to Berkeley.

I lied about Jannie. I was too ashamed of Jannie's strangeness to let anyone but Martin come to my house. Jannie screeched and flapped her arms and ran away every time she got a chance. She was like a perpetually terrified wild bird.

Jannie never spoke a word until after our mother died, and for a long time I hated that she was my sister.

My mother's strangeness was different, and worse.

Of all the kids I met in Germany, only Martin had ever laid eyes on Jannie and my mother, and I swore him to secrecy about what they were like. Martin and I made a blood pact, swearing each other to secrecy about other things too, and when Dad brought Jannie and me back to Berkeley, I started writing to him.

I liked getting letters back from him with his elegant German handwriting, and somehow our letter writing lasted for years.

It was only when I met Gina that Martin stopped being the one person in the world I told everything to, and that was partly because I couldn't think of a way to tell him about her.

CHAPTER 3

2002

Our father brought us home to Berkeley two weeks after our mother died. I was twelve and a half and Jannie had just turned five.

We had been away eight months, and when we walked into our house it felt to me like everything that had happened in those months had just been a bad dream. The house was the same as I'd left it the morning of the day Emmi had taken me out of my sixth-grade classroom just after lunch. Only my mother was missing.

My mother was missing from the kitchen, where I'd watched her knead dough. She was missing from the garden, where she had squatted to plant lettuce and arugula. She was missing from the rocking chair in the living room, where she had held Jannie, it seemed, for all of her years up until we'd left: the two of them rocking, rocking.

When we got back, Dad hadn't really devised a plan to deal with Jannie's weirdness. All the months we had been traveling, Jannie had been running around hotels and train stations screeching and not letting anyone touch her; we'd bought the Renault after she had run off a train one day at a station where we were stopped for only a few minutes, and Emmi and I had run after her, leaving all of our things in our compartment heading by themselves to the next stop as the train pulled away. The first thing Dad did after we returned was to take Jannie to a developmental psychologist at Children's Hospital who diagnosed her definitively with Autism Spectrum Disorder, and he speedily put a program in place designed to make Jannie as much like a normal kid as possible.

There were no summer plans made for me. I was more or less left to my own resources. My one friend who lived down the block had moved to LA and I didn't feel like looking for my other school friends from before. Mostly I stayed alone in my room lying on my bed and reading book after book. Fiction seemed to be my only solace.

I basically didn't talk to anyone about anything that had happened in the months that our mother had taken us on that frantic, maniacal adventure, the journey that ended with her death. And I pretty much stopped talking about anything else either.

As I grew more silent. Jannie was learning to speak. Dad hired a speech therapist for her and I would listen outside the room where they worked together, Jannie and a stout, gray-haired woman named Eleanor who gave her M&M's whenever she said anything that sounded vaguely like a word. I was astonished at what Eleanor found worthy of reward—"lay" for chair, "ta" for dog—and thought she was vastly underestimating Jannie's intelligence; but after a few weeks Jannie could ask for milk and grapes and her favorite metal truck. She could say "hi" and "bye," though she didn't necessarily remember when to use them, and she could say each of our names, including our new puppy, Lizzy, whom Dad had brought home from the shelter one night as a surprise. A few weeks after that, Jannie could even make a two-word sentence: "Lizzy outside."

I would sit on the sagging couch in the kitchen pretending to read, listening to everything that passed between Eleanor and my sister, fascinated and a little repulsed by the sounds that came from Jannie's throat, so different from her usual shrieks and whoops and grunts. I barely knew this sister whose mouth was beginning to shape itself around actual words. I felt that Eleanor, with her sappy smile and her exaggerated intonation, was taking my sister away from me and replacing her with a stranger; and I hated her for it.

* * *

The one word Jannie had said after Emmi died was the German word for "little roll," *Brötchen*. Now, when Jannie asked for bread, it was always *Brötchen*. It struck me one afternoon when Eleanor had nearly used up her stash of M&M's trying to get Jannie to say "Bread" in English, that *Brötchen* was Jannie's stubborn, personal way of remembering our mother. Eventually, enraged beyond my capacity to contain it, I threw my book on the kitchen floor, marched into the living room, and said to Eleanor, "You're probably too stupid to know, but Jannie is speaking German." When Eleanor, aghast, reported it to my father, I was docked a week's desserts; but I felt it had been worth it.

Something in me that summer did not want Jannie to speak. Something in me wanted everything to stay the same as it had been the day Emmi kidnapped us: my oma in Germany, my sister a wild child who didn't use human language; my dad thousands of miles away, where I didn't have to tell him anything true. And my mother alive.

I pretended to myself that summer and for months afterward that my mother was still alive and in Europe, that she had decided to send us home with Dad so we could get back to our regular lives while she worked at the fancy job she had found. I wrote her post cards, addressed them to *Poste Restante* in Paris and Rome and Hamburg, took stamps from Dad's desk drawer when he wasn't looking and walked Lizzy to the mailbox down the block to send them to her. *Dear Emmi,* I wrote, *Please tell Dad to get rid of Eleanor. She's getting worse and worse. She's turning Jannie into some kind of robot who says dumb things to get M&M's.* Or: *Dear Emmi, I'm worried about Lizzy. She's still just a puppy and she keeps getting ticks and Dad keeps forgetting to buy her a tick collar.*

At night I lay in bed thinking about the post cards with pictures of the bay, the university campus, the Golden Gate Bridge, that Dad always kept in one of the living room cabinets, piling up at the *Poste Restante* counters of post offices across Europe, waiting to be claimed. I liked to think of someone reading them as she sorted mail: an elderly woman in a starched blue uniform, chuckling to herself at yet another message from that girl who missed her mother, wondering when the mother's itinerary would bring her there to claim them.

My mother killed herself by driving the Renault into a tree one night on a road outside Badlein after we had been there almost four months. Jannie and I were asleep at our oma's. We knew it was suicide because she left a note.

All she said in the note, in English and German, was *I'm sorry.*

CHAPTER 4

2017 / 2002

Jannie and I have always been so different, few people looking at us even now would guess we are sisters. For one thing, I look like the German side of the family, while Jannie, with her dark curly hair and her deep-set brown eyes, looks just like our dad, the Jewish side. That made it easier for me, in those months in Europe, to stand slightly apart from her and pretend I didn't even know her. There were times when I felt so embarrassed by the way she behaved that I didn't want anyone to suspect I had anything to do with her. She and my mom were so glued to each other anyway that it wasn't that hard for me to sit in another row on a train and bury myself in a book or the passing landscape.

Once we were back in Berkeley, I distanced myself from Jannie in other ways. She had become Dad's project, and I was pretty much outside the loop.

* * *

By the time Jannie was seven, she had undergone a battery of assessments and been found to have a superior IQ, but her behavior was still really odd. She could speak as well as anyone else, but it usually didn't feel like she was speaking *to* you. She would spout lengthy disquisitions on whatever interested her—birds, most of the time—without caring at all if you were listening. She had begun going to a special school for high-functioning autistic kids in Marin; every morning at seven-twenty a van came to pick her up and she went off chirpily, her backpack stuffed with books about birds. Like me, Jannie read all the time; in fact, she had been diagnosed with something some autistic kids have, called hyperlexia: the ability to read at a way advanced level. But all Jannie read about was birds. She never read fiction, whereas I read book after book about others' fictional lives.

My own life felt like fiction, but not the kind I thought anybody would want to write about. I let Dad believe I had friends but just didn't feel like seeing them after school or on the weekends. It was easy enough to get away with, since Dad just kind of saw me as a studious, literary, no-trouble kid and accepted that at face value. He was so focused on Jannie anyway that he really had no idea what I was doing. He just figured I was okay.

Ultimately Dad turned a lot of responsibility for Jannie over to me. He had to be out of the house early to get to the school where he taught, so I took Lizzy for a walk while he got Jannie ready. Once he left, it was my job to make sure Jannie got onto her van. Then I would gather my own things for school.

In the time that had passed since my mother's suicide, I had never told anyone she was dead.

It had become clear to me that lying was an art, and that I had grown highly skilled at it. It had also become clear that one lie leads to another: before long, an entire world exists that is constructed of lies, and it can feel as real as the genuine world that runs parallel to it. It has walls, colors, feelings, dimensions you live within, as vivid as those in the world of truth.

The biggest difference between the two worlds, I had come to realize, was that in the World of Truth you lived with other people, while in the Lie-World you were alone.

The truth was I had no friends. None.

I told myself I didn't want them. I walked the corridors at school wearing an invisible "Leave Me Alone" sign; and everyone did.

* * *

The only person I wanted to communicate with was Martin. For the most part I told him the truth, though there wasn't really very much to tell. I felt like I didn't really have a life, so I wrote about Jannie's birds and the books I was reading and Lizzy's latest antics. He wrote me back about his family, his school, and his soccer team, which was the thing he was most passionate about. He would tell me about the intrigues going on with his friends on the team—how this one was upset that the coach didn't give him enough time on the field and that one had torn some cartilage in his knee and had to sit out for a while.

Then one afternoon in the winter of ninth grade I came home from school and found a letter from him that was different from all the others. Martin told me he had just been diagnosed with leukemia.

After that, for a while, his letters were shorter. He was having chemo and it made him tired. The worst thing was that he couldn't play on his team. I envied his sense of loss a little; I had nothing I cared about as much as Martin cared about soccer, and it was hard even for me to understand what it would feel like to be so committed to something—*anything*—that I would be sad to lose it.

I asked my dad if I could go to Germany to visit Oma and Martin. To my surprise, he let me. It was the summer before sophomore year.

* * *

It was shocking to see Martin.

He was ghostly pale and weak. His legs, sticking out of his soccer shorts, were as skinny as Jannie's, and most of his hair had fallen out from the chemo. One warm afternoon he and I sat on the grass talking about the World Cup when I noticed how much of Martin's scalp I was able to see.

"It's like you're bald but not bald," I said.

"It's stupid," Martin said. "Every time I take a shower and wash my hair, more of it falls out. I wish it were gone already."

His voice was so much fainter than it had ever been. I wanted to make him happy. I wanted at least to make him laugh. "I think we can do something about that," I said to him. He looked up at me from the blades of grass he had been pulling out of the ground, one by one, slowly.

"What?" he asked me.

"I bet we could pull the rest of your hair out as easily as you're pulling up that grass."

"You think so?" Martin asked, intrigued. On an impulse, I reached for his head and pulled out a handful of thin brown hair.

"Did that hurt?" I asked him, suddenly appalled at what I'd done.

"I felt it," he said. "But it didn't really hurt. It didn't really hurt at all," he said; and he pulled out a handful of hair himself.

That was how we did it. We took turns pulling tufts of hair out of Martin's scalp. At first we just let the hair collect on the grass beside us; I figured we would take it inside eventually and throw it in Oma's kitchen wastebasket. But a quick breeze carried some of it away and dispersed it in the neighbor's garden, and I had another idea.

"Hey," I said to Martin, "we could scatter it all. We could let the birds pick it up and use it for their nests. That way it won't just go to waste."

I stood up and brushed Martin's loose hair off my jeans. Martin stood for a minute as well, but he was way too weak to stand for very long and he sat back down. "You scatter it, Gracie," he said.

"No," I responded. "You can scatter it sitting down; but we both have to do it. It's a joint effort." I looked at him seriously, then threw a handful of hair toward the hedge. "Here, birds!" I shouted, opening my fists and releasing more hair I had just harvested from Martin's head.

Martin smiled at me. His smile was somewhere between conspiratorial and deeply sad. Then he pulled out another fistful of his hair and weakly waved his arm so the hair would land at least a few feet away.

Before long Martin's head was nearly completely naked. A few longish strands of brown hair clung to his scalp like dull tinsel on a discarded Christmas tree; his head otherwise looked like a sad pink globe.

He ran his hand over it. "What does it feel like?" I asked him.

"You can touch it," he told me.

"That's not what I meant," I said, though I did run my hand over his head. "I can tell what it feels like to *me*. I want to know what it feels like to *you*."

"It feels weird," Martin said. "Kind of cold. But there wasn't that much hair left before anyway, so it's not all that different."

"Let's go inside so you can see what you look like," I told him, pulling him up from the grass. Martin's wrists were so bony, and I was surprised at how light he was.

We went into Oma's house. Oma was napping upstairs in her room, so Martin and I walked quietly into the room where Emmi and Jannie had slept, where there was a mirror over a chest of drawers.

We stood in front of the mirror. There was tall Martin with his hollow cheeks and his pale, round head. And there was I, Gracie, several inches shorter, with straight, shoulder-length thick blond hair. Seeing the dismay in Martin's eyes, I put fingers from each of my hands in my mouth, stretched my lips wide and made a ridiculous face.

Martin laughed and did the same. We stood there before the mirror making one silly face after another, taking turns, imitating each other and going one better. After a while we were laughing so hard that Martin had to lie down on the rug,

I lay down beside him. We stared up at the ceiling. "Martin?" I said.

"What?"

"Your head looks like a soccer ball."

"It does not!" Martin said, jabbing me in the ribs. "Soccer balls are black and white."

"I *know* what a soccer ball looks like, dumb ass," I said.

I stood up and started ferreting through the top drawer of the dresser. As I suspected, it was still filled with Emmi's make-up: tubes and sticks and vials of black eyeliner, mascara, eye shadow. Emmi had always used lots of black make-up around her light blue eyes, and I figured Oma would never have thrown it away. An idea suddenly came to me.

"We could make your head look like a soccer ball," I said. Martin looked at me quizzically; then he understood what I meant.

"You're sure it's okay to use your mother's make-up?"

I looked him straight in the eye. "Martin, she's dead," I said. "She's not going to use it, I swear to you. Ever again."

A lot of it was dried up—it had been four years—but some was still good, good enough to make all the areas of black.

"What'll we use for the white?" Martin asked as I outlined the shapes of black on his head, and I thought for a minute. Once, when there had been a school fair toward the end of the time when Jannie and Emmi and I had lived at Oma's, we had bought face paint so Martin and I could paint our faces like clowns. I thought the face paint must still be in the closet of that room; and when I looked for it, there it was. I added a bit of water to it, and it turned out to be usable.

For the next hour Martin sat on a wooden chair while I carefully drew black pentangles on his hairless head, filled them in with Emmi's eye shadow and mascara, and then painted the white areas with the white face paint. By the time I was finished, Martin's head, from forehead to the nape of his neck, was painted like a soccer ball.

I still have the picture I took of it taped to my bedroom wall: Martin squatting so I could photograph his whole head, which hung over his yellow T-shirt and his skinny, dangling arms.

A few days later, Martin was too weak to eat and he had to go back to the hospital. I visited him there just once before I had to fly home. The nurses had washed off the soccer ball.

CHAPTER 5

2002

The night I came home from Germany, a woman named Kate came over for dinner.

Kate taught biology at the high school where Dad taught math. It turned out she had been coming over a lot during the summer I'd been gone, and I could tell from the way she and Dad looked at each other that they had begun a serious relationship.

Kate lived in an apartment in Oakland next door to a house where her sister Carrie lived with her family, and Dad and Kate and Carrie and Carrie's husband started going out together to dinners and movies, leaving me to babysit Jannie. As the year wore on—my sophomore year at Berkeley High—Kate spent more and more time at our house on weekends; and by the start of my junior year she was spending weeknights with us as well.

I had started out mostly liking her; then, as she was around more, her cheeriness annoyed me and mostly I tried to avoid her.

All through sophomore year, Martin and I had continued to write. By January he was declared to be in remission, and by spring he was playing soccer again, though his coach subbed him in for only minutes at a time.

By the start of my junior year, Martin's strength had come back and he was playing soccer as well as he'd done before the leukemia. I liked the process of sitting down at my desk at the end of the day and filling pages with the German-looking handwriting I'd learned from Emmi, and I loved getting letters back from him. Martin was the only person in the world who knew I was letting everyone think Emmi was still alive, and that made it possible for me to write him about the rest of my life with an honesty I could use with no one else.

Not that I had a lot to write about.

Dad got me a little flip phone when I turned seventeen that October; but when I left it on a BART train on a school field trip weeks later, I told him I didn't really need it replaced. I had no one to call. The phone's constant silence had only reinforced my aloneness, and I'd come to hate it.

I realized, though, one rainy afternoon in December, when I had stayed home from school with a bad cold and had been alone in the house all day, that I was actually lying even to Martin. I wasn't telling him the extent of my aloneness. I had begun pretending to him that the people I told him about were friends in whose lives I had some real part, pretending my days were as simple and normal as his seemed to be.

The irony of that didn't escape me. Martin had had cancer and his life was simple and normal? Why was it okay for everyone in his life to know that he'd had leukemia and chemotherapy, when I felt so desperate to hide my mother's suicide, my sister's autism?

It struck me once, reading some novel where the protagonist felt guilty for not having saved a friend who had died in an accident, that maybe that was it: had I felt responsible, especially during that disastrous trip through Europe, for keeping Emmi and Jannie safe? If that was true, I had failed utterly. The thought was so painful I immediately pushed it away.

I hated any time outside class at school, and I began hating coming home in the afternoons. I would drop off my backpack, clip on Lizzy's leash, and escape right away for a long walk until five-thirty, when Jannie's van would deposit her back at the house. I walked all over Berkeley: up to campus, down to the Marina. Dad never came home until six at the earliest, and then all we had to get through was dinner and I could go up to my room.

I watched myself, as though observing someone else, walking aimlessly all over Berkeley with Lizzy. Like a ghost whose own presence was invisible, I witnessed other people's lives. I watched people get into their cars, wait with frustration at bus stops, descend down the escalator underground to BART saying good-bye to each other as they left those with whom they had spent the day. I felt envious of their friendships, the predictable structure of their hours. I walked up to North Berkeley past well-tended gardens where mothers in long denim skirts pulled weeds with their toddlers. Each day Lizzy and I took a different route. We never came home before we had to, and I never told Dad or Jannie we'd gone anywhere except to the park I'd always taken Lizzy to. Neither of them ever bothered to ask.

CHAPTER 6

2002

One Tuesday afternoon in my junior American Lit class a girl named Jennifer gave a presentation about the poet Sara Teasdale, who had died by suicide in 1933 at the age of forty-eight. Jennifer passed out copies of a couple of Teasdale's poems as she spoke about Teasdale's doomed love for another poet, Vachel Lindsay, who apparently had loved her too but had not felt he could support her in the life she needed to write her poems. Both of them married other people. Eventually Lindsay killed himself and, two years later, Teasdale did the same.

The poems by Teasdale that Jennifer gave us made me shiver. *These could have been written by my mother,* I thought to myself:

There will be rest

There will be rest, and sure stars shining
Over the roof-tops crowned with snow.
A reign of rest, serene forgetting,
The music of stillness holy and low.

I will make this world of my devising
Out of a dream in my lonely mind.
I shall find the crystal of peace—above me
Stars I shall find.

I Shall Not Care

When I am dead and over me bright April
Shakes out her rain-drenched hair
Tho' you should lean above me broken-hearted,
I shall not care.

I shall have peace, as leafy trees are peaceful
when rain bends down the bough.
And I shall be more silent and cold-hearted
Than you are now.

"What a crappy attitude," said Eric from the back of the room, not far from where I was sitting. "It's like she's saying a big 'fuck you' to everyone in her life." We all appreciated the fact that our teacher, Mr. Bryzinski, whom everyone called Mr. B., let students use four letter words in class discussions as long as they handed in a paper about their derivations.

"She probably meant it as the biggest 'fuck you' to her boyfriend," Fania said. "Isn't that the kind of thing we all do—imagine that people who are mean to us when we're alive will be really sorry when we're dead? I think about what people will say at my funeral all the time."

The class laughed. "Tell me the date, I'll make sure I'm there," someone shouted out.

"Seriously, guys," Mr. B. said, "What do you think about suicide?"

"It's fucked," said Eric. "It's the most selfish thing anybody can do. It's like *poor me,* some kind of ultimate pity party, like after you're dead you can get all the attention from everybody you think should have paid attention to you while you were alive. As though you could even be there to enjoy it. And as though you were *so* important. What they don't count on is how fast people forget that you ever existed."

"Yeah," said another guy, deLeon. "How about all the people who die when they don't want to? Like the ones who die in wars. Or the ones the cops kill."

"My grampa died of cancer," delicate, soft-spoken Meilin contributed. "And he was eighty-two, and he still chose to have chemo because he wanted to stay alive for us. For his grandchildren. He didn't make it." Her voice broke as she said it.

"What do you think makes someone get to the point of wanting to kill themselves?" Mr. B. asked.

"Loneliness," said Jennifer. "Or a sucky relationship, like Teasdale's."

"It's like Eric said," called out his girlfriend Tanisha. Everyone knew that Eric and Tanisha were joined at the hip, so of course she seconded everything that came out of his mouth. "They want attention. It's the ultimate drama queen act."

"They want to be big shots in life but they fuck up, so all they can choose is death," Eric said. He was clearly controlling the discussion.

"Teasdale was in love with this dude who was married, and he probably didn't really want her in the first place. He was probably just making excuses, like, 'Honey, I'm sorry, I can't support your poetry. I don't have enough money to buy your pencils,'" said a boy named DeeJohn. He stood up and acted it out, and everyone chuckled.

"She made herself miserable," Tanisha said, running her hand through her hair. "She should have just moved on."

"Well, he—Vachel Lindsay—killed himself too," Jennifer said. "So maybe she thought she could follow him and they could finally be together in Heaven."

Eric put on a fake, saccharine smile. "Aw, how sweeeeeet," he said. Jennifer shot him a dirty look, but I could tell she felt hurt.

"People who commit suicide don't *go* to Heaven," Caitlin said. Her family were devout Catholics.

"People who commit suicide shouldn't even be buried," said Eric. "If they don't want to take up space on Earth when they're alive, they shouldn't be allowed to take up any space after they're dead. We barely have enough room for the billions of *living* people who are here!"

"The first poem is kind of sad," said Stefan, who everyone thought of as a math nerd. He almost never said a word in Lit class. "But the second one is, like, bitter. It really is like she's saying she doesn't give a shit if people are all broken up about her death. It's like she's getting back at them, even someone who might genuinely miss her. Like she's getting back at *life*."

"If I wrote poetry as shitty as that," Eric said, "I'd kill myself too."

Jennifer started walking back to her seat, as though in defeat. I felt kind of sorry for her. She must have liked Teasdale, since she'd chosen to present her for our unit on early twentieth century poetry. I found myself angry about the whole discussion, angry at Mr. B. for not steering it in another direction, furious at some of the kids, especially Eric.

And underneath the anger was a heaviness I found unbearable. Mr. B. was shuffling through his papers. It was nearly time for the bell to ring, and clearly he was about to tell us what we should prepare for the following day.

I couldn't contain myself anymore. I suddenly found myself on the verge of tears. "This whole discussion makes me want to scream!" I shouted. "What makes you idiots think you know anything about suicide?" I was surprised at how loud my voice was. "What do you know about why someone would want to kill herself? What do you know about what was going on inside them? What made them feel it was too hard to go on living one more day? Nobody just gets up one morning and says, 'Hmm, what'll I do today? Oh, maybe I'll kill myself. . . .' You have no fucking business talking about things you don't understand! You all sound so fucking superior! You sound like a bunch of wise asses, and I'm sick of you!"

Hot tears were streaming down my face. I threw my poetry anthology into my backpack and stuffed the two Teasdale poems in with it. I stood up just as the bell rang, walked out of the building without looking back into the room and, for the first time in my high school career, ditched class for the rest of the day.

* * *

A few days later I had just walked across the UC campus with Lizzy and was looking at the street vendors' stands on Telegraph Avenue when I heard someone call my name.

"Hey, Gracie."

I turned and looked. It was a punk-haired, skinny girl named Gina with a lip piercing and an eyebrow piercing who sat in the back of American Lit class and spoke even less than I did. In fact, even though Mr. B. clearly liked her writing and sometimes read it aloud, she was often not in class at all. "Hey, Gina," I said.

"What's up?" she asked.

"Nothing. Just walking my dog."

Gina bent to pet Lizzy's head. "Nice dog," she said.

"Yeah. Her name's Lizzy."

"Hi Lizzy," said Gina. She sounded dreamy and far away. Maybe she was stoned; I couldn't tell for sure.

"Were you in class today?" she asked.

I nodded. Gina looked across the street. She seemed as uncomfortable as I was.

"That talk we had last week—about the poet who offed herself?" Gina began, though she wasn't looking at me. "It was totally fucked."

"You thought so?" I asked warily.

"Yeah." She paused. "And I thought the stuff you said at the end—it was really good." Gina turned her eyes toward me and it suddenly felt like she was holding me hostage with them. Her intensity made me turn away; I shrugged, looked down at Lizzy. Gina went on.

"The thing I want to know is—you're usually so chill. Like you just sit there. How come you got so worked up over some poet nobody ever heard of?"

I shrugged again. "I don't know," I told her. Then, because she was still looking at me so intensely, I felt I had to say more. "The whole thing just kind of seemed . . . I don't know . . . unfair."

"Unfair to Jennifer?" Gina asked. I could hear her skepticism about that, as though she knew it wasn't at all about Jennifer but she was trying to give me an out.

"Kind of. I mean, I think she really liked that poet."

Gina nodded. "Are you friends with Jennifer?" she asked.

"Not really," I said. I felt like saying, *Haven't you noticed? I'm not friends with anybody.*

"Well, I never saw you get so worked up. I mean, I don't really know you . . ." she trailed off.

I nodded. People were sitting the doorway behind us, smoking. Torn sleeping bags, an empty whiskey bottle.

Gina looked away for a moment, then looked at me again in that super-intense way. "I liked what you said," she told me. "I thought the other kids were being total jerks. You were great. Really. They were all acting so wise-ass, like they knew what they were talking about."

I didn't know what to say to her, so I said nothing. Finally, "Thanks, Gina."

"Do you read, like, poetry?" she asked me. It felt to me like her question came out of nowhere, just to keep some kind of connection going.

"I read, yeah. Mostly novels. But some poetry. Yeah. Sometimes."

Gina squatted down to hold Lizzy's face in her hands. "You're a really nice dog," she told her. Still looking at Lizzy, she said to me, "I write poems. Kind of like . . . all the time. Maybe I'll show you some."

I was shocked. Gina had never said a word to me before. And I never said a word to anyone at school. "Yeah," I told her, not knowing what else to say.

I stood there looking down at the sidewalk. "Well, bye," I said to her. But I didn't move.

"Yeah, see you," Gina said. She didn't move either.

I started to leave. Then I turned. "Hey," I said, "I really *would* like to see your poems sometime. I mean, if you want to show me. . . ."

Gina nodded. "Sure," she said. "See you." But Gina was absent from school—not unusual for her—for the rest of that week, and I figured she'd forget about showing me her poetry.

CHAPTER 7

2017

Jannie has kept her word and is texting me daily about the gull.
It's clear to me that she's growing attached to her, though Jannie
would never put it that way. My best friend Maria comes with me one
afternoon to Jannie's place and we sit around Jannie's table drinking
tea—Jannie has learned that sole amenity, to offer tea to someone
who comes as a guest to her home—and talk about Jannie's work.
Maria is encouraging her to do a degree program so she can become
a vet tech for birds; I can see the anxiety on Jannie's face when she
thinks about it. "I don't know about a regular program," she says.
"But Jannie, you already know more than probably anyone coming
into that kind of program!" Maria pushes back. Jannie flaps a little—
almost unnoticeably, but I see it.

She comes to dinner with us at a place close to her apartment.
Then Maria needs to leave to get to a meeting. She gives Jannie a
hug and tells her she'll stop by the community college near where
she works and pick up some material about their vet tech program.
Jannie tenses, but knows enough to say thanks.

"What kind of meeting is she going to?" Jannie asks while I'm driving her home.

"It's a group she belongs to that works against police violence. "

"What do they do?"

"A lot of different things. They gather information. Help people find lawyers. Go to where the violence has happened. Help the families of people who've been killed."

"Kind of like what I do for birds, but for people?" she asks. She is struggling to put it together.

"Kind of," I say.

CHAPTER 8

2002

I t bothered me that Kate was around so much of the time.
It kind of surprised me, too. After Emmi died, our father had
never seemed interested in finding a girlfriend. He threw himself
completely into Jannie's "Program," as he called it, and he did that
really well. I assumed that, between Jannie and his teaching job, Dad
had no time for a girlfriend. He seemed to have little enough time for
me, which was fine since I mostly wanted to be left alone.

In fact, I was really annoyed by the attempts he would make to
reach me. "Want to go bowling with me and Jannie?" he'd ask on a
Saturday morning, coming into my room to wake me; and I would
decline, saying I had too much homework. "Gracie, let's all take Lizzy
for a walk on campus this afternoon," he'd say, and I would tell him I
was up to the important part of a book I was in the middle of reading.
Dad was easy to refuse; he never pushed it. It seemed like he was
inviting me to do things more from some sense of paternal obligation
than because he really cared if I did them, and he never looked disap-
pointed when I told him no.

So, in his typical fashion, Dad didn't really ever say anything to me about Kate. He would call her his "colleague" when he introduced her to other people. But I wasn't fooled. It was clear to me that he really liked her.

Kate was slender and tall like Emmi, but that was where the resemblance ended. Once, when I saw her wearing a sun hat with her brown hair tucked up into it, bending over a plot in the garden where she and Dad were digging up potatoes, I pretended to myself for a moment that she was my mother. That Emmi had never gone crazy and killed herself, and that this was an ordinary weekend in the life of an ordinary family where two ordinary parents worked together in the garden.

Kate had a wholesomeness about her that I couldn't stand. She had been raised on a farm near Fresno and she knew about plants. But her constantly cheerful, uncomplicated manner made me sick. One night when I was irritated with her for no particular reason except that she existed, I wrote to Martin, *If Emmi had ever met Kate, she would have hated her. At the very least, she would have been totally bored. But they're so completely different, I don't see how their paths would ever have crossed.*

I wondered what my father saw in Kate. How could he even be interested in someone like that? I started to call her, in my mind, Miss Rosy-Cheeks Farm Bred. I could kind of see what she saw in my dad: emotionally clueless as he was, he was extremely reliable. He took on projects and put all his energy into them. From the minute we'd come home from Germany, Dad had channeled everything into making Jannie into a regular kid. As much as possible he had succeeded.

After Eleanor—whom I'd had to forgive, since her sappiness and her M&M's had resulted, after a year and a half, in Jannie being able to speak—after Eleanor there was a special class in the district for high-functioning autistic children, and occupational therapy and physical therapy and horse-assisted therapy and a succession of social skills groups with other weird kids. And, when all that didn't seem to be enough, Dad managed to get the district to pay for the special school in Marin, forty-five minutes away.

Once, at a neighborhood potluck where Jannie was walking around with her cockatiels in a small, portable cage, I overheard one neighbor say to another, speaking of Dad, "He is tireless in advocating for that child." *Tireless,* I thought. *Advocating.*

I remember an argument between Dad and Emmi that happened shortly before Emmi took us to Europe. I had been sitting at the kitchen table, doing my homework. "She's autistic!" Dad was shouting at Emmi. "Just look at the criteria here in this book! Every one of them sounds like Jannie!" And Emmi was shouting back, "I will not have her labeled! Jannie is fine. She's shy and she hears two languages all the time. That's why she's not speaking yet!" "Gracie heard two languages and she spoke full sentences before she was two!" Dad had screamed at her, and Emmi had screamed back, "Jannie is not Gracie! Jannie doesn't need to go to a special preschool or any other kind of preschool! Jannie needs *me!*"

"You and Jannie are drifting into a world of your own." Dad's voice had quieted, but I could still hear him. "Every day the two of you drift farther away. I feel like there's no way for me to pull you back to shore."

"My job is to take care of Jannie!" Emmi had shouted at him.

"What about Gracie?" I'd heard my dad ask. Emmi didn't bother to answer.

"You just can't bear that I don't want to be married to you anymore," Emmi had said to him. Then I heard their bedroom door slam, and Jannie shriek. And Dad came into the kitchen to check on my math.

In the cosmic struggle for Jannie's soul, my dad had been right. It was not clinging to Emmi on that shaky little vessel edging toward some nameless horizon that Jannie needed. My mother was no navigator; her mind was windswept and lacked a steady compass. If Emmi had stayed alive, it's doubtful that Jannie would ever have stepped onto shore and joined us.

What Jannie needed was Dad and the matter-of-fact, methodical way he went about organizing her life. What Jannie needed was Eleanor and her M&M's. What Jannie needed were psychiatrists and prescriptions and special schools and therapy horses.

And after that, what Jannie needed was her flock of birds. They were what she loved most. Taking care of them, she was learning to be a responsible person in the world—accountable, thoughtful. Her birds spoke to her, responded to her, and she understood their language. Their short, concrete conversations were exactly like Jannie's. The birds accepted her. Were attached to her. Craved her attention. And she tended them with all her might and all her intensity, and her inscrutable mind became a veritable bird encyclopedia.

Jannie had said her first word after Emmi died. Horrible as it sounds, once our mother was out of the way, Dad was able to do what was needed for Jannie, and he did it.

Jannie spoke. Jannie stopped running away. Jannie sat at the table and ate with a fork and spoon. Jannie raised birds and studied them and learned everything about them. Jannie began to draw wild birds and her own birds.

What about Gracie? I heard Kate ask Dad one Saturday afternoon. Dad was planning an excursion for the following day, enumerating to Kate all the things Jannie would accept doing and all the things she would not accept. *What about Gracie?* in a voice that totally annoyed me; but I didn't think my dad ever asked that question anymore.

I was the Easy One. No trouble to anyone. I was the one who was willing to go along with the program or to stay at home reading. I was never consulted about plans because I never argued with what was planned. I just went along or stayed contentedly at home.

I wasn't autistic. I didn't have rituals or obsessions or strange aversions. I didn't flap my hands as though they were truncated wings. I didn't have a flock of birds I was always worried about. I didn't melt down into screaming fits if things didn't go exactly the way I expected them to.

What about Gracie? From Kate—who didn't even know the whole situation. Who taught high school kids and knew them to be anything *but* willing to go along with the family program. Who obviously hadn't learned yet that the world revolved around those who had the hardest time living in it.

CHAPTER 9

2017

J annie tells me she's had to reset the gull's wing because the bandages had begun to slip. *Enough to get a better look at the damage,* she texts. *It's bad. I don't know that she'll ever fly again.*

I'm in the faculty lunchroom, in the middle of a conversation with a friend in the Spanish department. But I text her back. *What does that mean for her?*

Maybe put her down. Maybe give her a little more time, then put her down.

Why do that? I ask her.

What, keep her for a while? Jannie texts.

No, why put her down if she's eating and walking?

I could never release her.

But can't she be okay like this?

How?

Eating and walking.

Bubbles, but no text yet.

I'm surprised at how passionately I want to advocate for this bird. *Can't you keep her?* I text, impatient.

Don't know. Have to think if it's fair.

Is it fair to bandage her and feed her and take care of her and then just kill her? I text my sister.

Another small oil spill in San Pablo Bay, Jannie texts, changing the subject. *Have to get to the Center. Other birds to take care of.*

I think of the gull, her wing newly rebandaged, walking around Jannie's bathroom, pecking at her food. Never before, I imagine, away from her flock, from the vastness of sky and water. But alive. Alert. Recognizing Jannie, trusting her, learning this new way of being a gull. Isn't that it? Don't we all have challenges like that at some point, that demand that we change our lives? Eating and walking.

Have to think if it's fair, Jannie texted.

I want Jannie to give her a name. I want to think of a name for her myself.

Scout? I think. My seventh graders, reading *To Kill A Mockingbird,* would love to hear that we'd named her that.

A few days later I ask Jannie if I can come over and see her and the bird. I pick up some Indian take-out and we sit at the tiny table in her kitchen, the gull strutting—happily, as far as I can tell—around us. When Jannie picks her up and holds her on her lap, the gull doesn't resist.

I tell Jannie the name I've thought of.

"Scout?" she asks. "Like Girl Scout?"

I tell her about the book. Jannie turns the name over in her mind. I can see her considering it carefully. I can see her knowing that if she names the bird, she'll be making a decision to keep her.

"Okay," she says at last. "Scout."

I remind Jannie that she wanted to ask me something about our mother; when I'd texted her back that next morning, she'd told me she had to do something for the gull and she'd ask me the next time we were together.

"Oh yeah," she says, as though whatever it was had slipped far to the back of her mind, buried under birds and oil slicks. "I wanted to ask you why she killed herself."

CHAPTER 10

2002

One rainy morning I got to school and found a white envelope taped to my locker door. When I stood in the corridor, rain jacket dripping, and opened it, I had no idea at first what I was reading.

Suicide.
  I can remember the
blood,
     gushing into the
       drain, staining
the tub,
    my soul leaving
      consciousness.
That was the first
   real time I
     knew nobody
cared about
   me.
      When nobody rushed

into the bathroom,
       when nobody
              dialed 911.

Finally when Bo
       called the cops
after taking one look
       at me,
              I was found
by the paramedics
       one minute away
              from escaping
       this mess of a hate-filled
world.

That was it. No signature. Nothing else in the envelope. The bell rang for first period and I stuffed the poem back into the envelope and then into the outside pocket of my backpack. Only while I was walking upstairs to Trig did I realize the poem must have been Gina's.

In Trig I took it out of my backpack and read it again. I must have read it four or five times. Was she making it up, I wondered, or was it really about herself? And who was it who didn't call 911? And who was Bo? *Escaping/ this mess of a hate-filled world,* Gina had written. Well, yeah, I thought: all the endless wars, all the innocent people killed by famine and war and police, all the people in prison, the hate crimes: was that what Gina meant?

I hadn't seen Gina in American Lit for a while. She had come a few times after we ran into each other on Telegraph, but there was nothing unusual about Gina cutting class. I wondered what she did when she wasn't in school: did she spend her day on the street? There were tons of homeless people and runaways and kids who didn't have anything else to do hanging out on Shattuck and Telegraph, minutes from Berkeley High: was that Gina's world?

She must have come to school this morning, I thought, if she left me this poem; but American Lit wasn't until the first period of the afternoon, and I had no idea whether Gina was going to stick around that long. When we'd seen each other in class after that time on Telegraph, we had acknowledged each other only with glances.

I found myself wired all through the morning. At lunch, since it had stopped raining, I walked to the far end of the yard, sat down on the stairs there, and ate my sandwich. I couldn't wait until American Lit and at the same time I kind of hoped Gina wouldn't be there. Maybe the poem wasn't even by her, I thought; after all, the whole class had had that discussion about suicide and maybe some other kid had decided to write a poem about it. It would be totally embarrassing to go up to Gina and say, *Thanks for the poem,* and then not even have it be hers. I could just see the look she would give me.

Maybe I just shouldn't say anything, I thought. After all, whoever had left me the poem had made the decision not to reveal who they were. But Gina had told me she might show me her poetry sometime, and she would certainly be wondering whether I'd bothered to read it if it *was* hers.

I sat there pondering what to do, eating my sandwich, when suddenly Gina was standing in front of me.

"Hey," she said. "I found you."

"Hey, Gina," I said. My mouth was full of peanut butter. Probably some was sticking to my teeth. I realized that, because it had been raining, I was wearing my dorkiest shoes, the waterproof rubber shoes Dad had bought me a couple of years before when we'd gone to Yosemite.

Gina was wearing flip flops, a tight-fitting black tank top over tight-fitting jeans with holes at the knees, and no jacket at all. "Did you get the envelope?" she asked.

"Yeah," I told her. "I found it this morning." Why did I always say stupid, obvious things to Gina, I thought. *Of course* I had found it that morning. I didn't know what else to say to her, but I knew I had to say something. "When did you leave it there?"

"Before first period." Gina said matter-of-factly.

I looked at my watch. Fifteen minutes 'til American Lit. "Are you coming to class?" I asked her.

"Probably," Gina said. She had sat down on the stairs beside me. She was quiet for a while, picking at the black polish on one of her toenails. "So," she said slowly, not looking at me. It came out "Sooooooo . . . ." "So what did you think?"

"I thought it was good," I said weakly. Probably the stupidest thing I could have said. "I mean," I started again, "I wondered . . ."

"If it's the truth?" Gina asked me. She was as direct as I was not.

"I guess, yeah," I said, wanting the bell to ring right that minute.

"Yeah," Gina said. "It is. I mean, I kind of wrote it about a couple of different times and I made it seem like it was all one time, but . . . yeah."

"You really . . ." I started.

"I really did try to kill myself. Twice. Once it wasn't . . . I wasn't that serious. But the second time, yeah. Yeah. I almost made it."

"Was that the time Bo . . .?" I began.

"Yeah, Bo." Gina laughed a little, but it wasn't like anything was funny. "Bo was my boyfriend. He's not anymore. We still kind of fuck . . ." she went on. "But we're not together."

"Oh," I said, wishing I were anywhere else. What was wrong with me? Why couldn't I think of anything to say?

The bell rang but both of us ignored it.

"That's why I thought that day in class was so messed up," Gina told me. "None of them knew shit about suicide and they acted so wise-ass."

I nodded. *Why can't I tell her anything real,* I thought, *Why?*

"What about you, Gracie?" Gina asked me. *She's not afraid of anything,* I thought. *And I'm afraid of everything.*

"You mean . . . "

"I mean, what about you?" Gina repeated, the emphasis on *you.* "Did you ever try to kill yourself?"

With all my might I was trying not to tell Gina about my mother. And yet I also wanted with all my might to tell her.

"No," I said." No, I never did." I thought for a minute. The second bell rang. Gina didn't move, but she stopped looking at me and looked down across the school yard. Kids moving toward the doors.

"No," I repeated. "But someone I know did. *Knew.*"

"Did they die?" Gina asked, looking at me again.

I nodded.

"Wow," she said. "Sorry," she said. She shook her head. Her eyes were soft.

"Yeah," I said, and picked up my backpack. Together we started walking to class.

CHAPTER 11

2002

Dad and Kate were going to somebody's wedding. We were all invited—Jannie and I were going too—and it made sense that Kate was invited since she was a good friend of the bride; but what bothered me was that we were going *together*. *Together,* the way families go to weddings. In the same car.

The night before the wedding, the Friday night just after Gina and I had that conversation, Kate came up to my room and sat down on my bed.

"Hey, Gracie," she started. "Whatcha doing?"

"Nothing."

She glanced at the book I'd put down on the bed when she'd come in. "What are you reading?"

"A novel."

"Nice title," Kate said, not buying into what should have been my obvious desire not to talk to her. "*History*. What's it about?"

"It's Italian," I said. "Translated."

"Is it for school?" she asked.

"No," I said.

"Wow," Kate said, picking up the novel, being careful not to lose my place. "This is a hefty novel. Most of the kids I teach don't have time to read books like this outside of their school work."

I shrugged. Where was this going?

Kate pressed on. "Yeah, mostly they're busy with sports or friends on the weekends. Parties. You'd never catch them sitting in bed on a Friday night reading a big-ass novel."

I hated the way Kate tried to seem cool by using kid vocabulary. "Too bad for them," I answered. "They don't know what they're missing."

I could see Kate take a breath, as though she were choosing exactly this moment to jump into an icy lake. "Do you ever wonder if *you're* missing anything, Gracie?"

"No," I said, looking away from her. I knew she wasn't going to stop. Dad would have let it go at this point. No; Dad wouldn't even have started.

"Sometimes I worry that you aren't having enough fun, Gracie," she went on.

"Fun?"

"I mean, you know—hanging out with people, doing stuff together . . ."

"I hang out with people all day at school. Five days a week."

"That's not really hanging out," Kate insisted. "I mean seeing people outside of school, going to movies together, parties."

"I hate parties," I said, picking up my book.

"There are lots of different kinds of parties," Kate said. She thought for a minute. "Look, Gracie, I don't want to get stuck talking about small points. What I'm saying is I see you always reading, studying, doing your homework. But I never see you bring another kid home. I never see you talking on the phone with anyone, anything."

"So?" I said. "Maybe I don't want to bring people home. Or talk on the phone."

I could tell Kate was getting frustrated. "I guess I don't understand what you *do* want," she said.

"Why *should* you understand?" I flashed back at her. "You're not my mother."

Kate walked out of my room. I could hear her turn the TV news on when she went downstairs. Dad was probably sitting down there in his armchair, reading the morning paper he hadn't had a chance to get to earlier. Jannie was in her room with her birds. What an unsatisfying family we must be for Miss Rosy Cheeks Farm-Bred, I thought to myself. Maybe if we're unsatisfying enough, she won't stick around.

* * *

Dad had promised Jannie that he'd take her to the marina to draw birds the next morning if she would agree to go to the wedding. It was the kind of bargain Jannie was good at and I was terrible at; I lied my way out of things whenever I could, avoided them; but all I got back in return was the reward of keeping my life shut exactly inside the parameters I had drawn for it.

I went with them to the marina to avoid being in the house alone with Kate. I knew she was hot on my trail and wouldn't let go of the subject she had brought up the night before. We packed up coffee and hot chocolate and muffins Rosy Cheeks Farm-Bred had, of course, baked at God knows what hour before dawn, and drove down to the bay through the fog.

There wasn't one thing about the whole excursion that I didn't hate.

Jannie climbed down to sit on a rock. It was a windy morning. She was wearing a blue down jacket and a gray wooly cap. Dad and I sat in the car in the parking lot about twenty yards from where she was, far enough so Jannie could have the privacy she had asked for but near enough so we could keep an eye on her. She was still just a little kid but she already thought of herself as a scientist, an ornithologist, and she wanted to sit on that rock alone, drawing pad on her lap, binoculars around her neck, to document the morning of the snowy egrets who lived in the little reedy inlet.

One of the egrets stood on a rock on a single yellow leg, the other leg tucked into her thick breast feathers. Jannie began to sketch. I watched her pick up the binoculars to get a closer look, put them down so she could add to her sketch, and pick them up again to make sure she had gotten it right.

Another egret landed silently on a rock near the first one. They seemed not to acknowledge each other; but neither did one seem disturbed by the other's presence—the negative space between that one and the first shaped by sky and the leaning of rock against rock. When the first egret set down her left leg, leaned her chest forward, her head forward, spread her wings and flew off—an arc of flight over the water and the arc of return.

It was cold in the car. Dad and I passed the thermos of hot coffee between us. I asked him if we could turn the heater on; I asked if we could listen to the radio. I was bored and sleepy and cold and still irritated by the things Kate had said the night before. She had opted not to come with us this morning—why did she *always* have to sleep at our house?—because she wanted to take Lizzy for a walk in the hills. We were going to meet back at the house, get dressed for the wedding, and leave around noon.

I marveled at the steadiness of Jannie's hand. From the car, I couldn't see her drawing; but I could see the total attention she gave it. She didn't seem bothered at all by the cold and the wind. She watched the birds, tracked each of their movements. I thought of the little girl she had been who couldn't stay still; I thought of Jannie's continuous escapes, her frenzied arm flapping, her total inability to focus on anything.

Dad was reading the newspaper he'd brought. I sat watching Jannie and was seized suddenly with a terrible sadness. *Emmi,* I said silently to my mother, *I wish you could see Jannie now. You thought she wanted only to escape this world, and here she is sketching it, marking its slightest detail. Making it come alive on paper. Studying it so closely. Loving the birds she's drawing, loving every line of their stillness, their movement.*

Then my sadness receded and revealed the anger lying beneath it like a creased, muddy shoreline. *And you're lying under the grass ten thousand miles from here. At least you didn't drag us down there with you.*

* * *

I had nothing I cared about the way Jannie cared about birds.

Nothing.

I did fine in all my classes, but I didn't really care about them. Trigonometry bored me. Chemistry bored me. American Lit I liked, and Mr. B. had written on one of my papers that he thought I could be a writer; but I wasn't someone who wrote all the time the way Gina did, and I figured that real writers had to be like Jannie was about birds, totally obsessed.

Martin loved soccer. He played it every afternoon after school and several times on the weekends. As soon as he was strong enough after chemo he'd gone back to soccer.

Dad loved teaching. It wasn't just his job; he was totally committed to the kids he taught, spent time with them after school supervising their clubs, helping them with homework that wasn't even in his subject. I envied his students, most of whom I had never set eyes on, because they seemed to get more of Dad's attention than I ever could. Dad and I barely exchanged sentences a couple of times a day, and I had to admit I was used to that and didn't even think I wanted to change it.

Kate loved to make quilts. She would bring bags of cut fabric to our house, lay them out on the living room floor, gently pushing Lizzy aside when Lizzy would grab a piece and run off with it into the kitchen, shaking it playfully. She would ask my opinion or Jannie's about where to place this piece of fabric or that: *Is this blue better next to the gray or over here, next to the orange?*

My answer was usually, "I don't know." Or: "They're both okay." Or: "It doesn't really matter."

What *did* I think mattered? Anything?

Maybe Kate had been right the night before. That *really* annoyed me. I couldn't stand Kate. Mostly I wished she would stay away because she intruded on the non-communication that had become my way of dealing with stuff at home. Kate saw things about my life and wanted to talk to me about them and I had to keep coming up with strategies to avoid her.

Kate got it. No one I knew at school was really my friend. Dad— probably prompted by Kate—had asked me a few weeks before, "Do you want to go out more, Gracie? Do you think I ask you to babysit Jannie too often?"

I'd answered, "No, it's okay."

End of discussion. Dad had walked out of my room. We were both relieved. Our habitual manner of failing to connect had been maintained.

Dad didn't need more than one kid to worry about, I reasoned; and besides, there was no one at school I wanted to talk to anyway. Well, there was Gina . . . but Gina cut class as often as she came, and I had no idea what to make of her leaving me her poem and finding me on the steps that day. I liked Nick, a kind of nerdy, serious literary type who had babysat Jannie for a couple of years until Dad thought I was old enough, but Nick was a sophomore at UC Berkeley now and even though he still came to see us sometimes, I didn't imagine he wanted much to do with a junior in high school. Everyone at school thought my mother was still living in Germany; and whoever even knew I had a sister thought she was some kind of genius and that was why she went to a special school in Marin. It would be way too complicated to undo lies like that, and what did I care anyway?

Sometimes it crossed my mind that maybe my story didn't need to be as hidden as I thought. Not everybody was normal, or had a normal life, whatever that was. Gina certainly had a story, though I didn't know what it was. And I knew there were other kids at school who had been through terrible things and still made friends. There was Josh, whose older sister had been driving drunk and died in an accident that killed the other two kids in the car as well. Helen's brother had been shot in a drive-by; even wise-ass Eric had a little sister who had nearly drowned in a pool and was permanently brain-damaged because of it. All those kids talked to other kids. Made friends. What was the matter with me, that I couldn't?

I sat there in the car, Dad turning the pages of the newspaper. I had no answer. I told myself I simply couldn't undo what I'd started to do at twelve, like going up to Josh and saying, "Hey, Josh, you know how I've always said my mom left my dad and got a job in Germany? Well, what really happened was she drove her car into a tree and committed suicide." As time passed and I kept doing nothing to contradict my lies, I felt I had condemned myself to live with them and leave it at that. I was trapped inside them and couldn't see a way out.

I couldn't even write any of this to Martin. I'd written to him that I couldn't find anything I really loved to do and that whenever I watched Jannie with her birds, I was torn between awe and envy. *Jannie is autistic and just a kid, and she's already a scientist, a bird expert, an artist,* I'd written. *I'm a sophomore in high school and I'm nothing.*

Du bist eine fantastische Lugerin, Martin wrote back. *You're a fantastic liar.*

I think everyone thought I was a snob. It wasn't that I didn't like people. I did. I was actually very interested in them. I figured out all the romantic intrigues around me. I knew who wanted to be in politics and who wanted to work with computers and who wanted to be a dancer. I just didn't feel like talking to anyone. I just felt my life was too different from the lives they were living and I had no way to bridge the gap. Even kids who had lived through stories as weird as my own seemed to have found their way back to the surface; but I had no idea how to do it.

I didn't even know if I wanted to be there.

I am as lonely as Emmi was, I thought. And a shudder of terror ran through me. Would I, too, wind up someday dead in a car I'd crashed deliberately into a tree?

A couple of days later, early the next week, Gina passed a note to me in Lit class while we were watching a video about Thoreau.

Who was it? was all the note said, and at first I had no idea what she was referring to.

CHAPTER 12

2002

Jannie's flock of birds was increasing and multiplying. She had recently talked Dad into getting her two young green-cheeked pineapple conures whom she'd named Pablo and Isabella and who were smart and sociable and mischievous and almost impossible to lure back into their cages once they were out.

We all had to learn to be meticulously careful about closing windows and doors, even though Dad had spent a few weekends putting screens on all of them; but Jannie often left for school with Pablo and Isabella flying randomly around the house. Just about every day a bird would swoop down on the food we were eating, land in our hair and get their feet tangled in it, shit on the carpet and perch tantalizingly, mocking us, on curtain rods and window frames, screeching their heads off. All Jannie's birds, but particularly the conures, stole whatever shiny objects we'd leave lying around. Sometimes they would stash them in their cages, but often we'd find that the rings, bracelets, glittery necklaces we'd removed and left lying on dressers, counters, or sinks had been carried off to some distant place in the house.

"It feels like your birds have only half their instinct left," I told Jannie one day, annoyed at not being able to find something, "Like they know how to pick things up but they have no idea what to do with them. Bird brains."

Jannie was insulted. Her face turned red and her eyes filled with tears. "Stop it!" she said. "You Person Brain! What kind of brains do you think my birds should have? Of course they have bird brains!"

Literal Jannie.

Dad tried to impose some discipline about the birds on Jannie, but Dad spoiled her so much that she didn't take his threats to bring the birds back to the bird store seriously. I found the birds totally annoying, and more than once—when one of her larger birds picked up a piece of aluminum foil I was just about to wrap a sandwich in, for instance—I screamed at Jannie, "Would you get your fucking birds into your room?"

I couldn't see what she saw in them. To me at that point in my life, Jannie's birds were exactly the way Jannie herself had been at her most severely autistic: screeching, flapping, always evading us. It was as though now that she had changed, Jannie wanted to ensure that there were vestiges of her former self still in the house. It was clear—Dad talked about it all the time—that Jannie's birds gave her a purpose and that taking care of them was teaching her more than anything else could have done.

I understood that. But, now, looking back on those years, I think I was also envious of how passionately Jannie felt about them.

One evening when it was just me and Jannie and Dad at dinner, Jannie started talking about how, every year, people went out to the Farrallone Islands, out beyond the Golden Gate in the Pacific, to stay for a couple of weeks and count birds. The islands were in the path of many migratory species and it was important to know exactly how many birds of each species stopped there to rest on their way to Mexico or South America.

A young woman who worked at the bird store was planning to go, and Jannie wanted to go with her. An argument ensued between Jannie and Dad, who told her she was much too young. "Why won't you come with me then?" Jannie screeched at him. "If you really cared about me you would come with me!"

I was shocked to hear Jannie say such a thing. It never seemed to me that it crossed Jannie's mind whether anyone human cared about her or not.

It never seemed to me that Jannie noticed if other people reacted to her at all. People were just obstacles in the way of Jannie's desires, or they were instruments she could use to achieve her ends. What they felt about her didn't seem to matter to Jannie, or even to register. But that evening, in the argument about the Farrallones, Jannie cried tears that did not seem to be only about not being able to go and count birds, but about not being understood. "You don't care, you don't care," she sobbed to Dad. "You don't even know how important this is to me. You think I'm just being weird. Weird Jannie! Weird Jannie!"

Suddenly Jannie started circling around the kitchen, screeching *Weird Jannie* in a crow-like voice and flapping her arms. She hadn't flapped in years, and this flapping seemed to me somewhere between deliberate, aggressive, and out of control. Lizzy tucked her tail under her legs and skulked out of the room. Like Lizzy, I could barely stand to witness what Jannie was doing. Dad just stood there looking helpless.

For once I found myself wishing that Kate was there to do something: calm down Jannie, comfort Dad. Something.

In the end Dad promised Jannie that we could all go out in a boat one day and sail to the Farrallones. Whether Jannie stopped screeching and flapping because she was pacified or simply because she was exhausted, the storm was over.

What I thought about more than anything when I went to bed that night was the way Jannie had wanted to be understood, and the way it drove her crazy to feel she was not.

Lying awake with my hand on Lizzy, I realized that I'd felt some affinity with Jannie that night which I'd never experienced before. I too felt unseen, unknown by just about everyone around me.

Dad was great at arranging therapies and programs and at keeping the refrigerator stocked with food and the laundry done, and he was great at helping his students with algebra and pre-calculus, but once feelings were in the picture, once he was asked to really listen to another person about what was going on inside them, he totally checked out. He had been that way with Emmi. He was that way with me. Up until now, Jannie had never asked anyone to understand her feelings; but I wondered what Dad would do if she started to.

I wondered whether Jannie cared if *I* understood her or not. I realized that I never thought about Jannie's feelings: I thought about her actions, thought about how much I was bothered by her birds and by her literalness. But I never tried to reach across the gap that separated Jannie from me. From everybody.

I watched her go about the tasks of her day, the seemingly scripted way she ate her breakfast, always the same: a bite of toast, a spoonful of medium boiled egg (it had to be perfectly medium, not the least bit too hard or too soft), a sip of ginger tea with one spoonful of honey. Toast egg tea toast egg tea. Never tea toast tea egg egg. Never anything different.

I watched Jannie slip her lunch bag into her backpack and zip up the backpack at precisely the same speed every day. I would silently scream at her to vary something, *anything*, and she never did. I began to see how my observing Jannie was a trick I had invented to distance myself from her, to widen that gap. To make her seem like a specimen to me.

I asked myself whether I loved my sister. And then I asked myself whether I loved anyone. Anything.

I loved Lizzy. Okay, *one* living being. I was pretty sure I had loved my oma, but I felt so far from her now, with our strained conversations over the phone and her mind growing so unclear she often thought I was my mother.

Maybe I loved Martin? But Martin was mostly a pile of letters I kept in a box under my bed, and writing to him was like writing to myself and putting it in an envelope.

I probably loved my dad. But how do you tell the difference between loving someone and just sort of counting on them?

And my mother. Had I loved my mother? She certainly wasn't the kind of person you could count on. Once, before Jannie was born, I had sat in a little boat off Muir Beach with my mother and watched her row. I had listened to her singing a song with a word she had changed to make me happy, and it had made me happy:

The water is wide
I cannot cross o'er
And neither have I
wings to fly

Give me a boat
That can carry two
And both shall cross
My child and I

I remembered the light wind, the smell of the ocean, the waves edged with sunlight. I remembered my mother's long, straight blond hair blowing across her face. Her slender fingers gripping the oars.

Was it love, to remember a single afternoon so clearly?

CHAPTER 13

2017

*J*annie, I wrote on a sheet of printer paper before going to bed on a Sunday night, *I'm going to write this to you instead of talking about it, because—just as I did when I was a kid—I think I can say important things more clearly in writing than I can when I talk.*

You asked me a couple of weeks ago why Emmi committed suicide. The short answer is that I don't know; I think no one can really know what it is in the mind of a person that makes it possible to hurt herself in ways most of us spend our energy avoiding. What it is in the mind of a person that aches so deeply that nothing—not even her children, not even her mother—adds up enough in the column marked "staying alive" to counterbalance the desire to be through with the pain.

What I can tell you is that Emmi was not really living for a long time before she drove that car down a precipice and into a tree. I remember her walking around Oma's house for weeks, muttering to herself about radioactivity and toxins and wanting to burn everything down; I remember being afraid that she would set fire to the house, and Oma reassuring me that she wouldn't. Looking back at that time now, I'm grateful that Emmi didn't take you and me and Oma into oblivion with her; and I can also see that, trapped as she was in the prison of her mind, she was desperate to escape in one way or another. I think that's what she was trying to do the whole time she was with us in Europe: every time she would take out the train schedule, I could sense the panic and hopelessness, the kind of imprisonment she was feeling. And when nothing else seemed to work to free her, I think she decided she needed to set herself free from life.

You were probably the person Emmi loved most in this world; but even that was not enough to keep her here. That's how much pain she was in.

I hope this is enough of an answer for you. If you want to talk about it, let me know.

Love,

Gracie

I put the letter in the mail on the way to teach the following morning. Two days later, Jannie texted me, *"Thanks."*

We haven't spoken about it again.

CHAPTER 14

2002

One Sunday soon after the Farallones episode, when Dad and Kate had gone to a concert, I asked Jannie whether she wanted to do something together besides sit in separate rooms in the house, which was what we always did.

"Do what?" Jannie asked. She was copying an illustration of a grebe from one of her bird books, curled in the oversized chair in the living room. I had been working on a paper about Woodrow Wilson at the kitchen table, and I was tired of it. I wanted to get out.

"I don't know," I said. "What would you like to do?"

She hesitated. Getting Jannie to do anything outside her routines was always a challenge. She bit her lip, thinking. "I'm not sure I want to do anything," she said at last.

I felt impatient. It was a beautiful day in February, one of those Berkeley winter-into-spring days when the plum trees are blossoming, the freesia and jasmine and daffodils and narcissus are making the air fragrant and there's a feeling of everything about to open up. "Well, I want to get outside, and I can't leave you here by yourself. How about we walk to the bird store?"

The bird store was about an hour's walk from where we lived, especially at the pace I would walk with Jannie. It was where Jannie always bought her supplies—bird seed, vitamin drops, cuttle bones. I knew I could get her out of the house with that as the goal. She agreed, put her drawing tablet and book away, and got her red sweatshirt.

I realized that this was the first time Jannie and I were ever going for a walk together, just the two of us.

She stayed at school so late now, with all her special therapies, that I was never alone with her on weekdays for very long. I always babysat her on weekends if Dad went anywhere, since I never had anything else to do. Mostly we just sat around doing our separate things.

That was the way of the whole household, except when Kate was there. Kate was able to pull Jannie and Dad and me together and make us engage with each other. I hated it.

* * *

The argument Jannie had with Dad about the Farrallones stayed with me. I had the nagging feeling that Jannie was trying to make herself more understandable to Dad and me than I'd given her credit for. Was that Kate's doing? Kate was so affectionate with Jannie, and she always spoke to her as though she was just a regular kid. Had Kate awakened something in Jannie that cared more about being connected to other people?

Walking with Jannie wasn't like walking with anyone else I knew. She was very slow, but she didn't stop to look at anything, talk to anyone, pet a dog or a cat we met on the sidewalk. There was a goal and that's what the walk was about. That and only that.

I kept trying to get her to look at something besides the street signs. She was reciting under her breath the names of the streets we would have to pass in order to get to the bird store. Dad had driven her there so many times that she had memorized the grid, and the only important activity now was checking off street names in her mind and counting how many we had left. "Hey Jannie, doesn't that dog look a lot like Lizzy?" I'd try; or "Look at that house? Isn't it painted a weird color?"

No response. If Jannie didn't consider a comment worth her attention, she never bothered to answer.

We were waiting to cross Telegraph Avenue when I heard someone call my name. I turned, took Jannie's hand so she wouldn't cross without me, and saw Gina standing half a block from where we were.

Oh, shit, I thought. I hadn't expected to meet anyone I knew. Then I remembered that I'd never replied to Gina's note about who it was who had committed suicide, and I almost thought I'd pretend I hadn't heard her over the sound of traffic.

Too late. Gina was running toward me and Jannie as though she wanted to make sure she reached us before the light changed.

She looked pale. She had dyed her hair fire-engine red. I realized that it had been a while since I'd seen her at school.

"Hey, Gina," I said.

"Hey Gracie."

"Have you been out sick?" I asked her.

"Kind of. Not really. I just . . . kind of haven't been making it to school." Gina looked at Jannie. "Is that your sister?" she asked me.

"Yeah," I could feel Jannie's impatience to get going.

"What's your name?" Gina asked Jannie. Jannie hesitated a moment. At her school the kids learned all the formulas for appropriate social response. Finally she said, "My name is Jannie. What's yours?" It came out formal and stiff.

"Gina." Gina smiled at the woodenness of Jannie's tone; but it seemed like a gentle smile. *It's so obvious how weird Jannie is,* I thought. And then it struck me: *Gina gets her.*

"Where are you guys headed?" Gina asked.

"We're going to the bird store," Jannie said. And then, "Your hair is really red."

I cringed.

"Yeah," Gina said. "It's redder than I thought it would turn out. Cheap dye. Are you going to buy a bird?"

Gina and my sister were having a conversation.

"No," Jannie answered, "just bird seed. I already have ten birds. Four parakeets, two Australian zebra finches, two cockatiels, and two green-cheeked pineapple conures. The conures are just babies," Jannie told her. I was about to say, "Jannie, that's enough;" but Gina seemed really into her.

"That's a lot of birds," Gina said, smiling. "Are they—like—friends with each other?"

"I don't really know," Jannie told her, confused. But she continued. "I don't let the finches out of their cage but the parakeets and the cockatiels and the conures all fly around the house."

"Do they land in your hair and stuff?" Gina asked. "That would creep me out."

I stood silently, listening to them. Gina didn't seem to have any trouble connecting with Jannie, and it made me feel a little bad that I'd thought she would.

"They do, but I don't care," said Jannie.

"The rest of us care," I couldn't help saying.

"Aw," said Gina, "They're just birds. They can't help it. They're probably just looking for trees."

Jannie smiled. "They know there are no trees in the house," she said. "There are plants, but they're really small." Understanding humor was not her strong suit.

Gina didn't take offense. "So . . . do they live a long time? Someone told me that parrots can live, like, seventy years."

"Conures can live to be thirty-five. That means when Pablo and Isabella die I'll be forty-five. That's four years younger than my dad," Jannie said.

"Really?" Gina seemed more interested than I'd imagined she would be.

"Our mom died at forty-two," Jannie volunteered. "She lived seven more years than a conure." She giggled.

My stomach sank. Here was Jannie, saying in her concrete way what I had been hiding all these years. I wondered if Gina had heard that I told everyone my mother had a high-powered job in Germany.

If she had, she didn't let on. Instead, "Really?" she said. "My mom's dead too."

I stood there, not knowing what to say. "We should probably go," was the best I could do. As soon as I said it, I felt stupid and insensitive. *That* was my response to Gina saying her mom was dead?

"Yeah," Gina said. "So . . . are you going to be at school tomorrow?"

"Yeah," I answered. "Are you?"

"I think so. Do you want to . . . maybe . . . hang out at lunch?"

I was taken aback. Here I had acted like such a jerk and Gina wanted to have lunch with me?

No one ever asked me to hang out. People sort of just assumed I wouldn't want to.

"I guess," I said. Then, sorry I had been so unenthusiastic, I corrected myself. "I mean sure, yeah, I can do it."

"I mean," Gina seemed suddenly shy, "I mean like, I don't know if you . . . have people you . . ."

"No," I said, and it came out more emphatically than I'd intended. "No. We can have lunch."

Gina smiled and nodded. "Okay," she said, "Meet you on the steps?"

"Yeah."

"Bye. Bye, Jannie." She said it as though Jannie were just a regular kid. I felt surprised and ashamed.

Did I think so little of Jannie? Did I expect so little of Gina?

Gina turned and walked north. I found myself wondering where she lived, what she was doing on the Avenue. I felt grateful that afternoon that Jannie was Jannie. Because she was Jannie she never asked me how I knew Gina, who was obviously—with her fire-engine hair and all her piercings and her not coming regularly to school—different from the kind of person anyone not autistic might have expected me to make friends with. Because she was Jannie, she never even noticed that that was the case.

Because she was Jannie, she never said a word to Dad or Kate about meeting Gina on the street. Jannie couldn't see what might be of interest about it.

Because she was Jannie, she had been able to tell Gina about our mom, which I never would have done. I could see the total lack of shock on Gina's face.

And I had learned that Gina's mother was also dead.

CHAPTER 15

2002

The history teacher kept us a few minutes late before lunch explaining something about World War I. I ran as fast as I could to the steps where Gina and I were supposed to meet. The day was gray with rain on and off. Gina and I had only American Lit together, so I had no idea whether she had actually come to school, or whether the rain would keep her from meeting me outside. When I got to the steps, out of breath from running, and didn't find her there, I felt a kind of letdown I wasn't used to feeling. I stood at the top of the steps and scanned the yard. Twenty-five-hundred kids were milling around, shouting to each other, laughing, running. I felt I might as well have been dropped from another planet; no one I saw meant a thing to me. There was no way I could join them and no way I cared to.

I reached into my backpack and pulled out the brown paper bag I'd packed my sandwich in. No Gina. What if she's gotten there on time, not found me, and decided to leave? A frantic feeling arose in my gut. Should I go looking for her? How could I find her among all those people?

I unwrapped the sandwich—cheese and lettuce—from its aluminum foil and I took a bite. It had started to drizzle again. There was a drier spot on the concrete a couple of stairs up, under an overhang, and I went and sat there. Just as I was looking in my backpack for the juice box I'd thrown into it, I heard Gina's voice.

"Gracie," she was saying. "Sorry. I just got here."

"Me too," I said.

"I just got to school, I mean," Gina said, sitting down next to me. "I kind of didn't make it this morning."

"Did you bring lunch?" I asked her.

Gina shook her head.

"Do you want the other half of my sandwich?" I asked. "It's nothing much, just Swiss cheese and lettuce. That's all we had in the house. It's all we ever have. Swiss cheese is the only thing my sister will ever eat for lunch, so my dad never buys any other lunch stuff." *How dorky can I get,* I thought, *telling Gina all this about the cheese in my sandwich?*

"Your sister's a cool little kid," Gina said. "I like her."

"She's okay," I said, offering Gina the half sandwich.

"You're sure you're not going to eat it?" she asked.

"Yeah, I'm not that hungry," I said. We sat together, looking out at the yard.

"Thanks for waiting," Gina said, sounding vulnerable in a way I hadn't heard her sound before.

"Sure. Mr. Hack kept us late and I was afraid I'd missed you."

We smiled at each other. "You have Hack?" she asked.

"Yeah. I had him last year too. He's not bad, but I don't really like American History," I ventured. Why didn't I have anything better to talk about?

"I have him too, but first period. I hardly ever get there," Gina said.

"Did he fail you last term?" I asked. "He really harps on attendance."

"I aced the final so he let me squeak through. I did all the reading."

I didn't know what to answer. Gina must be really smart, I thought, to ace the final without coming to class. I knew that everyone saw me as the girl who got As in everything, but I never thought of myself as that smart. I just studied a lot.

We sat eating our sandwiches in silence.

"So," Gina started. "So your sister said . . . your mom's dead?"

I didn't look at her. "Yeah," I said. Was it really that simple, after years of lying, to just say it?

"Was she the one who . . .?"

I didn't answer. I passed my juice box with its springy white straw bent at a ninety-degree angle to Gina. "Want some?" I asked her.

She took a sip. "It's so crazy, juice in a box," she said.

"Yeah."

It was raining more heavily now, and we moved farther back under the overhang. "My mom OD'd," Gina told me. "I was eight. I never found out if she really meant to die. She was doing so much heroin, she kept needing more and more. I found her when I came home from school."

"You found her dead?" I asked. "By yourself?"

Gina nodded. "She was all cold and stiff. The cops thought she'd been dead for, like, at least six or seven hours. Like it must have happened right after I'd left for school."

"Wow," was all I could think to say. "Where was your dad?"

Gina shrugged. "Nowhere. I don't know. It was kind of like now. Sometimes he was around and sometimes he wasn't."

I was silent.

"Did *your* mom do it on purpose?" Gina asked me.

She had figured it out. I hadn't even needed to tell her.

I looked at the kids pulling their jackets over their heads to shield themselves from the rain. *Probably all of them have mothers,* I thought. *Normal mothers who will make dinner for them tonight and ask them about their day.*

I kept looking at them, but I answered Gina. "Yeah," I said. "In a car." I hoped she couldn't hear me through all the noise of the school yard.

"She killed herself in a car?" Gina asked. "Carbon monoxide?"

"No," I answered, still not looking at her. "We were in Germany, at my grandma's. My mom took the car out one night and drove it down an embankment into a tree."

I had said it. I wanted to get up and run out of the yard.

As though she could sense it, Gina put a hand on my arm. "Shit," she said. "How did they know she did it on purpose?"

"She left a note. The cops found it. When they cleaned out the car."

"Wow," Gina said. "What did it say?"

"It just said 'I'm sorry.' In English and German."

"Wow," she said again. "How old were you?"

"Twelve and a half," I said. "And Jannie had just, like a few days before, turned five."

"She was so little," Gina said. I could feel her taking it in.

"Jannie was really different then, too," I said. "She couldn't talk, and she was always running away, and she screeched all the time. . . ."

"Did your mom do drugs?" Gina asked.

"I don't know," I told her. "She drank a lot."

We sat there not saying anything else. I didn't dare look at Gina. How could I just have told her all this, which I'd kept inside me for five years? I felt suddenly sick to my stomach.

At last Gina spoke. "I kind of figured it out," she said, "after that day, that talk in American Lit. When you got all intense at the end. I kind of thought you . . ."

I sat there wondering how to ask her to keep it secret. Gina turned toward me. "Hey, Gracie," she said. "Thanks for the sandwich. You know . . . all these kids in this school . . ." I could tell she knew I was anxious. "You know, she said, "I never talk to any of them. . . ."

I turned toward her and smiled a little. "Me neither," I told her.

The bell rang.

"You coming to class?" I asked her, and she nodded.

"What are we doing?" she asked.

"Steinbeck," I said. Gina reached for my hand as we walked to the building. "*Grapes of Wrath*," I told her.

"I love that word, *Wrath*," she said. She was holding my hand tight.

CHAPTER 16

2002

After that, Gina and I started meeting on the steps whenever she came to school, which wasn't regularly. We never actually said anything to each other about it; I would just go every day to that place on the steps and wait to see whether Gina would come. When she did, we sometimes talked a lot and sometimes just sat there talking only a little. Usually Gina brought only a bag of chips or a candy bar, so I would share my sandwich with her and we'd share the chips or candy.

One morning after we hadn't seen each other for several days I found another envelope taped to my locker with a poem in it:

Dope:

> *one shot*
>> *dizziness*
> *Two shots*
>> *emptiness*
>> *Passing out, maybe*
> *puking.*

Not mom.

   With mom

     it was hard to

  even tell

    anymore.

That's why

   she died.

I guess

    it's ignorant

      to blame myself

for what

   she did

    to herself.

That day Gina didn't come to the steps, and she wasn't in American Lit. Had she come to school just to leave me her poem? I wanted to talk to her about it.

I gave her our phone number. She wrote it down in the notebook she kept with her all the time, but told me she had no phone to call me from. Sometimes, she said, the manager of her building let her use his phone; but she didn't feel okay giving out his number.

Two days later she did come to find me at lunch. "Hey Gracie," she said. "I'm not really in school today. I mean, I'm not going to class."

"How come?" I asked.

She shrugged. "I don't know. I haven't done the work, so it's kind of dumb to sit there and not know what's going on."

"I could tell you what we're doing in Lit."

She shook her head. "It's okay. I just kind of wanted to see you."

I nodded. "Thanks for the poem," I told her.

"You read it?" she asked.

"Yeah," I said. "I thought . . . yeah, I mean, it was kind of . . . Do you really feel that way? I mean, do you really blame yourself?"

"For her dying?" Gina was watching an ant crawl on the lower step. "Yeah, like every day."

"Why?" I asked.

She shook her head. "I don't know. Like maybe I could have helped her more. Or I should have stayed home from school that day. Or I could have told somebody what was going on."

"Who would you have told?" I asked her.

Gina shrugged again. "I don't know. I have this auntie. She lives, like, in Cleveland now; but then she was just living in Vallejo or somewhere. She's my mom's sister. I could have told her."

"Told her what?"

"I don't know," Gina said. "Something. How fucked up my mom was. I mean, like she was shooting up all the time. Maybe my auntie would have cared."

"What about your dad?"

Gina laughed, but her laugh was more like a snort. "My dad? He's useless. He's worse of an addict than my mom was. He's just more selfish, and he does different shit, and so far he's been lucky it hasn't killed him."

I didn't ask Gina what she meant. I felt stupid, out of my element, as though I should have understood more than I did. As though if I were a cool kid I would know more about what Gina was talking about. More about drugs. *She knows I'm not cool,* I told myself; *and she still came to school today just because she wanted to see me.*

"Hey, Gracie," Gina started, "You know what's weird—I don't even know where you live."

"On Derby," I said.

"With your dad and Jannie?" Why was I surprised that she remembered Jannie's name?

I nodded. "And sometimes my dad's girlfriend. She actually stays there most of the time. She's really annoying," I volunteered. "She's so cheerful all the time it makes me want to throw up. I call her Miss Rosy Cheeks Farm-Bred . . . but just to myself. Her name's Kate. Sometimes I'm afraid I'll mess up and call her Rosy Cheeks to her face . . ."

Gina laughed a little but said nothing.

"How about you?" I asked after a while.

She shook her head, as though trying to shake something off. "We have a really small one-bedroom. My dad crashes in the living room, but he's only there some of the time. He got fucked up in Iraq, so he's on some kind of VA disability. That's what we live on, his disability. His leg got messed up, but his mind got way more messed up. He's out a lot, drinking and doing drugs." Gina waited a moment. "I like it better when he's not there."

I wondered what Gina ate, whether there was food in her apartment. What she and her dad talked about when he was there. *Not that my dad and I talk about anything much,* I thought.

We sat in silence for a little while. I thought of about a thousand things I could tell her, but I couldn't bring myself to tell her any of them. I hated myself for being so stingy and self-centered. Here she was telling me all this, and here *I* was, chewing my sandwich. "We have about five minutes 'til class," I said at last. "You sure you're not coming?"

Gina didn't answer. Instead she said, "Do you ever feel that way, Gracie?"

"What way?"

"Like I wrote in the poem. Like you should have done something to stop her."

"My mom? From killing herself?"

"Yeah."

I couldn't tell her. I felt like I needed to close up a seam that had split open. Gina was asking so many questions, and my habit of lying was too ingrained. I felt so confused; as soon as I spoke I regretted it.

"No," I lied to her. "Not really."

Gina sighed and stood up. There was a look on her face that was somewhere between sadness and anger, and I knew right then that my lie hadn't worked.

"Where are you going to go now?" I asked her.

She shrugged again. "I don't know."

We kept walking together in the direction of the building American Lit was in; it was clear to me that Gina didn't want to separate just yet, and I didn't either. But I didn't know what to say.

When we reached the building, I tried one more time. "You may as well come to class . . ."

"No," Gina said. "So . . . well, bye Gracie. See ya."

She turned. "Hey, Gina?" I called after her.

She looked at me. "Maybe you can come to my house some afternoon after school?" I said. "I mean, nobody's ever home until almost six. Not even Jannie. We could meet on the steps and walk together . . ."

"Sure," Gina said. But I wasn't sure she meant it.

CHAPTER 17

2017 / 2002

Last night I went to see a friend from work sing in a performance of the Brahms *Requiem*. The lines *Und alles Fleisch es ist wie Gras—And all flesh is like grass*—made me remember an afternoon during the months my mother took Jannie on me on that doomed trip.

We had arrived that morning by train in Paris, and were walking around aimlessly, as was Emmi's habit. By mid-afternoon we found ourselves, tired and hungry, in front of Notre Dame, where people were filing in for a concert. It was the Brahms *Requiem*, and Emmi told me it was one of her favorite pieces of music.

We sat in a pew between well-dressed Parisians, me in my overalls, Jannie with her hair unwashed for weeks. Emmi looking, as she probably was, drunk. Within moments of the concert beginning, Jannie started to shriek and Emmi told me I should stay in the cathedral while she took Jannie outside, and she would come and get me when the piece was over.

What made me trust Emmi puzzles me now; I was, in those months, never sure what she was doing, and certainly never sure she would come back from anywhere she went. But the music drew me, and I was glad she suggested I stay.

The choir began singing the dirge-like, cortege-like rhythms of *Und alles Fleisch,* and I—understanding German as I did—pondered what that might have meant. The image of grass growing in our neighbor's yard in Berkeley and being mowed down by their teenage son week after week came to me, and it seemed that maybe that was it: we grow and we are cut short. Again and again. No more important, no more remarkable, no more enduring, than blades of grass.

That phrase stayed with me long after the concert ended and I found Emmi sitting in front of the great cathedral, as she had promised she would, Jannie asleep in her arms. All flesh is like grass. That fragile, I thought last night at the much smaller Protestant church in San Francisco where my friend's choir performed it. That impermanent.

In those months when Emmi dragged Jannie and me through Europe, I kept writing post cards to my dad in Berkeley, telling him lies. Telling him nothing real about what was going on. Telling him we were fine and having a good time.

I never wrote him about Emmi's drinking. I never wrote him about the time Jannie ran through a café somewhere in Italy at such headlong speed that she knocked over a pile of glasses and glass shattered everywhere, and when Emmi tried to pull Jannie out of the corner where she had fallen, surrounded by shards of glass, Jannie bit her so hard she drew blood and both of them started shrieking and a whole crowd of people gathered around us, trying to calm them both, and I slipped out of the café and stood on the sidewalk wishing someone—anyone!—would take me home with them.

I never wrote Dad about Jannie's escapes. About how we were thrown out of one hotel after another when Jannie would run out of the room in the middle of the night, shrieking down the staircase, and Emmi would run shrieking after her, and everyone in the hotel would complain the next morning. I never wrote him about the time Jannie took off while we were in a park and Emmi left me there just in case she'd come back to where we'd been. I sat on a wooden bench for hours, long after dark, thinking I might never see my mother and sister again. And how at last when Emmi came back without Jannie I felt relieved, as though maybe finally we were rid of my crazy sister and my mother would be less crazy without her, and she and I would be close again and I would have my mother to myself as she'd been in the time before Jannie . . . And then Emmi told me that Jannie had been found by the police and she, Emmi, had only come back to get me so we could get into the police car that was waiting for us just outside the park; and the whole insane cycle began again.

I never wrote Dad about any of it. We were traveling from one city to another, day after day, with no plan and no reason, so there was no way he could have come after us. No way—it was the time before everyone had a cell phone—he could have found us. Emmi didn't want anything to do with him anyway; the task of keeping in touch with him was left up to me, and I understood that I needed to cover for my mother.

What if, even once, I had written him, *Dad, please do everything you can to track us down? Emmi is drinking all the time and either crying or raging or sleeping. Jannie keeps running away, sometimes for hours. I'm scared and confused and I keep thinking something terrible is going to happen.*

One night when we were at some hotel in France, Emmi left me and Jannie alone in the room and said she was going out for a minute to buy cigarettes. Jannie fell asleep, but I couldn't. Emmi was gone half an hour, then an hour, then an hour and a half. Had she been hurt? Killed? Had someone abducted her? Was she abandoning us? Would I have to go downstairs with Jannie in the morning and tell the man at the hotel desk that our mother hadn't come back, and would he please call our father in California?

I half-wanted that to happen, and I was half-terrified that it would. I lay in bed, holding Jannie for comfort. At last I heard Emmi's voice in the corridor, screaming at the concierge, who was slow finding the key to our room, since Emmi had apparently lost hers. Emmi was drunk, and the concierge was yelling back at her. I heard her puke in the hallway, and I turned my face to the wall.

I didn't want to see my mother when she walked into the room. I didn't want her to know I'd been awake and heard everything that had gone on in the corridor.

Why couldn't I bring myself to tell any of that to Gina? She must have thought my life was like 1950s TV: nice dad, nice dad's perky girlfriend, little sister who was cute and pretty even if she was a little weird. Nice middle class house on Derby Street.

There was, in the background, yes, a mother who had driven a car into a tree and committed suicide. But Gracie didn't feel guilty about it. Gracie never thought for a minute that she could have prevented it.

I was mad at myself. Here, for the first time in years, I had a friend, the first friend I'd made since Martin. And even to her I was unable to tell the truth.

I thought about Gina all the time. What was that look on her face between sadness and anger? My lying to her was useless; she guessed the truth anyway. Did it mean something that she hadn't held my hand as we'd walked to the building where Lit class was? Did she feel I had betrayed her?

I'll tell her, I promised myself. *The next time I see her I'll ask her over to my house and I'll tell her.*

But Gina didn't come to school for the rest of that week. It wasn't until that Saturday that I saw her.

Jannie was having a play date with a kid from her school, and she was going to be dropped off at home later that afternoon. Dad and Kate were at some kind of teachers' training, and I had the afternoon free until Jannie got home. I walked up to Telegraph with Lizzy, hoping to find Gina there, and I spotted her on the corner of Haste in front of Cody's Books.

Gina was standing with a group of street people who looked much older than we were. One of the women had a white bulldog with a rope for a leash, and he growled at Lizzy when Gina motioned me to come over. They were all smoking cigarettes.

"Hey, Gracie," Gina called. "Come over here." She could see me hesitate. "Don't worry about Rocky; he likes girl dogs. As soon as he smells her butt he'll be fine."

Rocky and Lizzy sniffed and circled each other. Gina offered me her cigarette but I shook my head no.

"Ida, JoJo, this is Gracie," she said to her friends. "Gracie goes to my school." I wasn't sure Gina knew the names of the other people she was standing with; if she did, she didn't introduce them. "What's up, Gracie?" she asked.

"Nothing," I said. "Just walking Lizzy."

"Just walking Lizzy?" Ida said.

I nodded. This was clearly not the time to invite Gina to come to my house. I felt very uncomfortable; I didn't belong in this world of Gina's. *Gracie goes to my school,* she had said: as though she needed to explain how she would even have the slightest connection to this preppy-looking blond girl who was obviously not a street person.

"Well, I should probably go," I said after a while. "I have to be home in a little while."

"Home," JoJo echoed. He was tall and wasted. I noticed his front teeth were missing. "You got to be home, girl? You got a nice home? You got room for us?"

"Hey," said Gina, pushing JoJo a little in a playful way. "Quit messing with her. She's my friend."

I walked home to Derby, running a little to make sure I'd get there before the Gersons brought Jannie home, thinking about what I'd seen. I was beginning to put together what I was learning about Gina's life. I wondered whether she spent most of her time on Telegraph with street people when she wasn't in school. I wondered how much her dad paid attention to her or whether their apartment was simply a place to crash. From that first day we'd met on the steps, Gina had never brought real food for lunch; I always shared what I brought, though she never asked for anything and she was always hesitant to accept what I offered.

It made me feel good to pack extra food in case Gina would show up. Kate probably noticed, since Kate noticed everything; but maybe she thought it was a sign that I had more appetite, though when Gina didn't show up I just threw the extra sandwich and fruit in the trash. I wondered what Gina ate besides the cheese sandwiches and apples I brought to school.

She's my friend, Gina had told JoJo. She had defended me to her friends, and I felt relieved.

CHAPTER 18

2002

I hadn't heard from Martin for months. Then one day I received a letter from him in his elegant German handwriting, which I tried to imitate but never could. The writing on the envelope looked smaller, shakier than usual, and I felt something was wrong even before I opened it.

Liebste Gracie, he wrote, *I have to tell you that the leukemia is back and I am in hospital for more chemotherapy. This time the treatment is very powerful and it makes me very sick. I am sorry not to have been able to tell you sooner, but I have been weak, even too weak to call you and talk. My mother finally brought me some paper yesterday and today is the first day I feel well enough to sit up and write to you. The worst thing is that my soccer team is playing a tournament this month and I cannot play with them. We have a good chance to be first but my teammates say they don't think they will win if I am not with them. I think they are just being kind, because Tomas is as good a goalie as I am, maybe even better, but I feel bad anyway because I would like to help them win. I need to go now but please write me soon. Your Martin.*

The news devastated me. Martin had been doing so well, had been declared to be in full remission! I felt terrible because I had not written to him for months. I had been so involved in my friendship with Gina—or in *thinking* about my friendship with Gina—that I had relegated Martin, I had to admit, to an outer orbit of my mind.

I hadn't wanted to tell him about Gina anyway. I suppose I didn't know how to explain my friendship with her. I didn't want to caricature Gina by telling Martin the concrete facts about her life; Gina was far more than that. She was hugely intelligent and she was a committed poet. And she was honest and defiant and straightforward in all the ways I was not. I didn't want to misrepresent her.

I had never mentioned Gina to my dad or to Kate, and I didn't feel like writing Martin about her either.

I was afraid Martin might be hurt that I had someone else I cared about. In the years since my mother killed herself, I had never made a single friend. I think I worried that Martin might write me something that would mar the good feeling I had about Gina, about my ability to talk to her in ways I couldn't talk to anyone else in my life, though even with her I still put up a wall.

It struck me that I had been lying to Martin as much as I lied to everyone else. And that, coupled with the fact that his cancer was back, made me feel even worse.

Dear Martin, I wrote him that evening, *I'm really sorry I haven't been in touch either. I had no idea you were sick again. I thought you were so busy playing soccer that you didn't have time to write. I figured once your tournament was over we'd start writing again.*

I've started to make friends with a girl named Gina who goes to my school, I began, and realized I didn't know how to go any farther. *She writes totally amazing poetry.* I decided to leave it at that. Another lie of omission, I thought. I continued a little, feeling I had to say something more, if only to fill up the rest of the page. Also, I didn't want to start leaving Martin out of whole dimensions of my life.

I had never been stuck for what to say to him before. I didn't want to hurt him and I didn't want to worry him. *I ran into Gina a few weeks ago when Jannie and I were taking a walk, I went on, and she and Jannie seemed to really connect. Of course, Jannie only wanted to talk to Gina about birds! But I was glad that Gina just accepted Jannie and told me later that she thought she was cool. Love and write to me, Gracie.*

I didn't hear from Martin for a few weeks after that, and every time I tried to phone him there was no answer at his house. I wondered whether my letter had reached him. I wondered whether he was hurt about Gina. I wondered what hospital he was at in Hamburg, where his letter was postmarked. I even looked up the names and addresses of all the hospitals in Hamburg, but there were so many I had no idea where to begin. I wrote down all the phone numbers but I couldn't imagine calling each one and asking if they had a patient named Martin Bachmann.

One day I came home to a postcard from Martin's mother. *Martin is still very ill,* she wrote, *but he asked me to write to you. He does not have the strength to write to you himself. He wants you to know that his team won the tournament and he wishes you would write to him. You may send letters in care of the below address, which is the home of a friend with whom Martin's father and I are staying in Hamburg. Martin will be so happy to hear from you.*

I copied the address and taped it to the wall over my desk. I wrote to Martin immediately, congratulating him for his team and letting him know that Jannie had won a prize at her school for an essay she'd written about the great blue heron. I told him Kate was living at our house practically all the time now and I wished she weren't. I told him I still found her efforts to get us to talk to each other so jarring, considering the way things had been before, that I wished she would stay at her own place more often.

At least, I wrote Martin, *I think she's good for Dad. She's completely different from Emmi. She really deserves the name Miss Rosy Cheeks Farm-Bred, which is why she annoys me; but she's not bipolar like Emmi was. I guess that's progress.*

I went on, *Maybe you'll meet her someday.* But the minute I wrote it I realized that that, too, was a kind of lie. Something inside me had already begun to know that Martin might never see *me* again, let alone Kate.

I didn't hear back from Martin. I started another letter to him a week later, deliberately leaving out Gina, telling him Kate had just planted spring vegetables in our garden, telling him about Jannie's birds and how they flew all over the house and stole anything shiny that was left lying around. I told him that Jannie had had her awards ceremony and was so proud of her trophy for the essay on the great blue heron that she told everyone about it, even the checkers at the grocery. It all seemed so chatty and cheerful it felt like I was turning into Kate. And it seemed, as well, even insensitive, given that Martin was lying in a hospital bed awaiting a bone marrow transplant. His mother had written me about that, and told me, "This will be his last chance."

I tore up the letter and started over. I wrote Martin about Gina and how she had offered me weed for the first time a few days earlier, and that I had smoked it and felt strange for a while afterward and hadn't really liked it. I told him I felt like a real dork, never having smoked weed before my junior year in high school. Then I had tried it a second time with Gina and one of her street friends, and it made me feel like everything was ten feet away and I could hear a kind of unsettling echo of my own voice from the inside when I talked. *That time,* I wrote Martin, *Gina walked me part way home when she realized I was feeling shaky; but I told her I was okay to walk the rest of the way by myself once we reached Shattuck Avenue. The real reason was that I thought Dad and Kate might be home, and I wasn't ready for them to meet Gina. I walked home,* I told Martin, *still feeling really weird and on top of that, feeling like a shitty friend. Gina had wanted to take care of me and I was—what? ashamed of her?*

I tore up that letter too.

I sat at my desk, biting my pen. *Martin,* I wrote on the third sheet of paper, *I'm worried about you. I'm seriously worried because I know if you were feeling any better you would have written to me by now. Your mom told me about the bone marrow transplant. I hope you get it soon and it cures the leukemia. Please get better so you can play soccer again. Please don't die, Martin,* I wrote, *because if you die I will lose the only person in the world who has really known me. Love, Gracie.*

I went out into the chilly night with Lizzy and walked two blocks to the nearest mailbox and threw in the letter, afraid if I didn't do it then I might think about it in the morning and never mail it.

CHAPTER 19

2002

Gina and I had started seeing each other nearly every day. If she didn't come to school and meet me for lunch on the steps, I took Lizzy up to Telegraph Avenue after school and looked for her. It wasn't hard to find Gina; she was usually hanging out with her friends on the corner of Haste or sitting in the park. Sometimes we stayed there. Sometimes we walked or took the bus to my house.

Sometimes we smoked weed. I was more used to it now and, if I didn't smoke more than a little, it didn't make me so shaky. Sometimes we stood around talking to JoJo, who had accepted me now, or Ida, who turned out to be in her fifties and had amazing stories about being a crab fisherman when she was young, before she'd gotten strung out on meth.

One afternoon at the end of the school day it started to rain heavily, unexpectedly. Gina and I had agreed to meet that day after each of our last classes. I had a big paper due the next day and had told her I probably shouldn't do anything but go home and finish writing it, so we had agreed to just see each other for a minute.

Within minutes it was pouring and Gina and I were soaked. "Hey

Gina," I said, "Let's just go to my house, okay? I can give you some dry clothes."

Gina hesitated. "What about your paper?"

I thought for a minute. "I'll have enough time to work on it after dinner."

We walked to my house as fast as we could, and let Lizzy into the backyard to pee while I boiled some water for tea. We were freezing and soaked to the skin. We went up into my room and I pulled open a drawer. It was stuffed with unfolded shirts and jeans.

"Here, pick anything you like," I told her.

"Wow, that's a shitload of clothes," Gina said.

From the first time she'd come, it was weird seeing my house through Gina's eyes. Today was the worst, though: All I could see were signs of comfort, signs that we were your regular normal middle-class family. Too much stuff. Too many clothes, too much furniture, too much food in the fridge we opened for snacks, too many kinds of crackers in the cupboard, even too many different brands of dog treats.

And it was weird seeing Gina in what she'd picked out: my black jeans and my SF Giants T-shirt. She was taller and skinnier than me, for one thing, and the jeans were a little short and baggy on her. We wore the same shoe size, and I opened my closet to find a pair of running shoes to lend her since hers were drenched; and I felt embarrassed about the number of pairs of shoes on my closet floor.

"What the fuck, Gracie, do you guys own a shoe store?"

"Some of them I've had since middle school. I've worn the same shoe size forever . . ." I fumbled for something to excuse the obvious fact that my family had enough money to keep buying shoes. Gina was already sitting on the floor, stretching her long legs and tying the laces on my eighth-grade orange Adidas.

She turned back toward the closet. "Hey, Gracie, what's in these boxes? More shoes?"

I walked over to the closet to see what she meant. Pushed against the back, behind the shoes, were three large identical packing boxes. "Oh, that's Emmi's stuff," I told her. "My dad sorted out some of her things that he thought I might want sometime. I don't even really know what's in there."

"You've never opened them?"

"Not really. I looked in one of them once, just took off the lid. It has some of her journals in it, a bunch of blue notebooks. And I think jewelry. Bracelets and stuff."

"Don't you want to know what's there?" Gina was incredulous. "I mean, when my mom died, she left nothing. Nothing. All she had was a couple of T-shirts and some jeans that were so old we just threw them in the garbage. Oh, and this," Gina showed me her hand. There was a thin green glass ring on her pinky. I'd noticed it before. "I took it off her hand before they took her body away. She always told me it was her wedding ring, and it probably was. I think my dad found it lying on the street."

I didn't know what to say.

"Shit, Gracie, I'd die to have three big boxes of my mom's stuff. I'd look at it every day of my life."

I looked at the boxes. Dad had brought them into my room one night shortly after he'd brought Jannie and me back from Germany. He had been putting most of Emmi's clothes and books in boxes for days, to give away. The boxes had stood in my closet for four years, unopened. I hadn't even thought much about them.

Gina sat down on my bed with me and took my hand in hers. "Gina," I said, "do you remember that time when you asked me if I felt responsible for my mom's death? If I blamed myself, or something like that?"

"Yeah," Gina said.

"And I said no."

"I remember," she said.

I took a deep breath and looked out the window. The rain was still pouring down.

"Well, I was lying," I told her. She nodded her head. "I was totally lying," I repeated.

Gina was silent.

"The whole time we were in Europe on that crazy trip," I went on, "I felt it was my job to keep my mom alive. Jannie too, but Jannie was like a part of my mom, like they were a single unit, like Jannie had never really left my mom's womb. And I felt outside, I mean *really* outside, of whatever dark place they were in together, and I felt I was supposed to keep them safe and alive."

Gina nodded and squeezed my hand.

"When I was little once, long before Europe," I continued, "I saw a movie about two little kids who were wandering in a field and suddenly they got stuck in quicksand. One of them, the smaller one, was sinking quickly—the other a little more slowly, but definitely sinking—and it seemed as though that was the way the movie was going to end, and I could barely watch it. I remember I was watching it by myself. Jannie was a baby and Emmi and Dad were upstairs trying to get her to take a nap, and she was screaming. And I didn't want to hear Jannie's screaming so I kept watching the movie even though it terrified me, and the children were sinking and the younger one's whole chest was in the quicksand. And suddenly this man came along on a horse and he saw the kids. And he had a rope hanging around his saddle, a strong rope, and he tied one end to the horse and somehow got the other end around the top of the little one's chest. And he told the horse to back up, and the horse did. At first nothing happened and I was afraid the horse, too, would be pulled into the quicksand; but then, little by little, the smaller kid began to come out; and when she was out the man threw the rope to the other kid, and he was pulled out too."

Gina was listening more attentively than anyone had ever listened to me.

"When we were on that horrible trip, I thought about that movie all the time. I kept having images of those two kids sinking, and the horse stepping backward, pulling them out. And I thought *I have to be that horse.*"

I started to cry. Gina put her arm around my shoulder. It was funny smelling my own laundry soap on her. "You smell like me," I said through my tears, and we both giggled.

"I wasn't sure I could do it," I started again, watching the rain, not daring to look at Gina for fear I would totally fall apart. "Be that horse, I mean. And, of course, I couldn't."

"You must have done it for a while," Gina said softly.

"Maybe. Maybe a little."

"And Jannie is cool. You kept Jannie from sinking."

I shook my head. "I didn't do anything for Jannie," I said. "My oma helped her, and then my dad when we came home."

"But sometimes, when your mom was drinking and stuff, you must have taken care of her. . . ."

I thought a moment. "I guess. Maybe sometimes."

"You're so hard on yourself, Gracie," Gina said, taking my chin in her hand and turning my face away from the window. "You're hard on yourself about everything."

I started to cry again, and Gina held me. "Gracie," she started after a while.

"Yeah?"

"If you want to see what's in the boxes, I'll do it with you."

I thought for a moment, then nodded. I looked at the clock on my night table; we had about an hour before Dad and Kate would be home. "Maybe one of them?" I asked tentatively.

She looked at me intensely. "It's up to you, Gracie. It's totally up to you. It's *your* mom."

We got down on our knees and extracted the box that was farthest back.

"You open it, Gina," I told her.

Gina opened it.

There was Emmi's green woolen winter coat, which took up much of the space. Under it, a long black velvet skirt.

"Wow," Gina said, "Your mom must have been quite the dresser." She held it up to admire it.

"You can have it," I told her. I suddenly felt nothing. Nothing at all.

Gina put the skirt down. "No, Gracie," she said. "I can't take your mother's skirt. It's yours."

"I'll never wear it," I said.

"That's not the point," Gina said, folding the skirt and laying it carefully, as though it could disintegrate, on my bed. *What a dumb idea this was,* I thought, and almost asked Gina to put the box back.

"Let's see what else is here," she said.

She pulled out a plastic bag filled with colored beads.

"Oh my god," I said, "Emmi's necklaces! I forgot about them! She wore those all the time."

"They're so cool, Gracie," Gina said, taking them out one by one, laying them alongside one another. "Look! Silver beads. I bet this one's from Mexico. And this one—look, it has little animals on it, like Native American totems."

"Emmi was kind of a freak about Native American stuff," I told her.

"She even had one of those flutes; I don't know what happened to it. She had this whole thing about the Navajo and the Hopi . . . you know, coming from Germany and all that, she could just romanticize it and, you know, appropriate it, without feeling guilty . . ."

"How was it for her that your dad was Jewish?" Gina asked. "How was it for *him*?"

I shrugged my shoulders. "I have no idea. I was too young to ask her, and my dad never talks about anything."

Gina was trying on one of the necklaces. She passed another to me. "Here," she said, "Let me see how you look in this one."

It was purple, amethyst. Long. I put it on.

"Is it weird for you, Gracie," Gina asked, "to be both German and Jewish?"

I shrugged again. "I kind of never think about it," I said. "But I remember wondering once whether the fact that Jannie has autism and I'm . . . kind of strange myself . . . was like a punishment, a curse, for my parents marrying each other. But that was when I was, like, ten, and I was reading *The Diary of Anne Frank*. Mostly I just don't think about it."

"There's a lot you don't think about, Gracie," Gina said. "Or maybe you think about it, but you never talk about it."

I had no answer for her. Gina was looking at herself in the mirror above my dresser.

"Hey, Gracie," she turned, "That necklace looks great with your eyes," Gina said. "Come look in the mirror."

I looked and remembered Emmi wearing it. Gina was piling on several necklaces now, one longer than the next. "Your mom had so many of these," she said. "Did she really wear them all?"

"Those look awesome with the Giants T-shirt," I said. "I remember her wearing some of them," I answered. "Maybe she'd stopped

wearing others. I don't know. They're all kind of too much. . . . Like
my mom. Kind of too much."

Gina slipped the necklaces back into the bag. "Stop being so . .
. sort of sarcastic, Gracie. It's like you're trying so hard not to feel
anything."

I said nothing.

"It's sad they're just lying here. They're nice," Gina said. "You
should keep some out and wear them. They're like, *abandoned,* in
here."

I thought a moment. "Like Jannie and me," I said. "Abandoned."

Gina looked at me in that intense way again. "You have your dad,"
she said. "He's an okay dad."

Gina's dad, I thought, was different. Not an okay dad. I suddenly
felt spoiled and self-indulgent next to her.

"Yeah," I told her. "He's okay."

"It must be really hard," Gina continued after a while, "to *know*
your mom deliberately left you. Like with my mom I can still hold on
to the possibility that it was an accident. Like she didn't really want
to kill herself, she didn't mean to OD. She loved me enough to want
to stay alive."

"Emmi wasn't in her right mind when she did it," I said, not looking at Gina.

"Of course she wasn't," Gina said.

We didn't say anything for a while. Then Gina looked at the clock.
"I should go," she said. "It's not raining that hard anymore, and your
dad and Kate and Jannie will be home soon."

I nodded. "You'll walk to your place?" I asked her.

"There or the Avenue," Gina said. "I'm not sure yet."

"I could lend you a rain jacket,' I said. "We have about a million."

Gina smiled. "I believe it," she said. "You should wear that necklace," she said. "It really does look good on you. With your blue eyes. It makes them look kind of violet."

I fingered the amethyst necklace. "Okay," I said. Then, "Gina? You know what hurts?"

"What?"

"I bet if I walk around wearing this, Dad won't even notice it. I bet he won't even remember it was Emmi's."

Gina shrugged. "It's a really nice necklace, Gracie," was all she said.

She stood up and walked to the doorway of my room. Lizzy, who had been in the room all the time, dozing on my bed, jumped off and walked over to her.

I went to the hall closet and took out an old nylon rain jacket. "Here," I said. "This should work."

"I'll give it back to you at school," Gina said.

"Hey Gina?" I started.

"Yeah?"

"Next time would you be willing to look at some of Emmi's journals with me?"

Gina smiled at me. "Sure, Gracie," she said.

We walked to the front door and I watched Gina go down the street. At the corner she turned in the direction of Telegraph.

CHAPTER 20

2002

I was right about Dad not noticing the necklace: for the next three days I wore it and he didn't say a thing.

Kate noticed it, but of course she had no idea where it had come from. "Nice necklace, Gracie," she'd said the first morning I'd put it on. "Is it new?"

"Not really," I said. "I had it lying around for a while." End of conversation.

Late the following week I came down to dinner and found that Nick, who had been Jannie's after-school babysitter when I was still in middle school, was talking to Dad and Jannie in the living room. Kate was putting together a salad, and, not feeling much like talking to Nick, I decided to help her in the kitchen.

"How come Nick's here?" I asked her.

"Your dad invited him. He thought it would be nice for you and Jannie to see him."

"What does Nick have to do with me?" I asked, irritated. "He was Jannie's babysitter, not mine."

Kate shrugged and went on rinsing lettuce. "He just thought it would be nice to have someone over."

I had no answer. I didn't particularly want to talk to anyone. I had been trying to write a paper for American Lit on Whitman, and I was having trouble with it. Also I was worried about Gina: I hadn't seen her since that time in my room nearly two weeks before, though the morning after I'd found a crumpled white paper bag with my shirt and jeans and the rain jacket in it next to my locker. She hadn't come to class that day, nor all the days since.

I had even gone looking for her on Telegraph and had run into Ida, and she'd told me she hadn't seen Gina either.

I noticed a ring on the window sill and realized it was the one that had belonged to Dad's mother, my grandmother Gertrude, who had died just before I was born.

"What's that ring doing there?" I asked Kate. It was a round, faceted blue sapphire surrounded by tiny diamonds that made a kind of flower pattern around it.

"Oh, I always take off my rings when I get my hands wet," Kate said casually. "Otherwise they slip off and go down the drain. Or the stones come loose."

"That's yours?" I asked her. "It looks like a ring my grandmother Gertrude left my dad," I tried to say equally casually.

Kate was silent for a moment. She kept washing the lettuce. "It *is*, Gracie," she said. "Your dad gave it to me for my birthday last week."

I didn't know what to say. I picked up the peeler and zipped the peel off a carrot. "It was your birthday?" I asked her.

"Last Tuesday," Kate said. "I didn't come over because I had a meeting that night and all these papers to grade. . . ." I could tell she was uncomfortable. "He brought it to school Tuesday morning wrapped in aluminum foil with the lunch he made me. He told me to save it for last. I thought it was going to be a cookie," she smiled.

"That was my Grandma Gertrude's," I said. I didn't know what else to say. "The grandma I never knew. They named me after her—Grace, since it started with a G."

I was suddenly furious. I hated that Dad had done something so playful and imaginative for Kate. I wanted to hurt her. "My dad tried to give it to Emmi once, but she didn't want it. It wasn't her style. She thought it was ugly."

I was making it all up. I was Gracie the Fantastic Liar again, and I didn't care.

Kate said nothing. She put the lettuce leaves in the salad spinner and spun them dry.

"Did *you* want the ring, Gracie?" she asked me finally. Her tone was sharp. I'd never seen her this way before. "Because if you did, you can have it right this minute."

"No," I told her. "You can keep it. I hate that ring. It's not *my* style either."

"It isn't . . ." Kate began after a while, "It's not—it doesn't mean your dad and I are engaged or anything. . . ."

I glared at Kate and threw the slices of carrot into the salad. "I don't give a shit if it does," I told her.

We chopped and rinsed in silence. A few minutes later Nick walked into the kitchen.

"Can I help with anything?" he asked. "Oh, hi Gracie."

"Hi, Nick," I said, not looking up.

"How are you doing?" he asked.

"Okay, I guess. Studying, writing papers."

"Junior year," Nick said, shorthand for *lots of work*. "It'll be over in a couple of months."

"If I survive it," I said. "You almost done?"

"Not too much longer. Two years of college down, just about."

I knew Nick was majoring in Lit. When he'd babysat Jannie I'd sometimes talked to him about the books I was reading. He'd turned me on to some of the best novels I'd read. He never treated me like I was three years younger than him, which I was. I'd always found him pretty easy to talk to, unlike almost everyone else.

I hadn't seen him in a long time, though, and on top of what had just happened with Kate, it felt awkward to have him there.

When we sat down at the table I couldn't take my mind off Kate's ring, back on her finger. I didn't say a single word to her all through dinner. Kate's fingers were long and thin, like Emmi's had been. I guessed my Grandma Gertrude's had been the same, since the ring fit Kate perfectly. My fingers were also long and thin, but I wore a thick silver and turquoise ring I'd bought with babysitting money one afternoon when I'd been with Gina on the Avenue. I told myself the sapphire and diamond ring wasn't anything I would ever have worn, but I was livid that Dad had given it to Kate, livid that Kate had accepted it. *If it belonged to anyone it should have been Emmi,* I thought. *That ring should be in the ground. It should have been buried with Emmi.*

Nick was talking about college. "You should come with me sometime in the fall, Gracie, and sit in on one of my Lit classes," he said, and I'd nodded. I wondered suddenly whether Nick had been part of a plan Kate had devised to get me to socialize with someone and to get me interested in college. Two birds with one stone. "Maybe," I told him.

When he left, he mentioned a party he and his housemates were planning to have on a Sunday evening in the middle of June. He called it a strawberry party because apparently they had a huge strawberry patch in the garden of the house they rented, and every year at the party the people in the house and all their friends made jam and strawberry shortcake. "You should come, Gracie," he said, "I think you'd like some of my friends."

What would they want with a high school kid, I thought; and I felt more confirmed in my guess that this was Kate's plan to get me out of the house more. *At least she doesn't seem to have a clue that I've been hanging out with Gina and her druggie street friends,* I thought.

"Sure," I told Nick. "Just let me know when it is."

I had no intention of going.

CHAPTER 21

2002

To celebrate Jannie having won the essay contest at school, Dad had let her convince him to buy her a third green-cheeked conure, one of the babies we'd seen that day at the bird store. She named her Annie, after her favorite teacher.

From the beginning I couldn't stand Annie. I conceded that she was charming: Dad and Kate really liked her. She was more social than Pablo and Isabella, who were more into each other. Annie wanted attention from humans all the time. She asked for it noisily, and she was totally willful.

She was also better at stealing than any of Jannie's other birds. When I went upstairs that night after Nick left, I couldn't find a silver chain necklace I'd put on the bathroom shelf. It was a necklace Gina had given me one day; she'd told me she'd found it lying on the street and she wanted me to have it in exchange for all the food I'd given her. I wondered a little if Gina had shoplifted it; she'd told me once that she shoplifted from time to time, and the necklace looked new and gleaming.

No one but Kate, of course, ever noticed it; and she never asked how I'd gotten it, though I had a story prepared about babysitting money if she did. I treasured the necklace because it came from Gina, and only took it off when I showered, afraid I would tarnish it. That evening, somehow, I'd forgotten to put it back on.

"Jannie!" I screamed at her through the closed door to her room, "Your fucking bird stole my necklace!"

Jannie had been asleep for some time. I pushed open her door and turned on the overhead light.

"What?" she sat up, silently blinking.

"Your bird stole my necklace," I said. "Let me look in her cage."

"She's sleeping," Jannie protested. "Her cage is covered."

"I don't give a shit," I told her. "She took my necklace." I walked in and ripped the cover off Annie's cage.

"Stop it, Gracie!" Jannie screamed at me. "How do you know she took it?"

"She always takes stuff. They all do. All your fucking birds. But she's the worst!"

"Leave her alone!" Jannie was sobbing. I rifled through Annie's cage. She fluttered, flew against the bars. "You'll hurt her!" Jannie screamed at me.

Dad appeared in the doorway. "What's going on?"

"Jannie's bird stole my necklace and I'm trying to find it."

"You have to do that now?" Dad asked. "It can't wait 'til morning? Jannie was sleeping."

"My birds were sleeping too!" Jannie sobbed.

"Just let me look in the fucking cage," I said sulkily, "since everyone's already awake." I kept rifling through Annie's bedding. All the birds in the room were now screeching and ruffling their wings. Jannie was screeching and flapping her arms. *Just like one of her birds,* I thought. Kate, in her plaid flannel nightgown, her hair loose, stood in the doorway behind Dad, saying nothing.

In the far corner of Annie's cage, buried under the bedding, I found the silver chain. I pulled it out, blew scraps of bird bedding off of it, and walked silently out of the room.

"Gracie—" Dad took my arm and tried to stop me but I ran down the hallway into my room, slamming the door. I could hear Jannie sobbing. Kate comforting her. Dad telling her gently that she needed to keep the door to her room closed if she wanted her birds to fly freely.

"That's not enough, that's not enough space for them," she was sobbing. "That's not enough."

I put the necklace back on. *Gina, where are you?* I asked silently. *Where are you?*

I still went every day to the steps, hoping for Gina to come. Mr. B. even asked me one day after Lit Class whether I'd seen her—how had he figured out we were friends?—and I told him I hadn't, and I was worried. That was more than I'd thought I'd admit to him, and I kind of surprised myself by tearing up a little. "I'll let you know if I hear anything, Gracie," he said. I went into a stall in the girls' bathroom and cried silently by myself.

I was afraid I had put Gina off by letting her come to my house full of stuff. By looking through Emmi's box with her. By disparaging my dad, when her dad was a million times worse.

Then, on a Thursday afternoon the following week, Gina was sitting in her seat in American Lit when I walked into the classroom. She looked thinner, and she had bleached her hair and then dyed it again. Some of it was bleached-out blondish; some was blue and some was bright green. She was clutching a sheaf of papers and seemed so agitated I thought she might be about to take off.

I walked up to her, trembling inside. "Hey, Gina," I said.

"Hey Gracie." She was smiling at me. "I got all my work done. Mr.

B. said if I handed it all in by today, he wouldn't fail me. I wrote a bunch of poems for extra credit. I copied out one for you," she told me, and handed me an envelope.

I slipped it into my backpack. "Is it okay if I read it later?" I asked her.

"Sure," Gina said. She sounded sad and tired.

"You okay?" I asked her. Other kids were beginning to file into the room and take their seats.

"Kind of," Gina put her head down and began rifling through her sheets of paper. "Sorry I've been MIA," she said quietly, not looking at me.

"That's okay," I said. Then, "I missed you." I couldn't believe I'd said it.

"I missed you too," she said. "You have time after school?"

"Today?" I asked.

"Yeah."

"Sure," I said.

"Meet on the steps?" Gina asked, and I nodded.

"Could we go back to your house?" she asked. I was surprised. Mr. B. was about to start, and he motioned me to my seat. Why hadn't he told me Gina had gotten in touch with him? He had promised. If he'd made a bargain with her about not failing her, they must have had contact. Had Gina asked him not to tell me?

"I don't feel like going to the Avenue," Gina added.

"Sure," I said again, and walked to my seat.

Before my next class I went into the bathroom, shut myself in a stall, and pulled Gina's poem out of its envelope.

Isn't it

    funny

how nobody can

        understand

    your inner

        struggle

when you spend

        so long trying

    to get them to

hear you?

        I guess

I have thought

    about the

easy way

    out,

        especially when

Dad is in his

    meth state.

But I try

    not to let

        him frighten

me.

    I like to think

I can be

    tough.

Gina's poem scared me. Now my whole body was trembling. I could barely sit through my next two classes, and when the last bell finally rang I raced to the steps to make sure Gina would find me the minute she got there. I was half afraid she wouldn't come.

She was running toward me, and waved to let me know she saw me.

"I read your poem," was the first thing I said to her.

"Yeah," Gina said.

"Are you okay?" I wished I could find something else to ask.

Gina's face darkened. "Does it sound like I'm okay?" she said bitterly.

"Sorry," I said.

Gina was silent for a moment. Then, "No, *I'm* sorry, Gracie. I didn't mean to get mad at you." She stopped, then continued. "I didn't mean to disappear on you. It had nothing to do with you."

I smiled. I was still stinging from her sarcasm, and I knew Gina could feel it.

"Things have been really crappy lately, Gracie. I've got . . . kind of a short fuse. I'm really sorry."

I nodded. "Should we walk?" I asked, and we gathered up our things.

We walked among the crowd of kids moving in different directions on the yard. Everyone going to their separate place. Like living cells moving under a microscope. It felt like we were totally outside that movement, as though everyone belonged to a distinct universe with its own mores and language, and Gina and I were mute voyeurs.

I didn't know what to say. Gina was clenching her hands. Opening them, then clenching them again. I remembered that that was one of the things Emmi had done in her last months, and it frightened me.

Finally, after we'd walked a block or two, she began, "I have to get out of here."

"What do you mean, Gina?" I asked. "Do you mean like it is in your poem, the easy way out?"

Gina said nothing. She looked at her hands, clenched and opened them. Looked at them intensely.

"What are you talking about, Gina? Do you feel like killing yourself?" I asked.

She said nothing. Kicked a bottle top that was in her path.

"What's happening with your dad?" I insisted. "What do you mean, when he's in 'his meth state'?"

Gina took a deep breath. "I can't really talk about it."

I stopped walking and turned to her. "Why not, Gina? I told you so much about my mom."

"So it's supposed to be, like, now I have to pay for what you told me?" she flashed. "You just told me *things*, Gracie. I have no idea at all what you *feel*."

Now I was angry too. "I just mean, Gina, if we're friends . . ."

She looked at me. "Are we, Gracie? Are we friends?" She sounded plaintive and lost.

"I really care about you, Gina," I told her, and there were tears in my eyes.

"Me too, Gracie," she said after a while.

We kept walking. "Is your dad beating you, Gina?"

Silence.

"Did you tell Mr. B.? He'd have to report it."

"So would your parents, right? If you said anything to them?"

"*Kate* isn't my parent," was the first thing I said. I felt stupid the minute it was out of my mouth. Then I said, more softly, "Yeah, they would, since they're teachers." I was silent for a moment. "But Kate and my dad . . . they don't even know you exist."

"That makes me feel really great," Gina said, the bitterness in her voice again. "Gina, Gracie's hidden friend. Get me out of there fast, before your parents come home. Oh, excuse me, *not* your parents.

Your dad and his girlfriend. You'd like to hide her too, like she doesn't really exist. And your sister, who you also seem to be ashamed of. Maybe Jannie's the one who should be my friend . . . or Kate . . ."

"Stop it, Gina," I said, tears running down my cheeks. "I'm sorry. I'm really sorry. I never meant you to feel like that. I just . . ."

"Just what? Didn't want to let your parents know that the one friend you've made is the kid of a meth addict? Who smokes weed and hooks up with street people?"

I was amazed that Gina kept walking with me.

"Why did you ever let me come to your house in the first place?" she pressed on.

"Why did you want to come *today*?" I asked her through my tears.

Gina hesitated. "I don't know. Maybe I don't feel like going up to the Avenue. Or maybe I just wanted to see if you'd let me."

"I want you to come to my house, Gina," I said. "I want you to come."

She said nothing.

"You can stay as long as you want," I said.

"No, Gracie," Gina said, very calmly. "No. I'll leave today before they come home. Just like I always do. Maybe another time I'll stay, after you've let them know I exist. Today I should get back to my dad before it's late, anyway. He kind of needs me to be there."

I was totally confused. "What's happening with your dad, Gina?" I asked.

"He's trying to detox," she said. "He's really sick. He's trying to do it himself, which is nuts. And it won't last more than a couple of weeks; it'll be a total waste. He's such a fucking addict."

"Does he do . . . anything to you when he's on meth, Gina?"

Gina stopped walking and looked at me. "Gracie, I'm not going to give you any information you'll have to pass on to your dad and Kate, okay? Or to Mr. B., who's asking the same questions you are. My dad is not beating me and he's not fucking me, okay? There's nothing to report."

"I wasn't asking you because of reporting," I said. "I was asking because I care about you. I want to know what's going on. I want to know what you're dealing with, Gina."

"My dad is a meth addict. When he takes too much meth he screams and breaks things. But look, Gracie—" Gina rolled up her sleeves "—there are no marks on me. My dad doesn't beat me."

I was silent. I wasn't convinced. If Gina wasn't being abused, what was the urgency about her leaving?

She went on as though she had heard my thoughts. "I can't stand living with him. He's not hurting me, but I can't stand it anymore. And anyway, there are . . . other reasons I need to get away from here. I want to live where I can just be a normal person. But now my dad is so sick from his detox attempt, I can't just walk out on him. I don't even know if I'll find him alive any time I come home."

"Where could you go, Gina?" I asked her. There was more to this than she was telling me, but she was obviously not going to say what it was.

"Remember I told you I have this auntie in Cleveland? I'm trying to get together enough money so I can go live with her. Or at least stay with her for a while."

"Can't she just send you the plane fare?" I asked.

Gina flashed around again, angry. "What do you think, Gracie? That everyone in the world has as much money as you?"

"I don't have a lot of money!" I almost yelled at her. "You know my house! It's not a big fancy house in the hills. My dad teaches high school!"

Gina stopped walking and turned to face me. "Gracie," she started, "you live in a house. You have a million pairs of shoes and jackets, your sister has a million exotic birds, your dad pays you to babysit her, he and his girlfriend go to concerts and drive cars. You're rich, Gracie Levine."

I had nothing to say. I was sorry I'd ever invited Gina to my house. But how could we be friends if our friendship was confined to school and the Avenue? Hidden, as Gina said.

It was the first time I'd ever thought about myself in terms of social class. I felt young and sheltered and ashamed. Gina was so much more sophisticated than I was.

"Does your auntie know you want to come stay with her?" I asked.

"I haven't really . . . been in touch with her for a while," Gina's voice was softer. "But I know she'd let me come."

"She's your mom's sister?" I asked, though I knew the answer.

Gina nodded. "Only she's much younger than my mom, and they had different dads. She was an addict too, but she did NA and got clean. I think she works in some kind of Walmart or something."

I didn't know what to say. I didn't want Gina to go anywhere. I suddenly felt that all I wanted to do was keep her with me, with all my might.

"Gina," I asked her, "Are you going to . . . take your finals?"

"I don't know," she said.

"I can help you with some of the stuff if you want. American Lit. Chem."

She looked at me. "I haven't been to Chem for like, half the semester. That's a lost cause. But American Lit, yeah. Sure. I did all my papers. Mr. B. likes my poems."

"He's read them?" I asked. "The ones about drugs? the one about . . ."

"Suicide?" Gina completed the sentence for me. "Yeah, a couple of those. I was pretty selective about what I gave him. He ran into me one afternoon last week on the street, totally by accident, and he told me if I turned in all my papers he'd forgive my absences. He told me you had asked about me . . ."

I nodded.

"But I asked him not to say anything to you," Gina said.

He'd honored her request over mine. Made a choice. I got it. "Was he, like—"

"Worried about me? Yeah. He was. I didn't tell him . . . everything that was going on, but he got that I've been feeling crappy. He said he would read everything I wrote. Anything. And he gave me the name of some clinic or something, to see a counselor. I wrote it down."

"Did you call them?"

Gina shook her head. "There's too much happening." I didn't ask what she meant.

"Gina, you know what's weird?" I said. "I have no idea where you live, except that once you said West Berkeley."

Gina looked at me. "Yeah," she said. "West Berkeley." She was silent again for a moment. "Okay, Gracie. I'll let you have my address. But don't just . . . don't just show up, all right?"

When we got to my house, we were both too drained to do anything except watch some mindless cartoon videos we had lying around since I was little. We sat together on the couch, Lizzy at our feet. We didn't mention Emmi's boxes or her journals. We had already been through enough.

At five o'clock Gina sat up and started putting her shoes on. "I'm going to go now," she said softly.

"Okay," I said. "You don't have to," I said.

She stood. Then she bent over and touched my hair. Then she kissed it. "Bye, Gracie Levine," she whispered to me. "I'll meet you on the steps tomorrow."

CHAPTER 22

2002

I wrote Martin's mother asking whether the bone-marrow transplant had happened. I heard nothing back. I told myself Martin had had the transplant and he was slowly getting better and his mom was too involved in his recovery to sit down and write me. The transplant had worked, I told myself. Martin was walking again. I pictured him in his hospital pajamas, taking slow, hesitant steps at first down the hospital corridor and then walking faster, then kicking a soccer ball all the way down the length of the corridor to a young pediatrician who kicked it back to him, annoying the nurses but making the other kids on the ward, sicker than Martin, smile. I told myself that Martin would write me, would be okay.

On the last morning of regular classes I found another envelope taped to my locker. Gina had come to school every day for about a week after that day at my house; but this week she hadn't appeared at all. I'd been too tied up studying to go looking for her on Telegraph; but I'd started to worry about her again.

I opened the envelope right away, standing there in the hall, my hands shaking, suddenly afraid it might be a suicide note. I was flooded with the memory of the night the police came to Oma's house and told her they'd found Emmi's note in the wreckage of her car, "I'm sorry" in English and German; and how I'd sat on Oma's big bed between Martin and his mother, my whole body wracked with sobs.

I unfolded the paper:

Loneliness.

> *But I guess when*
>> *the world turns*
> *to shit, though,*

you don't
> *really need to feel*
>> *welcome anymore.*

When Bo left
> *I realized I could*
>> *survive being*
the only person
> *who cared*
>> *about me*

anymore.

I didn't know what to make of it. I felt angry and hurt. Gina and I had gotten so much closer: didn't she know how much I cared about her? How could she just trash our friendship, trash *me*, as though I wasn't a part of her world?

Had she gotten back together with Bo—whoever he was—and been dumped? Gina had barely spoken to me about Bo. All I knew was that he was a dope fiend like her dad and he and Gina had been together on and off on the street for a couple of years. I had no idea how old he was: was Gina trying to cover for him because of that?

Because it could be reported? But Gina had barely talked about him recently; had she been afraid to tell me they were hooking up again? She'd mentioned that a while before, but as though it were something totally meaningless and impulsive. And was this poem her way of letting me know they'd separated for real and she was feeling alone?

It didn't surprise me that Gina didn't show up in Lit class that afternoon. I had waited for her on the steps at lunch, but she hadn't come. I thought I might ask Mr. B. if he'd heard from her, but there was a part of me that was afraid to find out.

What if this *was* a suicide note and Gina had killed herself that morning? What if she hadn't killed herself yet, but was planning to, and the poem was a way of trying to let me know so I could stop her?

How could I stop her?

I couldn't concentrate on class, but it didn't really matter since it was the last class of the year and people were just standing up and reading their favorite poems and Mr. B. spent a few minutes talking about the final.

When the bell rang and I was stuffing my books back into my backpack, he came up to me. "Gracie," he said, "do you have a minute before your next class?"

"Kind of," I hesitated.

"I can write you an excuse if you're going to be late," he offered.

"It's not a big deal," I said. "It's the last day, and it's just PE."

"I wanted to tell you how much I've liked having you in class," Mr. B. began. "And what an outstanding writer you are."

"Thanks," I said, looking at the floor.

"I hope you'll continue writing," he went on.

"I'm not . . . I'm not really any kind of writer," I said. "I just write papers for class."

"You write really fine papers, Gracie. Very mature. You use

language in a lyrical way. I think you're more of a writer than you know."

Is this all he wanted to talk to me about, I asked myself. "Thanks, Mr. B.," I told him. "I guess I better go." I slipped my backpack over my shoulder.

"Just a minute, Gracie," he stopped me. "You're still friends with Gina, right?"

"Kind of," I said. I was still feeling hurt by her poem.

"Has Gina ever shown you any of her poetry?"

"Yeah," I said.

"Do you know anything . . . about her situation?" I could see he was struggling to find the right word.

"What situation?" I asked. *Gina has about twenty situations we could worry about,* I thought.

"I mean . . . I think Gina is having a hard time at home," he said. *Understatement of the year,* I thought.

"Yeah," I said.

"And I'm concerned that she might be . . . depressed."

"Yeah," I said. I knew Mr. B. was on Gina's side, but suddenly I felt really protective of her and I didn't want to say too much.

"I don't really know anything about her home life," Mr. B. said, "And I don't want to lay this on you or make you feel you have to disclose anything to me you don't feel comfortable disclosing."

I took a deep breath and nodded. I could tell Mr. B. was uncomfortable too, and maybe regretting having gotten into this. I wanted to rip this morning's poem out of my backpack and have him look at it and try to figure out together what Gina had meant by it; but something kept me from doing it.

"Gracie," Mr. B., started again, "you don't really have a lot of friends at school, do you?"

"You've noticed?" I asked him. I was surprised. I wondered why he was suddenly talking about me and not Gina.

"I've had you in class every day for a year," he went on. "I had you in Epic Club. You stood out, Gracie. Your papers were astonishing. Everything you said about what we read was thoughtful. You didn't comment a lot, but when you opened your mouth, you brought the discussion to a whole other level. But I watched you walk out of class every day by yourself, your head down like it is now, never talking to anyone. I wondered what was going on with you; but, despite how insightful you were, I never felt any *passion* from you until the day we had that discussion about suicide."

"You remember that?" I asked, surprised.

Mr. B. nodded. "Of course I remember it. Gina came up to me a couple of days after that and showed me some of the poems she had written about her suicide attempts, and we talked about them. She had been very impressed by the way you'd spoken in class, and I told her she ought to tell you so."

"You mean *you* told Gina to make friends with me?" I asked. I felt betrayed.

"No," Mr. B. said firmly. "I just told her she should tell you directly what she was telling me *about* you. You couldn't have made friends with each other if there was no basis. But there was. You seem very different on the outside. But if Gina hadn't been absent so much she would have gotten an A-plus in this class, like you. Her papers were complex and original, outside the box. You're both phenomenal writers. And beyond that I actually think you and Gina have what it takes to understand each other pretty well."

I didn't know what to say. I looked up at the clock on the wall.

"I should let you go to PE, Gracie. Here." He tore a piece of paper from a pad on his desk. "Let me give you a note for Sally McLeod."

I took the excuse for PE and started for the door. Mr. B. walked with me. "Gracie," he stopped me again before I opened the door. "I just wanted to let you know . . . I was hoping Gina would make it to class today. I'm concerned about her. I won't be at the final; there'll be a proctor. If you see Gina, tell her she can come and talk to me any time, even over the summer. I'll be around, teaching summer school."

I nodded. I had a lot of things I wanted to say to him and I couldn't bring myself to say any of them. "Okay," I told him. "Bye, Mr. B."

"Bye, Gracie," he said. "Have a great summer."

I turned to him once I stepped into the hallway. "Thanks, Mr. B.," I said. He nodded.

* * *

The minute school was over that day I walked home and picked up Lizzy, then walked up to Telegraph hoping to find Gina. I didn't. I wandered among the clothing and jewelry stands, looking at this and that, thinking about the conversation I'd had with Mr. B.

At one of the stands I found a green chrysoprase pendant that was translucent, as though when you looked into it you were looking down into a deep green mysterious bottomless sea. It reminded me of Gina, and I bought it to give her whenever I'd see her.

CHAPTER 23

2002

Gina showed up for the Lit final a few minutes late. She touched my shoulder and waved at me a little on her way to her seat; but she must have finished early and slipped out, because when I looked up after I turned my exam in, she wasn't there. I went looking for her on the Avenue and couldn't find her.

I didn't see her the rest of finals week. I checked my locker every day, but there were no more envelopes. No more poems.

One evening that week Dad called me to the phone and said it was for me. No one ever called me, and I hoped desperately that it was Gina. But it was Nick, inviting me to the strawberry party he had told me about. "This Sunday night," he said. "Your dad says you'll be done with finals, so you have no excuse," he cajoled me affectionately; and something in his voice made me let go of my intention not to be there.

Still, when the time came, I hesitated. Dad was taking Jannie that night to some movie about birds, and the thought of being alone at home with Kate was worse than the thought of being at a party where I knew just one person; but what would a bunch of Nick's college friends want with a girl who had just finished her junior year in high school and wouldn't even turn eighteen until October?

I lingered at home in my room, re-reading all the poems Gina had given me. At last Kate called upstairs, "Hey, Gracie, you're late for your party! I can give you a ride over there if you like," and although Nick's house was walking distance, I took her up on it. *May as well give her the satisfaction of driving me to my social life,* I thought.

The party was going full swing by the time I arrived. Three or four dogs wandered in and out of the vegetable beds in the backyard. I was sorry I hadn't brought Lizzy. Metal and Indian flute and reggae and whatever other music people had brought were playing over the speakers in the backyard, and we flowed out of kitchen and house and garden until long after dark.

Then we ate: salads and grilled salmon, avocados and walnut bread, cheeses and basmati rice. And the strawberries were boiled in water and sugar, sliced onto shortcake, halved and laid out on platters, juicy and red and sweet. I stood at the kitchen counter and cut them; as I cut I talked to Nick, who stood for a long time in the corner of the kitchen where I was, asking about the books I'd been reading. Books were always the main conversation between us, but it still surprised me that, in the midst of all his housemates and college friends, Nick was standing there in his kitchen, talking at length to *me.*

Later I spoke to some of his friends as well. I was happy to see I could hold my own with people several years older than me, happy to find myself talking about books and politics and plans for the summer, even if I didn't have any plans. I liked Nick's friends. I liked being included by them, though I wondered if they were just being indulgent because I was a kid. I found myself wondering whether, in a little more than a year from now, I might be able to go to UC Berkeley as well and spend my days with people like that. For the first time in as long as I could remember I had a sense that my life could actually feel better than it usually did.

One of Nick's friends gave me a ride home after midnight. I lay in my bed, savoring the day, seeing in my mind, over and over, plump red strawberries falling to either side of a knife, red flesh exposed, brilliant red sunset light filtering in through the windows, the open back door to the kitchen. Thin basketball-player tall Nick with his reddish hair and stained apron talking to me about *Moby Dick,* Hart Crane's *Brooklyn Bridge.*

Red light and red strawberries, reddish hair and red-stained apron. *Juices of the earth and of summer*: the line came to me as I lay there and I thought I should write it down before I forgot it. Maybe I could even use it in a poem and show it to Gina. . . . It may well have been the first time I thought of something that sounded like poetry.

That was what I was thinking about when the phone rang, and I ran quickly downstairs to answer it.

It was Martin's mother, nine hours ahead into the day in Germany, calling to tell me that Martin's long struggle with leukemia had come to an end. He had died while I was standing in Nick's kitchen in all that light, slicing strawberries.

CHAPTER 24

2017 / 2002

Nick and I spoke on the phone the other night about how there are certain lines of demarcation in our lives, moments we can't possibly know will have the importance they turn out to have. Moments that divide one phase of our lives from another, moments that may seem ordinary but which, in retrospect, serve as milestones.

"That strawberry party at your house the night Martin died was that for me," I told him.

I could not have known it while the party was going on. It just felt like I was having a good time. I remember thinking at one point during the party how rare it was in the past four years that I felt good being anywhere besides my room.

And then Martin's mother called me and gave me the news.

Our conversation was brief. I don't even remember what I said to her. All I remember was Mrs. Bachmann's trembling voice saying, "Gracie darling, I have to tell you Martin died a few hours ago."

I sat on the floor of my room. My whole life suddenly felt as dead as Martin.

In the bedroom next to mine, Jannie and her flock of birds were sleeping. Across the hall, Dad and Kate were asleep. No one seemed to have heard the phone ring; no one had stirred. Thinking it might be Gina, I'd raced to answer it after the first ring. Now I felt guilty that Gina had been my only thought. Martin was gone and Gina was god knows where, maybe also gone. And the happiness that had been in me moments ago was gone too, absorbed into the dead night air.

Lizzy, who sometimes slept with me but sometimes slept on the ancient couch in the kitchen, must have sensed something, because I could hear her padding up the stairs. I opened my bedroom door and let her in, put my arm around her and sat there feeling nothing but a chilly numbness.

Then I felt like I had to get out. Escape. Suddenly I was compelled—maybe like Jannie and Emmi had been when the feelings inside them became unbearable—to leave, to get moving, to be anywhere else, as though by doing so I could elude the pain that was about to explode my insides.

I didn't want to take Lizzy. I didn't want to drag Lizzy into what felt unbearable to me. I had to tell someone what happened, but I didn't want to wake up my family. They weren't the ones I wanted to tell anyway. I had to get out.

I pulled on the pair of jeans and the sweatshirt I'd thrown hours earlier over my chair and walked as quietly as I could downstairs. I'd slipped the necklace I'd bought for Gina into the pocket of my jeans, a sort of talisman. *Martin was still alive when I put on these clothes*, I told myself, and shuddered. Lizzy followed me, curious and expectant; but when I reached the front door I told her to stay inside. I walked out into the darkness—it was maybe two in the morning—and kept on walking.

I don't know why I didn't decide to go back to Nick's. It wasn't that far from my house. There had still been a lot of people hanging around when I'd left, and some of them would still probably be there helping Nick and his housemates clean up. I might have gone back there, gone into the kitchen through the old screen door, stood there and told whoever was there that I'd gone home and gotten a call that my best friend in Germany had just died.

They would have dropped what they were doing and comforted me. Nick would have left a phone message for Dad, letting him know where I was, telling him they were letting me sleep in one of his housemate's rooms and I would be home in the morning.

Instead I walked in the direction of Gina's address. I had memorized it the minute she'd written it on the back of my Chem homework. But I'd never been there. She had asked me not to "just show up," and I'd obeyed.

I wanted to find Gina. I wanted to tell her about Martin.

I'd never spent any time in her part of the city, only ridden through it when we exited off the freeway. It was only a couple of miles from my house. As I walked, it grew cooler; the fog, which had come in thickly in the last few hours, had condensed to a fine, cold drizzle that soaked my hair. I wished I had put on something warmer than a sweatshirt.

I made my way through the dark streets, made darker by fog. A couple of cars passed. The streets were empty of anything except a few stray cats and some people sleeping in doorways under piles of clothes or torn sleeping bags. *You're rich, Gracie Levine,* I remembered Gina saying; what I saw drove in what she'd meant. There was a smell of cigarette smoke, a smell of weed, a smell of alcohol.

A few older men stood on a corner in the doorway of a liquor store that had shut its door hours before. One of them reached out and grabbed my arm as I passed. "Hey girlie," he said in a drunken voice, "Wanna fuck?" I wrenched myself away from him and ran as fast as

I could down the street, not knowing if I should disappear into an alley or if I'd be worse off there, trapped. I figured I was faster than him, and I got away. He wasn't really coming after me though. He was too dead drunk.

I ran anyway, past more sleeping bodies, not sure anymore how to get from where I was to Gina's street, wishing I'd stayed at home. Wishing I'd let Lizzy come with me. Wishing I'd gone back to Nick's. *Martin is dead is dead is dead,* I kept saying silently to myself, to force myself to believe it. *Martin is dead, my mother is dead, my oma is losing her mind and doesn't even know who I am. And Nick isn't really my friend, he asked me to his party because he took pity on me. Dad and Kate love each other and they love Jannie, but I'm just a problem for them. And Martin is dead and I was a horrible friend to him, and Gina is maybe dead too, or at least she's in some kind of trouble and I don't even know if she'll be home if I ever find where she lives.*

My heart was pounding. I was shivering from cold and fear. *Have a great summer,* Mr. B. had told me. I thought of Dante's *Inferno,* portions of which I'd read during sophomore year in his Epic Club. It felt like I was running through one of the circles of Hell.

There could be a new circle of Hell, I thought, for souls that keep themselves so apart from others that they end up belonging nowhere. To nobody.

And I was one of them.

* * *

At last I found the place where Gina had told me she lived.

The building was so wrecked it looked like one of those abandoned warehouses where people squat among rigged electrical cords and then go up in flames. I soon realized the building was actually divided into apartments that had doorbells with people's names on them in a doorway that stank of urine and rotting garbage. There were a few broken windows on the second story, one of which revealed a room with a light on and people moving around. I couldn't see them clearly.

I felt overcome by hopelessness. How could I expect to find Gina in this place? How stupid was I? There were a few names on adhesive tape over the doorbells, but Gina's last name wasn't there. That didn't necessarily mean it wasn't her place, because several of the doorbells had tapes with the names blurred or worn off.

I couldn't just randomly ring doorbells in the middle of the night. I stepped back to get another look at the window of the lighted room. There was an argument going on: raised voices, one man pushing another. I couldn't make out what was being shouted, but the violence of the argument made me more afraid that I already was.

I stood there, looking up. *Gina, if you're there, come to the window, I have something I need to tell you,* I said silently, hoping she'd sense my feelings as she often did; but she didn't.

The light went off. Whoever was in the room stopped their argument. The building was entirely dark. The street was dark and empty except for one emaciated cat poking through an overfull garbage can. I was afraid to start making my way home and afraid to stay where I was. *This is the world Gina lives in every day,* I said to myself, and shivered. *No wonder she wants to get out any way she can.*

It was still a few hours until daylight. I walked—no, ran—to the nearest street I thought would have some traffic, people starting their commute to Silicon Valley early, people leaving graveyard shifts. Trucks delivering stuff before the stores opened. But headlights, people who might see me if anything happened to me.

I wondered if Gina's dad had been one of the men in the argument. I wondered where Gina was sleeping, *if* she was sleeping. I wondered how I would ever find her again, now that school was out.

By the time I got back home I was soaked to the skin and so chilled I could barely use my fingers to get the key into the front door. Lizzy greeted me, wagging her tail. Everyone else was still asleep. I went upstairs to my room, taking Lizzy with me, and changed into dry sweatpants and the Giants T-shirt Gina had worn.

I started crying then, sobs I muffled because I didn't want to wake anyone. I didn't know if I was more upset because Martin was dead or because I hadn't been able to find Gina to tell her about it, and that made me feel really crappy. Do I care enough about Martin, or do I just want something to make Gina care about *me*, I wondered. Am I that self-centered?

Lizzy lay on the bed with me and moved her warm body closer.

I must have fallen asleep for an hour or two, because when I opened my eyes it was starting to get light, the foggy gray light of dawn in Berkeley summer. I came to consciousness and remembered that Martin was dead. I had walked for miles to tell Gina and hadn't found her. I didn't know whether I'd ever find her again.

I felt more alone than I'd ever remembered.

It scared me to lie there and keep seeing images of Martin pale and dead, and Gina sleeping in some dingy room with a violent argument going on around her, or sleeping in a doorway somewhere. Or worse. I stood up, slipped on my shoes, and said to Lizzy, "Come on, let's go for a walk."

CHAPTER 25

2017

Maria calls to ask me to go to a protest with her, and I do.
Yet another unarmed person of color has been killed by
police, this time—a couple of nights ago—a woman a security guard
thought was shoplifting from a chain store he was guarding.

He had called the police and they shot her as she was running
from them, panicked, through the darkened parking lot of the mall.
She'd called her sister to tell her she was being pursued, and the cops
had "mistaken"—as they claimed—her phone for a gun.

When they went through her purse and her pockets at the hospital, where she'd been declared DOA, they found no shoplifted items.

Maria is outraged. She knows the slain woman's sister, who frequently comes to the café where Maria works as a barista. The slain
woman had been diagnosed with autism and bipolar disorder; she'd
been in the midst of a manic phase and her loud talking at the store
had possibly piqued the security guard's interest at 9:45 in the evening after hours he'd been standing around, bored.

"Autism and bipolar disorder," I say to Maria over the phone.
"Sounds like my family history."

Maria chooses to answer me indirectly. "You've got to come with me to this one, Gracie. La Toya was her sister's main caretaker. She walked into the café yesterday afternoon and just collapsed in my arms. She must have sobbed for an hour. She needs all the support she can get."

CHAPTER 26

2002

It was five-thirty in the morning. I was surprised to find Kate standing at the stove in her blue terrycloth bathrobe, waiting for water to boil for coffee.

"You're up early," she said, not turning her head from the canister of coffee beans. She spooned some into the grinder and pushed down the lid. The sound of beans being ground was loud and jarring.

"Sorry," Kate apologized. "I keep trying to remember to grind my beans the night before, but I never do. When I'm at my own place it doesn't matter, because it's just me."

Kate looked pretty, I thought despite myself, with her long brown hair flowing loose around her face, halfway down her back. Most of the time she wore it clipped in a ponytail or pinned up. It crossed my mind that Dad was the only person who usually saw Kate like this, with her hair loose, and I felt a surge of jealousy—not of Kate, not of Dad, but because the two of them had a private life where they knew and saw things that were hidden from me.

I didn't want to think about it. "That's okay," I said. "I'm going out anyway."

"Out? With Lizzy? Now?"

"Yeah," I said, curbing the impulse to say "She's *my* dog." Why did Rosy Cheeks Farm-Bred have to be there, making coffee in my kitchen? I just wanted to get out the door without talking to anybody.

"Are you okay?" Kate asked. She'd turned to face me. "Did something happen at the party last night?"

I'd almost forgotten about the party. "No. Nothing happened."

"You're never up this early," Kate said, and her voice was gentle. Not insistent. "You don't seem like everything's okay, honey."

That was enough. The tears came again, hot and strong, and I couldn't stop them. "I'm sorry," I said to Kate, who had pulled me close to her. Her terrycloth bathrobe felt good against my cheek. It smelled good and warm and familiar and wholesome. I wanted her to hold me like that. And I didn't.

"What happened, Gracie?" she asked me again. She turned the burner off under the kettle. Her coffee settled in the bowl of the grinder. "Honey, what happened?"

"Martin died," I blurted out. "His mom called me after I got home from the party. He died yesterday."

Kate held me. "Oh, Gracie," she said, sounding stricken. And then, "I thought I heard the phone ring last night, but then I went back to sleep and I didn't remember . . . Oh honey . . ."

Lizzy leaned her body against both of us, then lay down on her rug on the kitchen floor.

"How did he die, Gracie?" Kate asked when my sobs had abated a little.

"His leukemia came back. They tried a bone marrow transplant, but it didn't work. That's all I know. His mom didn't tell me anything else."

"Did you know he was having a transplant?" I nodded.

"I had no idea, Gracie. I had no idea. Did your dad know?"

I shook my head. I knew Kate was being kind, but somehow it bothered me.

"I wish you had told us," she said.

"What the fuck could you have done about it?" I flashed at her, and started crying again.

Kate was silent. Then, "Gracie, Gracie," she said. She pushed a tear-soaked strand of hair away from my eyes. "I'm so sorry. So sorry."

We stood there in the kitchen, Kate holding me, not speaking. Dad and Jannie were still asleep. At last I stopped crying, and Kate led me, as though I were a little girl, to the sink, turned on the water so it wasn't too hot or too cold, and washed my face with her hand. I let her. Then she offered me one of the kitchen towels so I could dry it.

"Can I pour you some coffee?" she asked me. "It's pretty strong." I nodded.

Kate took a mug from the cupboard, poured in some half and half and the strong hot coffee. We sat down together at the table.

"Do you always get up so early?" I asked her.

She smiled. "Usually. I like getting up early. I know that sounds weird, but I like the quiet in the morning when nobody else is up. I get to start my day slowly and think about things. I like to take Lizzy out when it's quiet too. I think she likes it."

I nodded. "I never knew you took Lizzy out first thing in the morning."

"I do, when I'm here," Kate said. She said it almost apologetically, as though she were thinking she should have told me, as though she were afraid I might consider it a kind of betrayal, since everyone knew that Lizzy was pretty much my dog. Mine to walk.

"I'm sure she appreciates it," I said. "Thanks." Immediately I felt I shouldn't have thanked her, as though it were a favor and she, a stranger. But Kate smiled at me. "There's no such thing as too many walks for a dog who's part border collie," I told her.

I couldn't look at her. I felt like a horrible phony. What was this eagerness to seem like a gracious person? My desperation to find Gina still troubled me; did it really mean more to me to *tell* her Martin had died than Martin's death itself meant to me?

"Do you want anything to eat, Gracie?" Kate asked. "I could make some toast."

I shook my head. "I'm not really hungry," I said.

"Were you going to take Lizzy out right this minute?" she asked. "Because if you could wait, I could go upstairs and throw on some sweatpants and we could take her out together."

My automatic response would have been "No"; but something in me felt it would be nice not to be alone. "Sure," I said to her. "I could feed Lizzy while you get dressed. Lizzy's *never* not hungry."

We both smiled.

* * *

The streets of Berkeley in summer just after dawn are gray and still, as though the fog muffles the sounds. Kate walked beside me. Her hair was clipped back again. I realized we were nearly the same height. Why hadn't I ever noticed that? I'd thought of Kate as tall.

I held Lizzy's leash while she sniffed, stopped, made little leaps forward when a cat or a squirrel appeared from out of the bushes. There were very few cars on the road around our house, and only other dog walkers on the sidewalks. Everything looked so different from the streets I had walked to Gina's only hours before.

How was it possible, I thought, that people's realities could be so far apart when they lived so close together? I thought of Gina: what was going on between her and Bo? Between her and her dad? Was she thinking about me at all? Did she still want to be my friend? Or was our friendship irrelevant now that school was out?

I thought of Kate with her hair loose, Kate getting up every morning before dawn and making coffee in her bathrobe in the kitchen. Even the sound of the grinder never awakened the rest of us. Kate telling me she liked to get up early so she could think. What did she think about?

Kate never knew Martin's leukemia had come back, because I'd never told her. Even across the thin walls of our house, her world and mine were miles apart.

I thought about Jannie and how the world she lived in was completely unknown to me, and how I had so little interest in it. Mostly I thought of her birds as an autistic obsession; I never thought about how she might really have loved them.

And Dad? Mostly Dad stuck to our tacit agreement never to talk about anything real. I wondered what he and Kate talked about. I wondered if he ever told her he was worried about Jannie, who—despite all he did for her—would never not be autistic? About me? Gracie the Unrevealing? Gracie the Just About Friendless? Gracie the Fantastic Liar?

Kate and I walked silently together down one block and up another. Lizzy, too, seemed lost in her own reality: her dog-reality, her world made of smells and sounds indecipherable to the humans she was otherwise so attached to.

"Tell me a little about Martin," Kate said as we rounded the corner. "I don't know much about him."

"I don't know where to start."

Kate waited for me to say more. I didn't. I watched the fog blow across the tops of trees, hiding the houses in the hills. The image of the building where Gina lived came to my mind, the sounds of the violent argument I'd heard there. Was Gina's dad one of the men arguing? She had told me he raged and yelled and broke things. I didn't believe he was never violent with Gina despite her having rolled up her sleeves that day to show me there were no marks: no marks on her arms didn't mean no marks anywhere else.

Part of me wanted to tell Kate about Gina and part of me didn't. What would I say? *So Kate, I know you think I have no friends after three years of high school, but I actually do. Or at least did. For the past few months I've been hanging out with this girl whose mother died of an overdose and who cuts class all the time and lives with her meth-addict dad and writes poems about wanting to commit suicide.... And she actually made two suicide attempts and I'm afraid she might make another.... And last night I walked all the way to her house in a really scary neighborhood to tell her about Martin, but I had no way of finding her, so I walked back home.... And it makes me feel shitty to be thinking of Gina when Martin just died not even twenty-four hours ago....*

I suddenly felt dizzy and grabbed Kate's arm. "You okay, Gracie?"

"Yeah. I just felt a little woozy."

Kate stroked my hair. She was being so nice to me, why did I keep feeling like I had to maintain this wall between us?

"Martin was the best friend I ever had," I began. "We spent every day together in Germany in the months before Emmi killed herself. He loved to play soccer. He was a terrific goalie. His team won, like, major tournaments. He read all the time like me and he spoke perfect English—his mother was from England—*is* from England—and we always thought it was funny that we spoke each other's languages because of our moms. . . ." I didn't know what else to say.

"Do you want to keep walking or turn back?" Kate asked. I felt a small rush of panic. What if Gina was dead too? What if she'd already taken "the easy way out"? How would I even find out? I thought of how hard Martin had struggled to stay alive, how many grueling treatments he had undergone, how much pain he'd endured.

Staying alive was the hard way.

"What are you thinking about, Gracie?" Kate asked, and she touched my shoulder.

"Nothing," I said.

We had reached the park a few blocks away. "There's Lizzy's friend Charlie!" Kate said. "Lizzy loves Charlie. They play all the time!"

"You walk here with Lizzy all the time?" I asked. I felt jealous. Kate knew a whole life of Lizzy's I had no idea existed.

"When I stay at your house. When I stay at my own place I go to the Y."

I had never seen Kate's place. I didn't even know where it was. I wondered why she bothered to keep paying rent on a place she almost never used.

I watched the dogs play with each other in the wet morning grass. The line from Brahms' *Requiem* came to me: *All flesh is like grass.* Yes, I thought: grass dies away and new grass comes up from the earth. Flesh, which seems so much sturdier than grass, can be destroyed, mowed down. Easily. Recklessly: by cells that grow the wrong way, by a sharp knife to the wrist, a foot pressing down with its last resolve on the accelerator pedal of a Renault.

CHAPTER 27

2017

I haven't seen Jannie in a couple of weeks. She texts me every few days to tell me about the work she's doing with the birds injured by the refinery spill in San Pablo Bay. The spill has barely made the news; gallons of sticky oil in the bay and no way for most people to know about it. If it weren't for Jannie, I wouldn't know about it myself.

The gull whose wing we set is still alive, still walking and eating. "No flying yet," Jannie tells me when I call her tonight. If I didn't call her, she'd never call me except in an emergency; the phone is just not her medium. But she's willing enough to talk to me when I call her.

"Do you think she'll ever fly?" I ask her.

"I don't know yet," Jannie says, "but she gets around the house okay. I think she may end up just staying here."

"Does she just walk around freely? She's not in a crate or anything?"

"I sometimes put her in a crate if I have to vacuum or something. But otherwise she's okay just walking around."

Jannie talks to me about the oil spill, about the birds she and other people who work at the Center are trying to save. Their feathers are soaked with oil; Jannie and the others spend hours cleaning them, and often they still don't survive.

The spills happen all the time, I've learned from Jannie. Like this one, most of them aren't even reported. The Center finds out about the affected birds from people up near the refineries, often from those who fish in the bay.

I sit on my couch, looking out the window onto my quiet street. My sister, who used to run away all the time, who never spoke a word until she was four, who screeched and flapped her arms—my sister is now one of the steadiest and most reliable people I know. Her whole life is devoted to birds—but, by extension, to the environment. She is furious about the refineries and their carelessness. She, who for so long seemed barely even to know there *was* a world outside her own mind and the symbiotic bond she had with our mother, is passionately concerned about the quality of air and water. The teachers at the special ed school where she went in Marin even ask her to come and talk to the kids there about her work. I think about what Jannie said a while ago about her work and Maria's being similar, and I feel a rush of pride mixed with envy for them both.

I feel pitifully ineffective beside them.

"Jannie," I tell her, "if you're planning to work over the weekend, I'd like to come up with you and help out."

"Sure, Gracie," she says. Her voice is flat, but I know that it doesn't always convey what she's feeling. "We could use the help."

Outside my window, the street is empty except for an elderly man taking his elderly dog for what is probably their last walk before bed. I'm thinking about the oil spills. I'm thinking about how, in 1986, ten years before Emmi took Jannie and me to our oma's house in Badlein, all of Northern Europe—including the part of Germany where Badlein was—had been showered with radioactive particles from what was called "the accident" at Chernobyl. The air, the water, the soil, the grasses, the milk and meat from the animals who fed on the grasses—all of those had been contaminated.

Martin's mother had been very protective of Martin, who had been two in the immediate aftermath of Chernobyl, and even after ten years she had not wanted him to wade in the creek not far from our road, or dig with bare hands in the soil. Martin's father scoffed a bit at her, thinking already that Martin was too sensitive and too self-protective except when it came to soccer; and I, not knowing much about Chernobyl, many times on warm days during the spring I lived in Badlein, led Martin through the woods and into the creek. We found a dead bird once and buried it, with our bare hands, under a tree. At moments during the fifteen years now since Martin's death I have asked myself whether fallout from Chernobyl might have caused his leukemia. And—this is much harder for me—whether my encouragement of his wading in the creek and digging in the con-taminated soil might have also contributed.

I watch out the window as the old man and his old dog disappear around the corner. A light rain is falling. I pick up my phone, text Jannie, "I will be so happy to help clean the birds. Do you want me to pick you up? Do you want me to ask Kate if we can bring Justin?"

CHAPTER 28

2002

O nce everyone had left for the day I walked up to Telegraph to see if I could find Gina.

The streets looked so different in sunlight from the way they had looked earlier in the fog. I walked past the park, glanced at the tennis players who had replaced the ones we had seen on the court, the dogs who'd replaced the ones we'd seen playing on the grass in the morning.

That's how it is, I thought. *Everything, everyone gets replaced. Dad is replacing Emmi with Kate. I replaced Martin with Gina. I'll graduate from high school in a year and new students will come to replace me, Gina, Eric. Our dog Ruffi died and we replaced him with Lizzy. Someday Lizzy will die and maybe I'll replace her with another dog. Now that school is over, Gina has probably already replaced me with someone else.*

Telegraph looked almost festive. More sidewalk vendors had put out their stands for the summer school students, who lined the sidewalks looking clean-cut and confused. Street people were hanging out in the doorways as usual, like movie extras. I looked around for some of Gina's friends, and couldn't find any. I walked into a record store and flipped idly through some used CD's, came back out onto the street, tried on a ring from one of the street vendors, a silver ring made from a bent spoon handle, and reached into my backpack for the ten dollars it cost. The ring was decorated with some kind of flowery pattern I liked. *This is my Martin ring,* I told myself, and put it on the finger next to the one with the silver and turquoise ring. *Jannie's birds better not steal it.*

I was about to give up and turn down Haste to walk home when someone tapped me on the shoulder. It was Gina.

"Hey, Gracie," she said. Her voice sounded soft and apologetic.

"Gina!" I hugged her. "Oh my god, I'm so glad to see you!"

Gina shook her shoulders a little. She was wearing dark glasses and had a bruise on one cheek.

"What happened?" I asked her.

"Oh, I've been . . . kind of hiding out." She looked away. "I did okay on my Lit final. I had to leave right away that day though . . . Sorry I didn't hang out. . . ."

"No, I mean the bruise," I insisted.

"Oh, that," Gina said. "It's no big deal."

"Have you been . . . okay?" I asked.

"Well, I'm still here," Gina said, and I didn't know whether she meant she was still in Berkeley or still alive.

I looked at her. She was even skinnier than she'd been. The bruise looked pretty new, not yellowish. "Could we, like, go and sit somewhere? Like the café across the street? Do you have some time?"

"Yeah, sure, I have nothing going on." Gina hesitated a moment. "I don't have any money on me, though."

"That's okay, I've got some money from babysitting Jannie."

We walked across the street. Gina's hair was still dyed blue and green, but the colors had faded and it was stringy and oily, as though it hadn't been washed in a while. She noticed me looking at her. "I'm sorry. I'm kind of gross. I've been kind of sleeping out for a while."

"Sleeping out?"

"On the street. With my friends. Not here—the cops come after us. We go under the freeway at Gilman."

I nodded. I wasn't going to tell her I'd gone looking for her at her house last night. It seemed a thousand years ago anyway.

We stood at the counter of the café and ordered Italian sodas, then sat down at a table in the back corner of the café.

"So, what's up?" I asked her, feeling suddenly very awkward. It was dark in the back corner there and Gina took her glasses off.

Her eyes were bloodshot, and the one above the bruise was half-closed, her cheek swollen beneath it. "Sorry, Gracie. I know I'm really scary-looking, but it's hard to see with these glasses. Ida gave them to me and they're, like, a hundred times darker than I need. But they hide what I look like."

"It's okay, Gina," I reached over the table and put my hand on hers. "Who did it to you?"

"It doesn't matter," Gina said, looking down at her soda. "You don't know him."

Who was she covering for? I decided not to pursue it. "Did you take your other finals?"

"Not really. I probably failed everything except Lit. I just kind of bailed on everything else. Lit was the only class I cared about anyway; I went to school one afternoon, like a week ago or something, and asked Mr. B. how I'd done, and he told me I got an A."

"He really likes your writing," I said.

"Yeah," Gina looked down. She couldn't have had that bruise when she went to see Mr. B.; she'd have known he'd press her about who'd done it and report it if he needed to. So it must have happened very recently.

"He asked me about you on the last day of class," I told her.

"What did he ask?"

"Nothing. He was worried about you. He just wanted to know if I knew where you were. He said you could go talk to him any time you liked. But I guess he already told you that."

"Yeah," Gina said. She seemed not to want to talk much.

I went on. "He said you and I were, like, the two best writers in the class. Something like that. And he said that he was the one who told you to talk to me."

Gina looked puzzled for a moment. Then, "Oh, you mean after that time in class, the whole thing about suicide. Yeah," she said, "He thought we could be friends."

"Are we?" I asked.

"Are we what?"

"Friends?"

Gina sipped her soda. "I guess, Gracie. Kind of. . . ."

"Kind of?"

"Girl, you and I—we live totally different lives."

I nodded. There was nothing to say.

"But I really like you, Gracie," she said. "I like you . . . a lot."

"Me too, Gina," I said. How was I going to start telling her about Martin?

"It's just . . . I don't know how we can, like, do things together."

"We can do the same things together we do during school," I said. "I mean, I can come up to the Avenue and meet you. And you can come to my house. Dad and Kate are teaching summer school and Jannie's school is year-round. . . ."

"So I can be there as long as nobody knows? That's the deal?" Gina flashed at me.

"I didn't mean it like that."

"Then how did you mean it? I'm your hidden friend? Your token street person?"

I was angry. "I just meant that we'd have the place to ourselves. Shit, Gina," I said sharply, "if it's that important to you, you can come to my house for dinner. You can sleep over. You can have the whole family experience: shrieking, shitting birds and all. I'm serious."

Did I only just say this because I know she won't do it? I asked myself.

Gina didn't answer. Instead she looked down at the table. "I've been writing more poems. The one thing I brought with me from my dad's is this," she pulled her notebook out of a worn cloth bag she had set on the floor beside her chair.

It has to be her dad, I thought, *who hit her. Why else would she sound like she's left his place for good, to sleep under the freeway?*

"Wow, is that whole thing your poetry?" I asked, impressed.

"Most of it. Some of it is just . . . stuff. Nothing. Just stuff I write down. I kind of write all the time. But most of it's poems."

"Would you let me read some?" I asked. Gina nodded.

She pushed the notebook across the table in my direction. Before I opened it, I said, "Gina, remember that friend I told you about in Germany? The one who had leukemia?"

"Yeah," she said.

"He died yesterday."

"Wow, Gracie. I'm sorry."

"He tried so hard . . . to keep living. He had, like, all these fancy treatments and chemo and stuff. A bone marrow transplant, whatever that is. But he didn't make it."

Gina stirred the ice in her soda with a straw. "That's terrible, Gracie."

I didn't know what else to tell her. I didn't know what I wanted from her. It had felt so urgent the night before to tell her Martin had died. But maybe the urgent thing had just been to see her, to tell her something that would bring her closer to me; and I felt ashamed thinking that that could have been it.

Gina was so elusive. I suddenly felt like I didn't know her at all; but as long as I could keep sitting at that table with her, she was still here and still in my life.

"That's really sad, Gracie," Gina looked at me with an intensity that compelled me. Then, "Hey, Gracie . . . I feel like you want me to say something more, and I don't know what it is."

"That's okay," I said flatly. "There's not much to say."

We sat in silence for a moment.

"This soda tastes like cough medicine," Gina said after a while, and somehow that made us both laugh.

"What are you going to do?" I asked Gina.

"What do you mean? About what?"

"About school. About . . . where you live. About everything."

Gina shook her head. "I have no idea."

"Are you just going to . . . keep sleeping under the freeway?"

"Maybe. I don't know. I can't really go back to my dad's."

"Gina, please tell me if he's the one who hit you like that. We could do something about it. Please."

She glared at me. "I am *not* going to tell you, Gracie, so stop asking. But that's one good reason for me not to meet your parents—excuse me, your dad and his girlfriend—until this bruise goes away."

"Maybe things will be better for you if someone reports it," I said.

"What makes you so sure it's my dad who hit me? But if they see he's a meth addict, oh yeah, my life will get *so* much better. I'll get sent to some stupid foster home where the county pays someone who could care less about kids but just wants the money. Or they'll look at my truancy history and slam me in The Hall."

I looked at her, puzzled.

"The Hall," Gina said. "Juvy. Juvenile Hall," Gina clarified. "Oh my god, Gracie Levine, we *do* live completely different lives."

I sighed. "I'm sorry, Gina. I just thought . . . that maybe there would be some help . . . some help out there for you."

"No thank you" said Gina, shaking her head. "Foster care? The Hall? I'd feel like one of your sister's birds when they're in their cage."

"Okay, I get it," I said. I took a deep breath. Gina leaned across the table. I felt like telling her I had gone to her house the night before, and clenched my toes to keep from opening my mouth. Gina would feel invaded, as though I'd seen something about her life that she wouldn't have wanted me to see. And she had told me specifically not to go there.

Gina turned her notebook over and showed me the taped-together back cover. "My dad almost ripped this up, but I got it away from him."

That was all the information she was going to give me.

"My dad . . . he's been doing fucked-up stuff for a long time. It's not like it just started." She paused for a moment and then continued. "And then there's all this shit going on with Bo."

"What kind of shit?" I asked.

Gina shook her head. She wasn't going to say.

I stirred my straw in the melting ice in my glass. "So . . . are you still thinking about going to your auntie's?"

"I'm thinking about a lot of things. I don't know how I could do it, though."

"Go to your aunt's?"

"Go anywhere."

I sucked up the last of the melted ice with my straw, making a noise that made us both giggle again.

I looked at the first poem in Gina's notebook. "Wow," I said. "Gina, I'd give anything to be able to write like you."

"Are you kidding, Gracie? You're some kind of fucking genius. You could do anything."

"That's not the point," I said, almost in tears. "I mean, I can do stuff, but I never feel like I really care about doing it. But you . . . I can just feel how awful it would have been for you if your dad had really ripped up this notebook. For me . . . I don't even have one single thing I care that much about. And that feels like crap."

"Did you care about your mom?"

Tears stung my eyes. "I don't remember. I remember being terrified all the time about what she was going to do."

"It sounds like you cared about Martin."

"But I was a shitty friend to him." Now I was really crying.

Gina put a hand on my cheek. Her hand was warm and tender and smelled like cigarettes.

"My mom," she said after a while, "she may have been a junkie, but I loved her more than anything in the world. And I knew she loved me. We would sit on the floor and play cards and make jewelry out of paper and those cheap little plastic beads. When she died I just spent a month at home, crying my eyes out. Then my auntie moved in with me and my dad for a while and she made me go back to school. And then she left with her boyfriend and moved to Ohio."

"Why didn't she take you with her?"

Gina shrugged. "She was a junkie too, but kind of . . . Junkie Lite. More together than my mom. And anyway she was pretty young to take on an eight-year-old. She was only, like, twenty."

"I cried for a month too after my mom killed herself," I said to Gina. It was a lie. I had hardly cried at all, except for that one night when we found out it had been a suicide. I actually mostly walked around not feeling anything, like I was in a coma.

But I wanted Gina to feel like I'd done what she'd done. That I had feelings like a real person.

She nodded. "Do you ever feel mad at her?"

"At my mom? Not really." That was also a lie.

Gina looked down at the table, tracing the marble pattern with her finger. *Her fingers are so long and beautiful,* I thought. "I'm mad at my mom all the time," she said thoughtfully. "I loved her so fucking much, and she OD'd on me and left me with my dad. She knew what an asshole he was, and she just left me with him."

"But you said she probably didn't mean it . . ." I protested.

"The OD? Yeah, it was probably an accident. But she was still totally wigged out on drugs. If she really wanted to take care of me, she could have tried to get clean."

"Did she ever?"

"Try? I don't know. I was just a little kid. It wasn't like she was going to talk to me about it."

She was silent for a moment. Then she said, "Maybe she did try and it was just too fucking hard. My dad tried—remember I told you?—and he couldn't make it."

"Gina," I started, "What would you need to be able to get to your auntie's?"

"Money."

"That's all?"

"*That's all?*" Gina mocked me. "You *are* a little rich girl, Gracie Levine."

"I didn't mean it that way."

"What other way is there? How the fuck am I supposed to get the money? You have no idea what my life is like. You can walk up to the Avenue, hang out with me for a little while, buy me a soda, and then walk back to your nice clean house with your nice clean dad and his nice clean girlfriend. You can come and go as you please. In and out of my life."

Tears welled in my eyes. "*You're* the one who's so hard to track down, Gina! You have no idea how many times I've come looking for you. I *never* know where you are!"

Gina said nothing. She looked down at the table and smoothed the torn cover of her notebook.

I wanted to get up and go but I didn't want to leave her. I had no idea when I would find her again. At last I slid my chair back a little and said, "Are you sure your auntie . . ."

"Would let me stay with her?" Gina asked, and her voice was hard. Accusatory. "No. I'm not. I've been trying to get in touch with her, but I haven't been able to. Maybe she changed her phone. But we did speak like, maybe, a year ago, and she told me . . . I told her what was happening and . . . she said I should call if I needed her and I could always come . . . sleep on her couch."

I looked at my watch. Jannie would be getting home in about an hour, and I needed to be there when she arrived.

"Do you need to go?" Gina asked, sounding suddenly wistful and sad.

"Yeah. My sister is coming home soon."

Gina put her notebook back in her cotton bag. "Gracie?"

"Yeah?"

"I'm sorry this has been such a dumb-ass conversation. And I'm really sorry your friend died."

"That's okay, Gina." Then, "Gina?" We were standing on the sidewalk in front of the café now.

"Yeah?"

"Do you think there's a way . . . we could hang out?"

She shrugged again. "It's not like I don't want to. . . . But I . . . I really don't know what I'm doing from one day to the next. I guess you have to just kind of . . . come look for me. I know this guy on the Avenue who sells stuff and if I can get him something worth selling, he said he can get me some money and I can get out of here. But I don't know how that's going to happen. And some days I don't really see the point of anything anyway. I mean, like, maybe nothing really matters."

I didn't want to ask what she meant.

"All I know is one way or another I need to get out of here. Soon."

"Will you tell me . . ." I started. I couldn't continue. My eyes were hot with tears I didn't want to let her see. Martin was dead and Gina was going to leave.

"Tell you what?" Her voice was tender.

"Tell me . . ." I started to cry. "Tell me what you're doing? Where you'll be?"

Gina pulled me close to her. She kissed my hair again the way she'd done at my house that afternoon. "I'll try, Gracie Levine," she said. "I'll really try."

I nodded.

"Want me to walk you part way home?" she asked, and she took my hand.

The divide between Gina's world and mine was filled with late afternoon traffic: people heading home after work, people who knew who would be there to come to the door, make dinner, talk over the day's events. Gina would head back to a dark place where everyone she knew was lost; and I was heading back to my home, where I couldn't talk to anyone about the darkness I felt consuming me.

We stopped at the corner of Shattuck and Haste. I waited for the light and Gina waited with me. Then she looked at me, kissed my hair again, and turned. "Bye, Gracie," she said.

She walked a few steps and turned again to see whether I was still watching her. I was. She raised her hand in something between a wave and a salute. "I love you, Gracie," she called, and walked away.

CHAPTER 29

2002

I wished I had given her the chrysoprase necklace, which was still in the pocket of my jeans. I'd been afraid to give it to her, afraid to show her how much I wanted her in my life. Gina had told me she loved me, and I'd been too self-conscious to let her know what I felt for her.

What was wrong with me?

Everything felt wrong: Gina's dad had a daughter he didn't take care of and Martin's parents had done everything they could to take care of their son and now he was dead. And Martin had wanted to live so badly, and Gina didn't see the point in staying alive.

I thought again about people replacing other people, and wished for a moment that Gina could have taken Martin's death, if that's what she wanted.

What if it worked that way, I thought. In Mr. B.'s Epic Club we had read some of the Greek plays. Among them had been one about a woman, Alcestis, who wanted to descend into the underworld in her husband's place so he could remain alive.

What if someone had been driving in front of Emmi that night when she chose to veer off the road and plunge her car into a tree? Would the person in the other car have blocked her? Would they have been pushed into the tree instead, and then would they have taken the death that Emmi was aiming for? How different, after that, would her life have been? How different would my life have been?

For the first time since the night of her death I let myself picture that moment, the moment when Emmi turned the steering wheel of her car to the left and let the car career off the road to the steep drop into the woods.

What had she been feeling then? Frightened? Exhilarated? Numb? Or did she suddenly regret what she'd done and realize there was nothing she could do to change it? Did she die regretting it? Did she think about me and Jannie as the car plunged inexorably toward the tree?

At home, Lizzy came to the door. No one else was there. I sat down on the living room couch with Lizzy and cried. I cried about Emmi. I cried about Martin. I cried about Gina. I cried about the way everything is lost and replaced, lost and replaced again. And I thought of what Gina had said, *maybe nothing really matters.*

* * *

When Jannie came home she started chatting in her usual lively way about everything that had happened during her day, and I made an effort to listen without my usual impatience. Then she went into her room. I could hear her birds chattering just like Jannie, flying wildly down the hallway. I didn't intervene, though Dad—after the umpteenth incident where one of the birds had stolen yet another shiny thing—had imposed the rule that Jannie's birds could fly free only in her room. Jannie never paid attention to the rule when I was the only other person in the house, since she knew I just ignored it, not wanting to deal with her protestations.

I went up to my room, closed the door, and sat down at my desk. I wanted to write a letter to Martin's mother, and I had no idea how to begin.

Martin was my best friend in the world, I wrote. *I told him everything.*

I could hear Martin's voice telling me I was a fantastic liar, and I tore up the sheet of paper.

Another sheet. *Martin was my best friend in the world. For a long time I told him everything, and then I stopped telling anyone anything much, but the person I told the most to was Martin.* There. That was, at least, honest. I am going to be honest, I told myself. That will be my last gift to Martin, to be honest with his mother on the day after his death.

When Martin and I met I had no friends and it was the worst year of my life. Martin didn't care that my mother and sister were both totally crazy. He accepted me for who I was, and we liked a lot of the same things.

When my mother killed herself Martin knew the truth and it didn't scare him away from me. He wasn't afraid to be friends with a girl whose mother had committed suicide, which, for some reason, I thought would be like a curse branded on my forehead forever. I didn't want anybody else to find out. Martin was also really kind to Jannie when all Jannie did was run around screeching.

I want to tell you I'm sorry for two things, I wrote. *The first is easier because you know it already. In this past year I didn't write Martin as much as I used to. I really thought he was okay. I figured he was busy with school and soccer and I thought he would write to me more if he wasn't so busy. It never occurred to me that Martin had gotten sick again. I want to think that if I had known I would have written to him much more often.*

The other thing I'm sorry about happened a few years ago, and it's much harder to tell you. But I want to tell you now, and if you hate me for it forever I'll understand.

When Martin was almost finished with the first round of chemo, we were playing around one day and we pulled the rest of his hair out and I got the idea to paint his head like a soccer ball. It was totally bald, and I found some of Emmi's old make-up and some face paint and I painted his whole head black and white. Now I wonder whether the paint and make-up might have had too many chemicals for Martin to handle, and if I might have been a little responsible for his leukemia coming back. I was already worried the first time he got leukemia that it was because I convinced him to play in the woods with me and to dig in the soil and wade in the creek which may still have been contaminated with radiation from Chernobyl. I convinced him that you were being too overprotective and that the woods and the creek couldn't hurt us. He probably wouldn't have done any of it if I hadn't been his friend. I've thought about all that since last night when you called to tell me he died.

I just wanted to let you know that I'm really sorry. I'm sorry for everything, And I'll miss Martin for the rest of my life.

Love,

Gracie

I folded the letter, put it into an envelope, and wrote Martin's familiar address. *Will this be the last time I write it?* I wondered. Jannie was in her room. Dad and Kate had come home—I'd heard them walk in while I'd been writing—so I was free to go out and mail the letter.

I clipped on Lizzy's leash and walked down the block with her to the mailbox. I stood in front of it for a long time, watching cars pass. Lizzy lay down at my feet, sniffing the sidewalk.

Then I took the envelope in both my hands and ripped it into a hundred pieces.

I walked with Lizzy to the Walgreen's a few blocks up. I still had some change in my pocket from the sodas Gina and I had had; it seemed like months ago now, but it was only a few hours. I picked out a Hallmark condolence card with a drawing of a single sailboat on front, sailing on what seemed like an eternally tranquil lake. I wrote, under the printed message *(My deepest sympathy)*, *Love, Gracie,* and walked back home. I'd put a stamp on it at home and mail it in the morning.

The shards of the letter sat like confetti in the pocket of my jeans until late that night, when I threw the jeans in the wash, forgetting about them. Then they were nothing but crumbs of lint on clean blue denim.

CHAPTER 30

2002

J annie came down with a fever and cold the next day and stayed home from her summer program. Dad asked me to babysit her, and I felt a little relieved to have an excuse not to go up to Telegraph and look for Gina. I felt guilty that I was even thinking of Gina two days after Martin died; but I was stirred up by her having told me she loved me, and troubled by what she had talked about in the café.

It made me remember what I had felt in the last weeks of Emmi's life: a terrible dread that had no content, just the sense that something awful was about to happen. I'd walked into the bathroom to pee one night and found Emmi in the bathtub with Oma washing her hair as though she were still a little girl. The bathroom stank of vomit and it was clear to me that Emmi was totally drunk and had puked all over herself. I'd gone back to bed and, horrified enough not to want to step back into the bathroom, had wound up peeing in my pajamas.

Emmi was crazed in those weeks to make Jannie talk. One morning she'd come home from the bakery with some little rolls, *Brötchen,* and wouldn't let Jannie have one until she could say the word. She had screamed at Jannie and held Jannie's little chin in her hand, moving it up and down like the hinged chin of a marionette. Jannie had shrieked and sobbed until Oma had put an end to it, washed Jannie's face and given her a roll.

And that was the first word Jannie ever said, but not until the day of Emmi's funeral.

Then there were hours on end when Emmi would pace around the house, unable to stay still, raving about how toxic the environment was and how the only thing that would help would be to burn everything down. I'd become terrified every time she lit a cigarette; was she going to set fire to the house?

I couldn't stop her. I couldn't reassure her.

Could I stop Gina? If I helped her get away from here, would that keep her from killing herself?

By afternoon the fog had burned off and Jannie was feeling well enough to agree to take Lizzy for a walk up to the park on Oregon Street. She brought her sketchbook and colored pencils; Jannie loved to sketch the seagulls who scavenged for food in the park. That afternoon, though, Jannie asked to draw me.

It surprised me. Most of the time I felt Jannie didn't even notice me. Or anyone human, for that matter.

I sat for her on the grass, holding still, a little self-conscious. Jannie drew, erased, drew again. Then she pushed the sketchbook toward me so I could see.

What I saw astonished me. Not only at Jannie's skill, which was considerable; but at how much I looked like Emmi, as though Jannie had drawn a picture of Emmi at almost eighteen. Looking back, I think that portrait of me was the beginning of a concerted effort I've made ever since *not* to look like my mother. It wasn't only the features, but a particular look in the eyes which Jannie had captured, and which I remembered.

Distant. Disengaged.

Was I really as remote as Emmi had been? Was I that, in Jannie's eyes? In Gina's? Gina had called to me that she loved me and I had said nothing. Nothing.

Walking home, I asked Jannie what she remembered about Emmi.

"Her red sweater."

"That's all?" I asked.

"I think so," she said. "I can't tell if what I remember is Emmi or just the pictures we have of her. But I do remember her red sweater and how I used to lie with my cheek against it. It was fuzzy."

"Do you think that's why you like your red sweatshirt so much?" Jannie had worn that red sweatshirt since she'd been four. We'd bought it on that trip, on the very first day, when Emmi had realized she hadn't brought any warm clothes for us. It had been huge when Jannie had first put it on; now it barely zipped, was threadbare in places, and the sleeves were at least four inches from her wrists. Still, Jannie could not be convinced to part with it.

She was puzzled at my question. "No, Gracie," she said, as though I'd just asked the stupidest question in the world. "It's a sweat*shirt*. Emmi's was a sweat*er*. They're totally different."

Then, out of the blue, the way Jannie tends to bring up things abruptly that would never occur to most people to bring up at all, she asked me, "What if Emmi didn't really die in that car crash, but just pretended she did, just made it look like she was dead, the way Lizzy does when Dad tells her to play dead? What if she just got up from the car when no one was looking and she walked down the road and decided to live a whole different life? And she got married again and even had different children? How old would her children be now?"

I pictured Emmi before her coffin was closed. She had make-up on to cover what had happened to her face, her whole head, in the crash.

I didn't want to be having this conversation. But Jannie insisted.

"They would be really little," I said, "like the oldest would be maybe four at the most."

"So what if they're four and two? But she gets sort of tired of them and one day she says to herself, 'Hey, I wonder whatever happened to my old kids. I think their names were Jannie and Gracie.' Do you think she'd remember our names?"

"Sure, Jannie. Of course she would."

"'So whatever happened to my old kids, Jannie and Gracie,' Emmi says to herself one morning in Germany. And she gets on a plane and comes to Berkeley and she comes to our house. Do you think she'd remember where our house is, Gracie?"

"Maybe. If she didn't, she could look it up."

"How?"

"I don't know. Maybe Dad still lists it in the phone book." I was getting annoyed.

"What's the phone book?"

"It's a big book almost no one ever uses anymore, that lists everyone's phone numbers and some addresses."

"Then it should be called the phone and address book," Jannie said, triumphant.

"This is a dumb conversation, Jannie," I said.

"No it's not!" she protested. "So Emmi finds our address and she comes to our door. But then she stops just under the living room window, right where she can see us."

"And we all just happen to be in the living room?"

"Yeah. It's a Sunday." I wondered if Jannie had been making this story up in her head for years.

"I'm drawing a yellow male finch from a photograph in my Peterson's. Dad is grading math papers. Kate is there, sewing a quilt. You're reading and Lizzy is lying on the floor. Even though Emmi doesn't know Kate and Lizzy, they're part of our family."

"And Emmi sees us all through the living room window?"

"Yes. And she stands there watching us for a long, long time. We're not doing anything very interesting, but she keeps watching us. Maybe she wonders who this dog is, and who's this woman sewing a quilt? Maybe she can even hear us talking. And every few minutes she thinks, *Now I'm going to ring the doorbell. . . .* But she doesn't do it."

"She doesn't?"

"No.

"Why not?"

"I don't know. She just doesn't."

"And then what happens?" Jannie shook her head.

"She gets back on the plane and goes back to Germany."

I looked directly at my sister. I was startled at this fantasy of hers. At how elaborate it was and how deeply sad. "Why, Jannie?" I asked her. "Why would she bother to come all that way just to stand outside our living room window? Why wouldn't Emmi want to come inside the house and see us?"

It suddenly felt totally real to me. Jannie's face darkened. "I don't know," she said, an edge in her voice. "She just looks at us and sees us and then she goes back to Germany."

"Is she happy to see us, Jannie?" I pressed her, as though Jannie had some personal knowledge of Emmi that was real and true. It crossed my mind how close they had been. Like two pieces of hard candy stuck to each other.

"I don't know," Jannie said, and I thought she was about to cry—not out of sadness but out of frustration because I was pressing her to go beyond the story she had made up.

"Do we ever know she was there?"

Jannie was quiet for a moment. A wind was coming up and she pulled her too-small red sweatshirt around her skinny chest. "Maybe Lizzy knows she was there, but she's the only one. And Lizzy doesn't bark at her or anything. You know how Lizzy can sometimes not bark when someone's outside?"

I nodded.

Jannie shivered a little. "No. No. We never see Emmi. We're just sitting in our living room, doing what we do. We're just all busy with our stuff. We never think about looking out the window. We never know Emmi was there."

CHAPTER 31

2002

Jannie went back to her summer program a couple of days later and then it was Friday and then it was the weekend and I hadn't seen Gina or heard anything from her. I had a disturbing dream one night that Kate was Martin's mother and Martin was a little kid, maybe about four, and she had brought him to live with us and he was a lot like Jannie had been at that age and I hadn't wanted anything to do with him. I found myself more and more annoyed with Kate; the nicer she was to me—and she'd been particularly nice to me since Martin died—the less I could stand it. And I was annoyed with myself for feeling that way.

One morning the next week I heard Lizzy barking downstairs. When I went down to check I saw someone standing, back turned, in the front yard, and realized it was Gina. I didn't think she had rung the bell. I thought immediately of Jannie's fantasy about Emmi, and I opened the door as fast as I could.

"Hey, Gina?" I called, stepping onto the front porch. "Did you ring the bell?"

Gina hesitated a moment, then turned. "Not really," she said. "I was just . . ."

"Come on in," I said. "It's freezing out here." Another foggy, windy Berkeley summer morning.

"I just wanted to leave you some copies of stuff," she hesitated.

"Poems?"

"Yeah."

"Come inside. Do you have some time?"

"Kind of," she said.

"Did you have breakfast? I was just going to make myself some cereal."

"Sure," Gina said.

I poured us each a bowl of cereal and milk. It seemed so normal having Gina there, just sitting across my kitchen table eating Cheerios. And at the same time it felt tense, as though anything might be about to happen.

"So," I said. "Do you know what you're doing yet?"

The bruise under Gina's eye had grown yellowish. She wasn't wearing her dark glasses and the yellowish tinge made her look unwell.

"No. Not really."

She took a sheaf of papers out of her bag and pushed them toward me. "Here, Gracie. This guy at the copy place copied them for me for free. It was after hours and his machine was kind of broken, so some of them are a little messed up. But I think you can read them."

I nodded and looked at the first one. She was quick to say, "You can read them later. When I'm not here." She smiled.

"Gina," I started, "if you can stay for a little while, we could look at some of my mother's journals. You know—all those notebooks in those boxes up in my closet."

"You really want to do that?"

"Yeah, but not by myself."

Gina looked at the clock on my kitchen wall. "Sure, I can stay a little while. Maybe we could at least look at one or two."

I opened my closet and pulled out one of the boxes. I looked at the dates on the outside of the notebooks—Emmi had marked them all in Sharpies on the outside with the dates they were begun and ended. "Here," I told Gina, laying them out on the floor. "Let's just close our eyes and pick them at random, okay?"

Gina nodded. The one she picked was from the year I was two. The one I picked was from just before Emmi took us to Europe.

"Oh my god," I said, "This one is from just before she kidnapped me and Jannie."

"That's how you see it? *Kidnapped*?"

"Well, she took us without telling Dad she was doing it, or where she was taking us. I think that counts legally as kidnapping."

"I always thought kidnapping was when it was someone else's kid."

I shrugged. "Were you just going to drop the poems on my doorstep and leave?" I asked.

"Kind of," she said. "Hey, Gracie? I have some weed the copy guy gave me. We could smoke a little while we read."

I nodded. Gina took the weed and her bong from her bag, and we passed the bong back and forth.

"Did Lizzy's barking scare you off?" I asked her.

"Maybe," she said. "Not really. I just kind of . . . thought I should go."

"You didn't even leave the poems. You were just going to walk off, like, without leaving them?"

Gina didn't answer. I could feel the weed beginning to get to me. I opened the window behind my bed to dissipate the smell.

"You know Lizzy," I said. "Sometimes she barks and sometimes she doesn't."

Gina giggled. "It wasn't so much about Lizzy. . . . I just suddenly looked around at your house and at all the houses on your block, and I had this feeling like, *What am I doing here?* So I guess I kind of felt like running."

I nodded.

Gina's eyes always got red right away when she smoked.

"Yeah," she continued, "and I didn't even know if you were home, or if Kate or somebody would find the poems, and I didn't want anyone but you to read them. . . ."

We sat together on my bed, mildly high, leaning against the pillows, turning the pages of Emmi's journals. "Hey, Gracie, your mom really thought you were cool. Listen." She read me a passage about how I was learning to talk, how many new words of mine Emmi was aware of, how we had had a conversation about Ruffi, our dog, and whether Ruffi felt sad when it rained.

"And this one, Gracie," Gina said a few minutes later. It was about how having me be her child had made Emmi happy. "She really loved you, Gracie. She wrote, 'This little girl is the best thing that ever happened to me.' Look!"

I almost didn't want to. I was sunk deep in Emmi writing about wanting to leave Dad. She named all the things that annoyed *me* about him; but she didn't name any of the good things about Dad, and I suddenly felt really protective of him.

"What's yours like, Gracie?"

"It's like, about how really unhappy she was with my dad. And how worried she was about Jannie. I don't remember Jannie so well when she was so little, but Emmi wrote that she almost never slept for longer than forty-five minutes, and she made Emmi afraid to be with her. Except that Emmi was with Jannie all the time. Once Jannie was born, she was all Emmi thought about."

"Gracie, you're always saying you don't know what you felt for your mom. Or what you feel for her now. But look—from everything she wrote in this journal, you were totally close to her. I mean, you must have loved each other a lot, at least when you were little."

I suddenly wished I had never asked Gina to read these with me. I wished I had never opened them myself. I didn't want to feel sorry for my mother. I didn't want to feel sorry for my dad. I didn't want to know how happy I'd made Emmi when I was small. How attached to each other we'd been.

It was all too confusing. I liked being there next to Gina, our shoulders touching. I liked listening to her turning pages, making little noises under her breath when she came to a good part.

After about an hour Gina closed the notebook she was reading. "I have to go, Gracie," she said. "I need to . . . like . . . I'm meeting someone on the Avenue. It's not like an exact time or anything, but . . . I told him I'd look for him."

"Bo?" I asked. Gina grimaced.

"Oh fuck, no! I'm done with him. Totally done. This guy I'm meeting . . ." she hesitated, stopped.

"Who is he?"

"He's kind of someone I've known for a while. He wanted—*wants*— to go after Bo."

"Go after him?" I asked.

"He has a gun," Gina explained. I felt so out of it.

"He wants to go after Bo *with a gun*?" I heard myself say it. *Gracie, you are unbelievably naive*, I thought.

Gina stood up, took a deep breath. "I don't think he'll, like, really do it. But he told me he wanted to and I . . . I want to try to talk him out of it."

"Be careful, Gina."

Gina slipped her feet into her flip flops. "He thinks he's . . . protecting me."

I nodded. "Do you need protection?"

Gina didn't answer at first; then she turned to me. "Gracie, if I tell you something, do you promise not to tell anyone?"

I nodded.

"Not Mr. B. Not your dad and Kate. Not anyone," she said.

I nodded again.

"Okay. Bo was the one who did this to me," she pointed to the bruise under her eye, "and my dad and I had a screaming fight about the fact that I was still seeing Bo. He's not much of a dad, but he did really get on my case about Bo. And Bo is older than me, he's nineteen, and he's already done time in the Hall; he'd be considered an adult now and he could go to prison if anyone finds out about this. But he'd kill me—I mean literally *kill me*—if he finds out I ratted on him to anyone."

I nodded. I felt chilled and sick to my stomach.

"Gracie, I got so mad at my dad I told him I was not going to stay with him anymore and he just screamed at me, 'Go ahead, get out, go sleep on the street . . .'"

"Was that the fight where he ripped your notebook?"

Gina looked down at the floor. "Yeah," she said. And then, "I didn't tell you anything about this, Gracie. Any of it. Okay?" She looked at me hard.

I nodded.

"That's for *your* protection, Gracie," she said quietly, and she stroked my face. "I'd feel terrible if anything happened to you because of all my stupid shit."

"I get it, Gina."

She started walking toward the door to my room. "Hey, Gracie?"

"Yeah?"

"Thanks for letting me read your mom's journals. Thanks for . . . like, asking me to come inside and like, be in your room and stuff."

I shrugged. I didn't know what to say.

She took my hand as we were going down the stairs. "You see why I want to get out of here," Gina said. I nodded.

"I just don't know how I'm going to get the money to do it," she said.

We stood at the open front door to my house. Lizzy stood in the doorway with us, not knowing if I was about to take her out or what. She tentatively wagged her tail and licked Gina's hand, and we laughed.

Neither of us wanted to end our time together. Gina reached over and touched my face. "Tell me what you think about the poems, Gracie, okay?"

"Sure," I said. "Hey, Gina?"

She looked at me in that intense way of hers.

"I . . . Be careful, will you? I really care about you. I mean . . . I really . . ."

She stood there looking at me, not speaking, and smiled a little.

"I'll be okay, Gracie," she told me, and walked away. Then she turned again. "You be careful too," she said.

CHAPTER 32

2002

When Gina turned the block and was out of sight, I felt an emptiness that was something like loneliness and something worse. Like everyone and everything I cared about was missing or endangered, and I was the last person standing.

It had probably been a mistake to read Emmi's journals; it had brought me closer to Gina, so I dreaded her imminent leaving more acutely. It had also brought me closer to Emmi, which was probably the last thing I wanted; it opened in me a chasm of grief I hadn't wanted to know was there.

I thought about calling my oma in Germany, but it never really felt good to talk to her any more anyway. She could barely follow a conversation, and I doubted she'd even remember who Martin was if I told her he'd died.

I lay across my bed and picked up the book I'd been reading the night before. I heard a fluttering of wings and realized Jannie hadn't gotten all her birds into her room that morning. Annie was still flying around, and had probably been hiding out somewhere in the house the whole time Gina and I had been there. *At least that fucking bird didn't fly out of the house when we were standing there with the front door wide open,* I thought; for a moment I figured I'd try to get her back inside Jannie's room, since Dad had made her agree to keeping them there under penalty of giving some of them back to the bird store; but the weed Gina and I had smoked made me feel suddenly overcome with sleepiness, and I thought instead I'd go into the bathroom and throw some cold water on my face to wake myself up. I wasn't really in the mood for chasing down Jannie's crazy bird.

On the shelf above the bathroom sink I saw Kate's ring—my grandmother's ring, that Dad had given her. Every time I saw that ring on Kate's finger I felt a little shudder of anger and resentment. I didn't want to get used to the fact that Dad had given it to her.

I knew Kate always took the ring off when she washed her hands or took a shower or washed the dishes; she'd told me she worried that the ring would slip into the drain or the stones would loosen and fall out. But this morning, obviously, she had forgotten to put it back on when she'd left the house.

I examined the ring. It looked shinier than it had a few weeks before; clearly Kate had polished it. It shone in the sunlight that had broken through the fog and was coming in through the bathroom window.

I picked it up. I put it on my finger. I really didn't like it. The sapphire was too big and the diamonds were kind of gaudy; the ring looked cumbersome and ostentatious. I was used to my silver and turquoise ring and to the silver spoon ring I'd bought the day Martin died. And in any case, I couldn't just walk around wearing the ring Dad had given to Kate.

I didn't feel like putting it back on the shelf, though.

I clenched the ring in my fist and went downstairs. My heart was pounding. *What am I going to do with this?* I asked myself. I didn't even know why I had taken it off the bathroom shelf. I just did it. I was stoned and upset and that's what I did.

I didn't want it for myself. But I didn't want Kate to have it either. That was the main thing, I told myself. I didn't want Kate to have the ring.

It would be so easy to hide it and let everyone think Jannie's bird had stolen it. Annie was the one who stole more than all the others combined. But by now we knew the places in the house where she and the other birds tended to hide things, and it wouldn't be easy to keep the ring from being found.

It felt almost as though I were someone else. As though I were being driven by something I didn't understand. I felt frightened and almost dizzy. I couldn't even fully take in the fact that I was filching the ring; it was as though someone else was doing it and I, Gracie, was watching it happen.

I was *not* going to bring it back to the bathroom shelf. That was certain.

I could bury it, I thought suddenly, in the backyard. *That's where this ring belongs anyway: buried under the earth.* No one would think to dig up the yard to find a ring they assumed a bird had stolen.

I left Lizzy in the house, not wanting her to watch what I was doing. My hands shook as I dug a small, deep hole in the corner of the yard under some juniper bushes. The topsoil was soft; I dug with my fingers at first, but after a couple of inches I reached a more clayey soil and went into the basement to get a trowel. I felt shaky and afraid someone would see me, some neighbor or the mailman or someone; but I kept telling myself there was no one around. It was the middle of the day and I was in my backyard, fenced and sheltered by tall trees. I dug with the trowel the rest of the way down, finally reaching a place with spindly, hairy little roots and a couple of worms.

I laid the ring in the hole and began covering it with soil and stones and more soil and more stones until the ground looked like it had before and seemed undisturbed. I made a mental note about exactly which bush the ring was under so I could find it again if I ever wanted to.

Then I went inside, gave Lizzy some kibble, and went back upstairs to my room and took a nap.

When Jannie was dropped off that afternoon I didn't say anything about Annie flying free. She went upstairs and released the rest of her birds. I gave her a snack and then each of us got a book and settled into the living room chairs.

When Dad and Kate got home they were greeted by the conures.

"Jannie, birds in your room!"

"They're okay, Dad," Jannie said, not looking up from her book.

"They're *not* okay flying around the house. You know the rule," Dad told her.

"Okay, fine," Jannie said, annoyed, and threw down her book. She began whistling to call her birds down from the curtain rods.

After a little while Kate called from upstairs, "Hey you guys, I think one of them took my ring! It was right on the bathroom shelf!"

I buried my face in my book and said nothing. Jannie was still whistling at her birds.

"Jannie! Sam! Could somebody help me look for it?"

I kept on reading. It was not unusual for me not to participate in such things, and I figured nobody really expected me to.

The search for the ring went on through the house as I buried myself in my book. All the regular places failed to reveal it. By now Dad was angry with Jannie, which almost never happened, and Jannie was crying and flapping her arms. Kate kept insisting it wasn't Jannie's fault, and Dad kept saying it was, and Kate started saying that she had been careless to leave the ring where she did, to which Dad replied angrily that it was true. I'd never heard Dad yell at Kate before. He shouted at me as well.

"Gracie, it was your job to get Jannie to put her birds in her room!" I didn't answer. I didn't even look up from my book.

"Gracie! You could have put the birds in her room yourself!"

"You know I can't get those stupid birds to do anything!" I shouted. Jannie was crying hot tears of frustration. "They are *not* stupid!"

"The least you could do, Gracie, is get up from your book and help us look for it."

"Sorry," I said sarcastically. "How the fuck should I know where some bird put a ring?" I was so accustomed to lying that the anxiety I had felt all afternoon was now absorbed in the story that Jannie and her birds were, in fact, responsible for the missing ring. If I took one small step inside my mind I could almost believe it myself.

I picked up sofa cushions, looked behind drapery, behind books on bookshelves.

Now Dad was even more angry with Kate. "You know she's not always responsible about the birds," he raised his voice. "That ring is worth something, Kate. You shouldn't just leave it lying around."

"I *said* it was my carelessness, Sam!" Kate responded, equally angry. Jannie was sitting on the couch in the kitchen, sobbing. Lizzy, upset by the unraveling of everything, had posted herself next to her, slowly wagging her tail, pressing her nose into Jannie's lap.

At last the search was abandoned for the afternoon. We were all exhausted. Kate went over to Jannie, held her head, told Jannie she was sorry for having caused this mess by leaving the ring on the bathroom shelf. She asked Jannie what she wanted for dinner. Jannie said she wasn't hungry and Kate told her she could choose not to eat but she needed to sit with us all at the table once dinner was served.

We all sat without speaking around the bowl of pasta Kate made. Jannie ate nothing. She sat watching her pasta get cold. I had a few bites but didn't feel like eating much either.

"Can I be excused?" I asked.

"No!" Dad shouted, "No, you cannot be excused!"

"Sam, this has nothing to do with Gracie," said Kate. "Leave her alone. She's been through enough these last weeks."

The more she defended me, the more I hated her.

"I'll look for the ring in the morning," Kate said softly. "Sometimes things turn up when you're not so desperate to find them."

Dad turned to Jannie. "Jannie," he said to her. "It's clear to me that you can't manage all these birds. We'll have to do something with some of them."

Jannie got up from her chair and overturned it with a loud thud. Then she started kicking it with all her might, screaming "No! No! No!" She stormed into the hallway, then came back into the kitchen and took the plate she had been eating from and threw it on the floor.

It shattered. Shards of ceramic and gobs of tomato sauce everywhere.

Now Dad was able to stop her. He grabbed Jannie by the shoulders and lifted her in his arms. She was sobbing and kicking him now. "Don't do anything to my birds. Don't do anything to my birds. Don't do anything to my birds."

I sat watching. Listening. As though it were all happening behind a wall. I felt nothing. It was as though another Gracie had stolen the ring, and, as Kate said, I'd had nothing to do with it.

"We'll talk about it in the morning," Dad said, stroking Jannie's hair. At last she quieted. Without a word, Kate took Jannie's hand and led her upstairs.

I could hear her running a bath. I could hear her talking gently to Jannie as she bathed her.

It made me remember my oma bathing Emmi the night I found them in the bathroom in Badlein.

CHAPTER 33

2017

Maria and I take my dog Carson to run at McClure's Beach after a week of rain. I rarely get to the coast anymore now that I'm teaching full time, and I always feel guilty about Carson spending so many hours inside by herself. In Lizzy's last years, when I was working nights at the bookstore and taking classes for my credential and trying to write poetry, I would pick Lizzy up at Dad and Kate's and drive her out to the beach at least once a week. Sometimes Nick would come with me and we'd talk about how we felt like a family.

The last real walk Lizzy took was at Abbott's Lagoon on a bright October day when the three of us traipsed back slowly, the sun setting in the Pacific behind us and the moon beginning to rise in the east, ahead of us. Three days later Lizzy had the stroke that effectively ended her life.

She had accompanied me through all the difficult years.

It was soon after her death that, lonely and bereft, I moved in with Nick, and the sixteen months we spent together in his tiny Oakland apartment were in no small way owed to Lizzy's passing.

I'm talking about those months to Maria as we walk on the windy shoreline. Nick has been saying he'd like to try living together again when his poet-in-residency in Washington State ends in May; and though my habitual ambivalence seems to have receded from other areas of my life, I'm continually ambivalent about committing myself to Nick.

Maria pushes me, as is her wont. "What if you just tried it again, Gracie?" she asks. "I mean, your place is big enough for him to move in. You wouldn't have to change much, and it wouldn't be like the two of you bumping into each other all the time in that tiny place he had. The worst that could happen is that it didn't work, and you wouldn't have lost anything."

I ponder what she's said as I throw a long piece of greenish-brown kelp for Carson. Maria makes it sound so easy. Maria and Jannie are so totally clear about what they're committed to.

"I think what you need to ask yourself," Maria goes on, "is: Is there any real danger in it? Or is this just Gracie being Gracie?"

CHAPTER 34

2002

I woke a few mornings later to the sound of Jannie shrieking "No! No! No!" again downstairs.

The ring had not been found. I thought of it in its dark wormy hole, covered by soil damp with fog.

Dad had told Jannie he would take some time to think about what "consequences" to impose on her. Jannie's school was big on consequences and I had even overheard Dad tell Kate, in the argument that had gone on late into the Night of the Missing Ring, that he was going to take up the issue of Jannie's birds with her head of school.

Kate had protested that the loss of the ring had been her fault and not Jannie's. Dad had disagreed, telling Kate that Jannie had been warned over and over not to let her birds fly out of her room. "The conures are going back to the store if the store will take them," Dad had said. "They're young. They'll get adopted easily."

"Sam," Kate had implored. "Jannie adores those birds! It would break her heart to lose them. Think about it for a few days. You're being too hard on her."

"Don't you care about the ring I gave you?" Dad asked Kate. I could hear the pain in his voice. Was *that* what this was about? I wondered. Did Dad feel Kate didn't care enough about *him*?

I couldn't fall asleep for hours. I hadn't intended to set all this in motion. I hadn't intended *anything*. I'd been stoned and confused. I'd just taken the ring on an impulse. It had clearly meant even more to Dad to give that ring to Kate than I had imagined. Was this going to cause a rupture between them? Did Dad doubt that Kate loved him? Dad, whom Emmi had left in such a horrible way: was it hard for Dad to believe that Kate wanted to stay with him?

Dad was always so indulgent with Jannie that his harshness shocked me. Jannie was going to lose her conures and it was *my* act that caused it.

Not hers. Or Kate's.

I was destroying my family. I was hurting Jannie.

Something I didn't understand kept me from just getting out of bed and going into Dad and Kate's room to confess.

I could put a halt to this now. I could tell them what I'd done. But I couldn't. I couldn't.

And I didn't.

I rationalized: Jannie did let her birds fly around all the time when she wasn't supposed to. Kate did leave that expensive ring of my grandmother's lying around. Jannie really couldn't manage the number of birds she had. It was Dad's inability to say no to her that started all this in the first place.

Maybe Kate didn't care as much about my dad as he did for her. Maybe the ring really wasn't such a big deal to her.

It would be totally possible for me, anyway, to dig up the ring any time I wanted, plant it somewhere in the house when nobody was around, and let someone find it. I considered that for a while. I could do it maybe in a few days, a week. I even began to feel sorry for

Jannie's conures, convicted of a crime they hadn't committed and about to be banished.

But I did nothing.

Even though I felt a fear and heaviness I couldn't even name, I didn't go into the backyard when I was alone in the house the next day or the day after that to retrieve the ring.

I had even begun to think about something else I might do with it.

* * *

That Saturday morning while I still lay in bed, Dad had told Jannie the consequence he was imposing. The head of school, who was around for the summer program, must have agreed that Jannie needed a consequence; but Kate had definitely succeeded in getting Dad to mitigate the sentence.

The three conures, Pablo and Isabella and Annie, were, indeed, to be exiled; but only provisionally. They were to spend the next two months at the home of a colleague of Dad and Kate's whose wife volunteered at a wildlife museum and did foster care for birds. Dad and Jannie would drive the conures out there this morning so Jannie could see where they would be.

They would be able to come home only if Jannie remembered to keep her other birds in her room all the time. If Jannie slipped up even once, Dad told her, the conures would be permanently given away.

Jannie sat at the kitchen table, her little body wracked with sobs. "I can take care of them. I can take care of them."

I had never seen Dad so adamant. "Prove it to me with your other birds and you'll get them back."

I came into the kitchen, poured myself a bowl of cereal and milk and took it into the living room. Jannie was trembling. Was I that hard hearted?

I was. I pretended to be reading the newspaper.

"Now come upstairs with me," Dad was saying to Jannie, "and we'll get their food together and anything else they need. You can write a list of instructions for Mrs. Hilverson so she knows what to do for them. I told her we'd be there at eleven o'clock."

"I can't even visit them!" Jannie wailed, looking at me as she walked upstairs. I said nothing.

"We'll be back in a couple of hours, Gracie," Dad said. "Do you have any plans for the day?"

"Not really," I said, not looking up.

CHAPTER 35

2002

O nce they left the house, I kept assuring myself the conures would be all right, the way Dad was assuring Jannie. I felt restless and agitated and I didn't know what to do with myself. After a while I put the chrysoprase necklace in my pocket and walked up to the Avenue to see if I could find Gina. Lizzy insisted on coming with me, so I took her and left a note that we would be back in a few hours.

I walked up and down Telegraph for a long time. No Gina. I looked inside the windows of cafes. Nothing.

When I got home, Dad was in his basement workshop rewiring a lamp. Jannie was drawing, sitting at the kitchen table. She looked small and vulnerable. I felt sad for her and sick to my stomach about what I had done.

"You got the birds out to Mrs. Hilverson?" I asked.

She nodded.

"Was she nice?"

"She was okay," Jannie said. "She has a canary named Pepper. He's yellow with black markings."

"So the conures will have some company," I offered.

"Conures don't really care about canaries," Jannie said, and went back to her drawing. "Don't really care," she repeated to no one in particular.

"Oh," I said. I felt like everything I was doing was making things worse.

* * *

I lay on my bed upstairs, staring at the ceiling. There was nothing I wanted to do, not even read. I was Gracie the Fantastic Liar. Gracie the Thief. Gracie the Cruel. Gracie the Destroyer.

On my walk back from Telegraph I'd thought of a plan for the ring:

The right thing, I knew, would be to dig it up, wash it off, hand it to Kate and confess to them all what I'd done. Kate would get her ring back, Jannie would get her birds back, Dad could be angry at me and not Jannie and Kate.

I knew that was what I should do. But I wasn't going to do it.

Gina had told me she knew someone who "sold stuff" and could get her some money if she had something worth selling. I didn't want her to move away; but I was terrified she would kill herself or—now that I knew something about her story with Bo and with someone who might go after Bo with a gun—be killed.

If I could give her the ring and she could let the guy she knew sell it, maybe she could get enough money to go to her auntie's. That was certainly better than winding up dead.

I figured I'd tell Gina my plan the next time I saw her. If she agreed, I'd get her the ring.

* * *

The summer days went by. Jannie was being scrupulous about leaving her birds in her room. I felt numb and heavy, tired all the time. I had no desire to do anything at all. I took naps and lay on my bed, languidly rereading novels I'd read years before. In some way I found it comforting that the events in the novels would turn out exactly as I knew they were going to. I read and slept, read and slept. I stopped looking for Gina. Why bother?

Dad and Kate seemed to have calmed down about the ring, or given up on it. Kate, who was on a week's break between summer sessions, came up to my room one day and convinced me to go to a fabric store with her so she could buy what she needed to start a new quilt.

"I can teach you to quilt," she offered. To her surprise and mine, I agreed. For some reason I didn't understand it seemed like it could be calming to cut pieces of cloth, lay them next to each other, stitch.

I thought of the ring buried in the garden. In one of my naps I dreamed it was Martin buried at the bottom of my garden under the juniper bush, and I couldn't tell anyone because he wasn't supposed to be there.

I wondered where Martin had been buried. Was it in the same little cemetery in Badlein where my mother was buried?

Martin, who had friends from school and friends from his soccer team, would have had a much bigger funeral than Emmi's. The pastor who had presided over Emmi's funeral would have said some words over Martin's poor emaciated body and everyone would have cried and the story of Martin's life would have been told, first by one person and then by another. Martin would have had a funeral where those who loved him reconstructed his life of sixteen years and his death, which no one had wanted to think could happen. There would have been flowers and music and Martin's father would have held Martin's mother's elbow as they walked out of the church together ahead of the others into the hazy sunlight of late afternoon.

And then, little by little, Martin would be left behind where he was: under the grass that was like all flesh. In the past. In oblivion.

One day, I thought, Martin's mother will walk into his room and take down the soccer posters, clear out the drawers and make room for her own winter sweaters. Put Martin's clothes in a bag to bring to the church to be given to charity. One day Martin's bedroom will become the room where Martin's mother, like Kate, does her quilting. The sewing machine will be carried up from its corner in the kitchen by Martin's father. Machine, sewing table, basket of thread, notebook of patterns will all be transferred up to Martin's room. Martin's things, I thought, will be replaced by all these.

All flesh is like grass.

And one day Martin's mother will see a bright-colored rug in a department store in Hamburg. She will bring it home, take the old brown rug from the floor of Martin's bedroom and notice how shabby it has become, how faded and threadbare. She will roll it up and put it in the trash bin outside; and what has been Martin's bedroom will be transformed by the new red and orange and yellow rug.

And Martin—as patches of quilt to be hand-stitched fill chairs and sewing table and bed—will come more and more to be numbered among the missing.

CHAPTER 36

2017

Text from Nick:

Thinking of coming down for the weekend.

I text back:

Justin's staying with me. Dad & Kate going away. Maria and I are taking him and Jannie to a movie Saturday night.

Nick:

I can have dinner with my mom Saturday. Make her happy. Come over later?

Me:

Sure. Can you hang out with us Saturday afternoon? Justin has little league at two. Want to come root for his losing team? He's shortstop.

Nick:

Sounds like fun.

Me:

It'll be good to see you.

Nick:

Only six more weeks of this teaching job. I can't wait to get home.

Me:

☺

CHAPTER 37

2002

The ring still lay in the ground. Was it rotting there? Had worms loosened the stones, turned the ring to a bunch of tarnished holes? I couldn't bring myself to dig it up and look. I couldn't bring myself to walk up to Telegraph. I could barely bring myself to walk out of my room. The one thing I did all day was quilt with Kate.

It felt oddly good to quilt alongside Kate. Maybe it was my own depression coloring everything, but Kate actually seemed less cheery herself. I wondered if something about the tension between her and Dad over the ring had worn off a bit of that veneer, subdued her a little. I liked her better that way.

I realized I wasn't thinking of her so much anymore as Miss Rosy Cheeks Farm-Bred. I just thought of her as Kate.

She didn't pressure me so much to talk. I figured that, unlike Dad, Kate could see I was feeling awful and, without making me tell her about it, she was just trying to be nice to me in ways I could tolerate.

Kate told me stories from her childhood or about her friends. "So I told you about Karen's boyfriend, the one who worked for a newspaper? Well, he was out on this assignment to cover a fire, and it turned out that the people whose house burned down were cousins of his whom he hadn't seen in years. . . . And now he's putting them up at his house until they find a new place."

Or: "Did you see that new golden retriever down the block? She was supposed to be a guide dog for the blind, but she failed their course because she was too friendly. So the guide dog foundation put her up for adoption and the Humboldts adopted her. "The funny thing," Kate went on, "is that their grandma, who lives with them, is blind, and the dog totally adores her and leads her around."

One day Kate told me about something she'd read in a book about primates that she was planning to assign to her honors Bio students. It was a story about a chimpanzee named Bibi who was in an experiment where chimps were taught sign language. Then, after years of being there and working with the same trainers, the experiment ran out of money and all the chimps were dispersed to different facilities. Years later one of the trainers from the original experiment happened to come to the place where Bibi had been sent. She hadn't signed for years, but she recognized him immediately and ran, crazed, to the bars of her cage, jumping up and down, signing her name again and again.

I thought about the chimp, so desperate to be known. Underneath everything I did to hide myself, was I also like that, desperate to be known?

Had Emmi been like that? Was Jannie? Gina? Dad?

Kate?

Everyone?

* * *

I could tell that Jannie, too, was not quite herself. She missed her conures; and I think she had been wounded by the harshness Dad had displayed to her for the first time in her life. She had started flapping her arms again, and spinning around on the swivel chair in her room.

She was excited about one thing, though: she had been chosen as one of nine kids to go with her summer program on a backpacking trip in the Sierras at the end of the summer. Jannie had never spent even a single night away from us, but she said she felt ready. She knew all the other kids who were going, and her teachers would be leading the trip. Her way of preparing was to read everything she could about the birds of the western Sierra.

One afternoon, Kate took Jannie to the camping goods store to pick out a backpack and sleeping bag. It was a cold, gray afternoon. I felt groggy—I'd already taken two naps that day—and thought I would try and wake myself up by going out for a walk. I snapped Lizzy's leash on and took her out.

I walked around aimlessly for a while in my neighborhood; but then, almost as though I were on automatic pilot, I found myself walking toward Telegraph. I wasn't even sure I wanted to see Gina. It had felt kind of soothing, easy, *not* to see her. Not to think of her so much, even. To just hole up in my house and sew together pieces of cloth.

It had been weeks since I'd been there. The summer students had left and the place looked like a street in a war zone. Strung-out street kids sat in the doorways, old blankets and sleeping bags wrapped around themselves against the wind and chill of Berkeley August. *Maybe it always looked like this,* I thought, *and I just never noticed how sad it was.*

In a corner of the park I saw a group of kids sitting with two dogs on rope-leashes. I recognized one of them as Rocky, the dog I'd met the first time I'd run into Gina on the Avenue; and right away I realized that one of the girls in the group was Gina.

I couldn't avoid her.

She looked so different at first that I thought I'd mistaken someone else for her. Her face had grown thinner but was swollen again, very swollen, on the side that had been bruised before. Her hair was dyed parakeet green again. It was oily and stringy. When she started walking toward me I noticed she was limping.

"Gracie?" she called, as though she wasn't sure who I was either. Her voice sounded slurred and distant. "Want to get stoned?"

I ignored her question. "How are you, Gina?" I asked. I didn't know what else to say.

"Oh, I'm spectacular," she said sarcastically. "Seriously, Gracie, we've got some good weed." She pushed a joint at me. I sat down and accepted it. Just not to say "No" to her. Just to have a reason to sit there with her.

Lizzy seemed restless, but at last she sat down as well.

"I came looking for you a bunch of times," I said. The others she had been talking to were ignoring us.

"Yeah?" Gina said. "I guess you didn't find me."

I shook my head. "What happened?" I asked her.

"Oh, you mean this?" Gina touched her face. She pulled up the long skirt she was wearing and showed me her leg, which was also swollen and bruised. "It was way worse before. I still can't wear jeans—they hurt."

Gina inhaled the joint deeply and passed it to me again. I took another toke, and another. I hadn't gotten high since the last time I'd seen her, and this weed seemed more powerful than what we'd smoked before. It got to me quickly, made me feel crappy. But I didn't want to refuse her.

"Was it Bo again?" I asked.

Gina didn't reply. She shook her head slightly, as though to let me know we couldn't talk about it here.

"I've been really worried about you," I said. "I didn't know if you had left, or what."

She said nothing.

"Gina," I started, "do you still know that guy, the one you said could sell stuff and get you money for it?"

She thought for a moment. "I don't know who you're talking about," she said, and thought again. "Oh yeah. Yeah, I remember. Kind of."

"Well, I think I have something for him to sell. I tried . . . I wanted to find you before, to tell you, since you told me that all you needed to get to your auntie's was enough money. But I couldn't find you."

"I've kind of . . . been trying not to be found," she said. I felt she was telling me more, but I didn't understand. "It has nothing to do with you, though." She closed her eyes for a moment. "Hey, Gracie," she said, her voice tender, "do you want to go over there?" she asked, pointing to a corner of the park that was empty of people. "That way we could have a little more privacy."

I was trembling a little. The weed. I hated that it had that effect on me. Other people smoked it to feel *good.*

"Are you still thinking of going to your auntie's?"

I could hear a faint echo of my voice, and it made me even more anxious.

"My auntie's?" Gina repeated. "I don't know. Maybe. I want to go *somewhere,* that's for sure."

"If you had some money could you do it?"

"Maybe. It depends."

"I have this ring," I started. "It belonged to my grandma. My dad gave it to me," I lied. "And I don't really need it. I don't even like it. But it's got some diamonds and a sapphire in it, and my dad says it's worth something. If you want, I can give it to you. And you can give it to that guy . . . to sell."

Gina looked at me. "Your dad gave it to you?" she asked. It felt like she was looking through me.

"Yeah," I lied. I looked away from her, pretending to be concerned about what Lizzy was sniffing. "Leave it, Lizzy," I said.

"And you really don't want it?"

I shook my head. Gina kept staring at me. She was very stoned.

"You have really blue eyes, Gracie Levine," she said at last, slowly and dreamily. I giggled nervously. I was pretty stoned too, but not as stoned as she was. "They're really really blue."

She was looking deep into my eyes. She was silent for what seemed like a very long time. Then she leaned over and kissed me on the lips.

I was trembling all over from the weed and from the kiss. I didn't know what to think. What to do next. I touched Gina's face where the bruise was. Gently, with two fingers.

"I love you, Gracie Levine," Gina said to me.

This time I said, "I love you too, Gina."

Did I? Did I love her? What did that mean? What did *she* mean?

"Gina," I started.

"What?"

"That must really hurt," I said softly. I had meant to say something else, but I couldn't remember what it was. The weed was stronger than any I'd had.

"Not as much as right after it happened."

"Was it Bo?" I asked her again.

Gina nodded.

"Why did he do it?"

"Because he's an asshole," Gina said bitterly.

"I thought you weren't going to see him again."

"Yeah. Well, I told him that, and this was his answer."

"Where is he?" I asked her.

Gina shrugged. "He comes and goes. He always finds me, Gracie. No matter how much I try not to let him. It's like . . . he has radar or something."

I touched Gina's face again. She looked at me and suddenly I saw my mother's face. Gina had my mother's face. *Am I that stoned?* I asked myself. It scared me. Gina looked smaller and so vulnerable, like a child.

"That's why I need to go somewhere far away," she was saying. I could barely hear her through the haze in my head.

"I'll try to help you, Gina. I'll bring you the ring and that guy can sell it and then you'll have some money to get away."

The wind had come up and it was chilly. Gina was wearing only a tank top over her skirt. She had goosebumps on her arms and she was shivering.

I felt a tenderness for her, seeing how cold she was, that I didn't remember ever feeling before. For anyone.

"You're freezing. Do you want to wear my sweatshirt?"

"Really, Gracie?" she asked. I took it off and Gina put it on over her head.

"You can keep it," I told her suddenly; and I felt embarrassed the minute I said it. Was I being Gracie the Rich Kid?

"I mean," I told her, "I have another one just the same at home." It was a lie.

"You mean it, Gracie? Do you just feel like, *Oh poor Gina,* or what?"

"No, Gina. I really mean it. It's just a sweatshirt. If you want it you can keep it."

Gina took my hand and held it. Her hand was bony and cold and holding it made another wave of tenderness overcome me.

"It's nice," Gina said. "It's fuzzy."

We sat there on the grass, looking at each other. She kissed me again. Then I leaned toward Gina and kissed her.

"Gina," I started. I kept losing track of what I wanted to say.

She looked at me.

After a while I asked, "Are things . . . any better with your dad?"

She shook her head. "Why would they be any better? Things are always the same with him. Always the same." She seemed to close up. "I haven't stayed with him for a while," she continued. "It's not even safe for me to stay there. Not because of my dad; but because Bo knows where my dad's—where our place is—and there are people out to get Bo, and the whole thing is a fucking mess."

I said nothing.

She continued. "But I go see my dad. I guess I feel sorry for him. He tried to detox again and he got really sick. I had to get the building manager to take him to the ER."

"Wow," I said. I pulled up some grass, tossed it a few feet away. Lizzy watched, curious.

Gina seemed to close up inside herself just then. I wanted her back. I wanted the moment of closeness we had just had to come back. What had it meant that we had kissed? Anything?

"Are you . . . are you writing?" I asked her. I rubbed her leg below where the bruise was. She took my hand and kissed it.

My head was spinning. From the weed. From everything.

"Oh yeah," Gina said. "I write all the time. That's all I do." She pulled her thick, torn notebook out of the worn cotton bag she always carried. "Here, I can show you one." She began leafing through the pages. "I wrote it just a couple of days ago."

I took her notebook and read it.

I find myself
way too often in a
state of worry
a state of confusion
and usually anger.
Where my feelings swirl
around me, whispering
my fears into my ear
frightening me to the
point where I
collapse.
Yell at myself
over
and over again until
my voice is hoarse
and Dad comes home
and my fears just spiral
back to me
as I hear his
boots pound against the
hardwood floors

"Wow," I said again. "This is really good, Gina."

"I could copy it out for you," Gina said. "If you want it."

"Really?" It was clear she wanted to give me something. She took a pencil out of her bag and started copying. Her head down, her hair, which had grown longer in the front, falling across her face. She kept brushing it away from her eyes with her left hand. I didn't stop looking at her.

Would Gina have kissed me if she hadn't been stoned? Would I have kissed her?

"Hey Gina," I said after a while. "I should go. I have to get home. But I can come back tomorrow or . . . whenever . . . and give you the ring."

"Sure, Gracie," she said slowly. "I just . . . I'm never sure where I'll be. But . . . yeah, just come look for me."

I started to stand. Gina took my hand again and held it. Her hand was still cold and tense. We looked at each other.

"Hey, Gina," I said. "Bye, I guess."

"Bye, Gracie. Bye, Lizzy."

I turned and started walking.

"Hey," Gina called. I looked back at her. Her face started turning into Emmi's again, and it scared me. *I'm just stoned,* I told myself. *It's just the weed. I smoked too much of it.*

"Thanks, Gracie," she called to me. "Thanks for the sweatshirt. I like it. It's really warm."

"Sure, Gina." I felt scared and shaky and I wanted to get home quickly and wash my face.

CHAPTER 38

2002

"**W**here were you, Gracie?" Jannie ran to the door to greet me the minute Lizzy and I got home. *Shit, they're home, I* thought. *Kate's going to know the minute she sees me that I'm stoned.*

"I got a sleeping bag that's good for twenty-five degrees Fahrenheit!" Jannie was telling me excitedly. "And it's the same color as a Stellar's jay!"

"Can you show it to me later?" I asked her, running upstairs. "I need to take a hot shower. I got really chilled."

I took a shower and sat in my room until dinner and came down with sunglasses on to hide my red, dilated eyes, claiming a migraine.

I didn't go up to Telegraph the next day. I just lay in my bed all day, reading. I didn't feel well. I wasn't sure whether the weed was still affecting me or whether it had really shaken me to see how vulnerable Gina was and to have her kiss me. To have kissed her. To see her face keep changing into Emmi's face. To take in the whole twisted knot of my feelings for her.

All I knew was I didn't have it in me to go looking for her that day.

That night, when I was still lying on my bed staring up at the ceiling, I overheard a conversation between Dad and Kate. They thought I was asleep. I had gone back upstairs right after dinner, claiming I still had the migraine.

"Do you think Gracie's okay?" she asked Dad.

"What do you mean? She's getting headaches, but otherwise she seems all right. She may be a little bored, but all kids her age get bored in the summer. Too old for camp, too hard to find summer work. She does take care of Jannie a lot in the afternoons . . ."

"I don't think it's just boredom," Kate responded. "Have you noticed: not a single friend of Gracie's has crossed our threshold . . ." *She's never known Gina came here,* I thought. *All those times, and Kate never suspected.* "Not a single one. She never goes to anyone's house. She's been quilting with me, but apart from that and reading, she hasn't done anything all summer. And she seems to sleep an awful lot."

"Kids her age sleep a lot," Dad dismissed it. "Hormones. But didn't she go to that party a few weeks ago at Nick's? They seem to be friends."

I could picture Kate shaking her head the way she often did. "That was in June," she said. "Gracie hasn't seen Nick once since that night, and that was the night Martin's mother called to tell her Martin was dead."

There was a silence. "Do you think she could be depressed about Martin?" he asked.

Dad gets the Nobel Prize for Cluelessness and for Discovering the Totally Obvious, I thought.

"I think there's something on her mind that she isn't telling us," Kate replied. "She and I have talked a little about Martin. Of course she's grieving, but I don't think that's the whole story. Kids Gracie's age don't spend the summer sitting around making quilts with their dad's girlfriend. They're with their friends, they're driving around, they're staying out half the night . . ."

"Gracie has always been kind of a homebody," Dad said. "Maybe a little livelier before Emilie took them to Europe. But since Emilie died Gracie has never had a lot of friends."

"She doesn't have *any* friends," Kate corrected him. "Martin was *it*. Unless she's hanging out with people we don't know about."

"What do you mean by that?" Dad asked.

Yeah, what do you mean, I thought from my bed.

"Sam, my sister Carrie called me this morning. She told me she had to go pick up a book at Cody's yesterday afternoon, and she parked on Bowditch near People's Park, and she noticed Lizzy in the park next to Gracie. Gracie was with a bunch of kids. My sister said she couldn't be sure, but she thought she saw Gracie smoking a joint. She wouldn't have even noticed her if it hadn't been for Lizzy."

Shit, I thought. *I was with those kids for, like, five minutes before Gina and I went and sat somewhere else. How random is that? And what makes me any of Kate's sister's business?*

"So what?" Dad replied. "Gracie is almost eighteen. She's a good kid. A straight-A student. She takes good care of Jannie and Lizzy. She's bound to experiment with a little weed. . . . Do you know any kids who haven't?

Kate was silent for a while. Then, "I don't know, Sam. There's something going on that I'm not at all sure about. And the last few weeks, Gracie has seemed really off."

"She says she's getting migraines. Maybe she should go see the doctor? Emilie used to get migraines."

Oh great, now I'm like my crazy mother, I thought.

"I'm worried about Gracie," Kate said. "That's all. I don't know. I think she's depressed. Maybe she's doing drugs, maybe—I don't know what. Maybe she's just grieving for Martin. But I'm not sure that's the whole story."

"Do you think we should ask Nick over for dinner?" Dad asked her, avoiding everything Kate had just told him. "Nick is friends with the whole family. Jannie adores him."

"But what about Gracie?" Kate flashed back. "Do we know whether Gracie adores him?"

Dad didn't reply. *There they go*, I thought. Another fight.

"Sam, Jannie's going on her camping trip in a few weeks, and I have no idea whether Nick is even around. I can tell you this: having him come for dinner won't solve anything. But sure. Go ahead. Invite him over."

I lay in my bed, uneasy. I didn't want to see Nick. Could that be a sign that I really was depressed? Nick was kind of like a good older brother; I'd been happy to have the conversation he and I had had at his strawberry party; but now I could care less if I ever saw him again.

Was I depressed, then? I didn't want to see Nick. I didn't want to go looking for Gina. I didn't want to dig up the ring. I was becoming an expert at doing nothing. I was coming to understand that if you did nothing about an issue for long enough, it would begin to lose its charge. It would begin to be absorbed in some gray sludge of troubling issues accumulating just under the surface.

I certainly didn't feel good.

The truth was I didn't feel much of anything. Kissing Gina had left me confused. Did she like me in *that* way? Did *I* like *her* in *that* way?

Maybe. And maybe.

But Gina's life was up in the air. Obviously she was having a hard time getting away from Bo. I hoped that my seeing her with Emmi's face was just a weird stoned fantasy and not some kind of premonition that she would wind up like my mother.

Maybe I should go and talk to Mr. B., I thought, lying awake long after Dad and Kate had stopped talking. Maybe I should tell him how worried I was about Gina, worried more than anything that she would wind up dead, either by suicide or at the hands of someone she hung out with who had a gun. Or that Bo himself would kill her.

Mr. B. had said he'd be around all summer. He really liked Gina and would certainly want to help her.

The strongest feeling I'd had in weeks was my tenderness for Gina, holding her hand that afternoon in the park. Mr. B. would certainly want to know she was in trouble. But I couldn't imagine myself going to school, looking for him, talking to him. It felt like it would take way more effort than I was capable of.

Why hadn't I dug up the ring? I had hours and hours alone at the house. Was I afraid that digging it up would put the seal of finality on my theft? As long as Kate's ring was still buried I could tell myself it was possible to bring it back into the house and let it be found.

Was it guilt that kept me from bringing it to Gina? Or was this just another instance of my preferring to do nothing?

CHAPTER 39

2002

Nick was coming to dinner.

I spent the afternoon in the kitchen with Jannie and Kate, making lasagne. I was nervous; I didn't really feel like seeing Nick. Or anyone else, for that matter. I wasn't sure what to say to Nick or anyone else anymore. *What have you been doing this summer, Gracie? Oh, nothing much. I've been walking my dog. I've been sleeping twelve, maybe fourteen hours a day. I've read about a hundred novels, all of which I read in sixth or seventh grade. I've gotten stoned. Quite a bit, actually. Oh, and I stole a ring my dad gave Kate and I let everyone think it was Jannie's birds who took it, so now Jannie's conures are in exile and Jannie feels like shit. And I've been planning to give the ring to a friend whose dad is a junkie and whose boyfriend is beating her, and she might commit suicide unless she can get out of here, and some-one connected to her boyfriend (or whoever he is to her) might kill him or her or both of them; and maybe the ring could help her if someone can sell it for her. . . . But I haven't gotten it together to give her the ring. . . . And she kissed me, and I don't know if she meant it just as a friend or something else. And I kissed her, and I don't have any idea what I*

207

want with her either, and I don't even know when I'll see her again, but I think about her all the time. . . .

Great summer.

Jannie was chatting eagerly to Kate about the birds she'd been studying, birds she might see when she went on her camping trip. I didn't have anything to say. I sat at the kitchen table tearing a bunch of spinach leaves into little pieces to be sautéed. Kate came over and put both her flour-coated hands on my face, laughing.

"Gotcha, Gracie!" she said. Jannie laughed. I was annoyed, but they both seemed so happy. "Look at yourself!" Kate brought over a hand mirror that always stood on the window sill over the sink. "Gracie the Flour Princess! Queen of Lasagne!"

I looked at myself and smiled. Then all of a sudden I burst into tears.

"Hey Gracie, what's wrong?" Kate asked gently, surprised. "I'm sorry. I didn't mean to hurt your feelings."

"Kate was being silly," Jannie said in a soothing voice. Amazing autistic Jannie.

"It's not about that," I said, still crying. "I don't even know what it's about."

Kate, standing in front of me, pulled me toward her and held my head. I cried even harder.

"Gracie?" Jannie asked out of the blue. "What was the name of the girl we met that day we took a walk to the bird store? The one with the spiky hair that was the same red as a macaw?"

I'd forgotten that Gina's hair had been dyed bright red that day. I was startled. What had made Jannie think about Gina just then? I stopped crying and looked at her.

"I have no idea what you're talking about," I said, and the sharpness of my tone didn't escape Kate.

"Jannie was just asking," said Kate. "Hair the same red as a macaw? Wow. Cool."

Jannie thought for a moment. "Oh, I remember," she said. "Her name was Gina. Her G has the same sound as my J for Jannie, but it's the same letter G as Gracie. So she's a little the same as both of us." Jannie was obviously pleased with her analysis.

Kate looked as though she were about to ask me something but she turned back to the strips of lasagna she was shaping from the fresh pasta machine.

* * *

By the time Nick came, the house was filled with the smell of baking lasagna and garlic bread. Jannie raced upstairs to get her *Birds of the Western Sierra* to show Nick.

"Look!" she said, excited. "I may get to see all these! Blue grouse, mountain quail. Band-tailed pigeon, Williamson's sapsucker, American dipper!" the more she named, the more excited she got. "Townsend's solitaire! Northern pygmy owl! Calliope hummingbird! MacGillivray's warbler!"

Nick turned the pages as Jannie spoke. He had a mild interest in birds himself, and had taken her for a few bird walks in the East Bay hills. They lingered over the photograph of a slender gray bird with a longish tail. "That's a Townsend's solitaire," Jannie told him authoritatively. "Do you know that a Townsend's solitaire eats nothing but juniper berries all winter long? And if anyone tries to get the berries one of them is guarding, there could be a really big fight! A really big bird fight!" The thought of this sent Jannie into peals of giggles. "But in the summer they eat insects too."

"Wow," said Nick, suitably impressed. "Just juniper berries. Doesn't sound like a very balanced diet to me."

"It wouldn't be for you!" Jannie couldn't stop giggling. At last she settled. "Their Latin name is *Myadestes Townsendi*," she told him. "Doesn't that sound silly? Townsendi? Like I would be Jannieay Levini, and you would be Nickoles Claytoni."

They laughed together. I felt envious of how easily Jannie connected with Nick. I had no bird books. No funny Latin names to talk about. Nothing interesting to show him.

We ate. Dad asked Nick about his studies. When he told Dad he would take nineteenth-century American poetry in the fall semester, Dad said, "That was Gracie and Jannie's mother's field. She came here from Germany to study Emily Dickinson."

"Who's Emily Dickinson? Emilayey Dickensoni?" piped up Jannie, on a roll.

"Hey, she wrote some far-out bird poems," Nick told her. "Listen!" He straightened his back and began to recite.

A bird came down the walk
He did not know I saw
He bit an angle-worm in half
And ate the fellow raw

"Well, of course he ate it raw!" Jannie giggled again. "Birds can't cook!"

I thought what a relief it would be to see the world in concrete terms like Jannie did. While she pondered the impossibility of a bird frying an angle-worm, I thought about Emmi sitting in the Bancroft Library reading Emily Dickinson. Ten thousand miles from Germany, lonely and intense.

The talk turned to what I had been doing all summer. I had rehearsed my answer, though my voice trembled a little as I spoke. "Kate's teaching me how to quilt," I said. "And I've been writing."

That was a total lie. I knew it would catch Nick's interest. And maybe it would even placate Kate. Maybe she would think I was doing something productive with all that time in my room.

"Writing?" he said. "What are you writing?"

I shrugged. I hadn't rehearsed this part. "Oh, just about my friend Martin, who died of leukemia." Lie.

"Your friend from Germany?" I was surprised Nick remembered. I guess I'd talked about Martin during the years when Nick babysat Jannie.

I nodded. "He died the night of your party. When I came home I got a call from his mother."

"I'm so sorry," Nick said. "I wish you had told me. I kind of wondered what became of you after the party. We'd talked about going for hikes."

I remembered that part of the conversation. It seemed as though it had happened centuries ago. "Sorry," I said. "I guess I got kind of busy."

"No, I'm sorry," Nick said. "I could have called *you*."

"No problem," I was quick to say.

"You don't have to call each other!" Jannie giggled again. "You're both here, sitting at the same table."

"Right," Nick smiled. He held his hand to his ear as though it were a telephone. "Gracie, hi, this is Nick," he said. Jannie giggled again. "I was just wondering whether you'd like to go for a hike."

I was drawn in despite myself. Nick was so easy going and accepting. "Maybe," I said, holding my hand to my ear.

"What kind of answer is that?" Nick smiled. "I'm going up to Chico for a few days this week to spend some time with my brother. How about the weekend after next?"

"Okay," I said to him. The weekend after next seemed far enough away so I could figure out how to get out of it.

Just before he had to leave, Nick asked if I wanted company taking Lizzy for a walk around the block. He knew I did that every night, and I couldn't think of a good way to say no. The truth was I didn't want Nick's company or anyone's. I just wanted not to be asked anything. Not to have to talk.

We started down the block. "I'd love to hear more about your writing, Gracie," he said.

"There's not a lot to hear," I said.

"Still. I'd be happy to see any of it you wanted to show me."

"It's not ready to be seen by anyone," I said.

"Sometimes it can help to have someone take a look. It can sort of clarify the direction it's taking."

There is *no "it,"* I thought. But I nodded.

"Have you ever tried fiction?" Nick pressed on.

All I ever try is fiction, I thought. But I said, "No. Not exactly."

"I've always thought you could be a writer," Nick said to me.

"Why?" That made three people who thought I should be a writer. Mr B. Gina. Nick.

"You tell stories really well when you want to tell them, I mean, like, in conversation. But it has always felt to me—since I first started babysitting for Jannie when you were, like, thirteen—that you have a thousand inner thoughts for every one you actually speak out loud. You're kind of private and secretive. And you read all the time. And it feels like you're looking inside things, inside people. Looking *through* them. Looking through situations. Like you're always trying to figure things out. Fiction writers do that. Poets do it too, in a different way."

I had no idea what to answer him. Had Nick always been observing me that closely?

We walked half a block in silence. "Maybe," I said finally. "I mean, maybe I could write stuff other than memories of people who died and papers for school. I don't know."

We had come back around to where Nick's old Toyota was parked. We stood in front of it for a minute while Nick tried to remember the title of a book he wanted to recommend to me. Then, "I really meant it about the hike, Gracie. I'm going to hold you to it."

"Okay," I said. Maybe I'd actually do it, I thought. Maybe.

"And the writer thing . . . I really meant that too. I'm not bullshitting you, Gracie. I think you have it in you."

I nodded. "I'll have to think about it. I mean the writer thing." Lizzy was standing between us, leaning against Nick's jeans. Nick took his keys out of his pocket. "So call me, I guess," I said to him. "About the hike."

CHAPTER 40

2002

W as I a writer? Or was I only a liar?

I remembered that line that had come to me before Martin's mother had called, about the juices of summer and of the earth. I took a sheet of paper and wrote that down. Then I wrote down a few things I remembered Martin and me doing together. Just notes about how we exchanged vows of everlasting friendship when we were twelve and made what I'd called, pretending it was a real thing, a Blood Pact: we made little pricks on our arms with a pin and mingled our blood together. Martin's blood that was not yet infested with leukemia.

Maybe I could actually write a story about it, I thought. Change things a little, make Martin's death something hinted at and then revealed. I stayed up until after midnight, writing down notes.

When I got into bed, what I thought about was Nick. Would he really call me? Was he planning to do it because Dad and Kate had asked him to? Or did he really want to spend time with me? What could he possibly see in me? I was still in high school. And I had nothing interesting to say.

* * *

I wasn't sure I could trust Nick *or* my ability to write; but something about talking with him seemed to have given me a boost of energy.

The next morning Dad and Kate would have an all-day meeting at their school. I made a plan for myself to dig up the ring as soon as they and Jannie were out of the house.

I stayed in bed that morning, listening to the sounds of them all getting ready to leave the house. For the first time in a while I'd awakened early, but I didn't want to risk anyone—Kate especially— picking up on the mixture of excitement, stealth, and anxiety I felt; so I thought it better to pretend I was still asleep. They were all used to my sleeping late anyway.

When I finally heard Dad's car pull away, I showered and went down for breakfast. I wanted to dig up the ring and get away as soon afterward as I could, so I made myself completely ready. I even washed my cereal bowl and my cup.

I went down to the basement to get the trowel. Then I went outside, Lizzy following.

The soil was harder than I had remembered it, and for a moment I was afraid I was digging in the wrong place. I dug deeper, I hadn't recalled burying the ring that deep, though, and wondered whether some natural shifting of the earth had occurred to settle it father down. Even though no one was home, I was anxious. What if the neighbors saw me? What if Dad and Kate had forgotten something and came home to get it before their meeting got too far along?

Just when I was thinking I should dig a little to the left, I saw something that looked like a bit of dull aluminum foil. I dug one more trowel's worth and uncovered the ring.

There it was, its shininess gone but the stones still in place. The sapphire and diamonds were caked with dirt and looked smaller than I had remembered them. I wondered whether they would really be worth much after all. Maybe I had caused all that pain for nothing.

I put the ring in the pocket of my jeans and piled soil back in the hole. Lizzy watched, curious. *Why would anyone bother to bury something like that?* she was clearly asking me, thinking humans were an odd species indeed.

I walked over to where the garden hose was and turned it on the ring. I worried for a moment that the water might loosen the stones, remembering why Kate had left it on the sink in the first place. But the stones seemed all right and I rubbed the ring on my T-shirt to shine it up a bit. After a while it looked better. I put it in my pocket and got Lizzy's leash.

Again, I decided not to bring the chrysoprase necklace. It seemed enough to give Gina the ring. I didn't want her to think I liked her too much. But I was also afraid that she didn't really know how much I liked her. The necklace, I decided, I would give her as a going-away gift if her friend managed to sell the ring and give Gina enough money to get to her auntie's.

She wasn't anywhere on Telegraph. It felt like a very long time since I'd seen her. I went to the place where we'd last been together in People's Park: three older men were sitting there, drinking from a bottle wrapped in a paper bag. I wandered up and down the Avenue, back and forth, for a full two hours, hoping to find someone who could tell me something about Gina. But I didn't.

I walked into a café to get a soda and a cup of water for Lizzy, tying her up outside. I sat at one of the outdoor tables. Lizzy sat at my feet. I kept feeling in my pocket for the ring, as though it might evaporate. No one I recognized walked by. At last I felt too impatient to stay there and decided to leave Telegraph and walk down to Gina's building on the west side of town. I was afraid that if I didn't get the ring to Gina today, when I had the energy for it, it might never happen.

* * *

The streets in daylight were way less ominous than they'd been in the dark, but I could see the full extent of the poverty and broken-down-ness of everything as I approached the place where Gina's dad lived. Maybe Gina had gotten sick and couldn't sleep under the freeway anymore and had to go back home? Maybe Bo had beaten her even worse than before, and she had to go back to her dad's to recover?

I realized I knew practically nothing about Gina.

In daylight it didn't seem to take that long to get to her place. Lizzy and I stood in front of the building I'd stood before a number of weeks earlier. The doorway still smelled of urine and rotting garbage, and the names of the tenants were still written blurrily on strips of adhesive tape over the six scratched metal doorbells. Gina's last name was not visible among them.

I was faced with the same problem again, and the same sense of helplessness; but at least it was only the middle of the day and Lizzy was with me. Even if Gina wasn't there, I might be able to find out something about where she was.

I stood there for a long time, debating which bell to ring. Finally I picked one that said *Floyd*.

No answer. I rang it again. Nothing.

The next one I rang said *Davis*. Again, nothing.

I decided to ring one of the bells that had no name taped above it. This one was responded to by a buzz on my first ring. I was so surprised by the buzz, which I figured must have meant that I was supposed to push the front door open, that I didn't do it fast enough. I rang a second time.

A second loud buzz and a woman's voice calling something I couldn't understand.

Lizzy and I were inside Gina's building. How we were supposed to find the apartment the woman had answered from, I didn't know; but we started up the stairs with their moldy-smelling worn carpeting. "Hello!" I called. No answer. "Hello?"

Just off the second landing a woman stood in the open doorway of her apartment. She was large and wore a pink bathrobe and flip flops. Her curly gray hair was bleached partly blond and looked as though she hadn't brushed it since waking up.

"Was that you who buzzed me in?" I asked her.

She looked puzzled and annoyed. "I thought you were George. George!" she said bitterly, almost spitting on the hallway carpet. "He buzzes to let me know he's coming up. You know George?"

"No," I said. "I'm sorry."

"It's okay, girlie. Why don't you come in? I need to sit down. Can't stand up too long."

I followed her inside her apartment. "Name's Margie," she told me.

"Gracie," I said.

"I won't remember it," she answered.

I noticed she limped when she walked. We sat down at her small kitchen table. Most of the things in her apartment were pink.

She scanned my face, lit a cigarette she took from the pocket of her bathrobe. "George," she repeated. "He takes care of the building. He's supposed to come fix my toilet and he told me he'd be here at eleven. Look!" she said, tapping her watch. "It's two in the afternoon and he's still not here!"

"I'm sorry," I said again. "I didn't mean to disturb you. I'm looking for someone."

"Who are you looking for, girlie?" she asked. Lizzy slunk behind me, as though she were wary of being seen.

"Gina?" I said tentatively. *Please let her know who Gina is,* I said silently.

"Gina," repeated the woman, inhaling. She looked up at the ceiling. Flicked her ash in a pink plastic ashtray that said *Viva Las Vegas* in gold script. "I don't know no Gina."

"Gina Powell?" I asked, as though her last name might clarify it.

"Powell," she thought for a moment. "George would know. He's the manager. You can ask him yourself if he ever comes to fix the goddamn toilet."

I imagined myself waiting for George for the rest of the afternoon with this woman in her apartment with her stuffed-up toilet. I sighed. Lizzy looked up at me.

"Wait a minute," the woman said. "You mean the skinny kid with the hair she colors red? Green? Her old man has a bum leg?"

I was thrilled. "Yes! Gina! Yes!"

"At my age I forget what people are named. I already forgot what *you're* named, and you just told me two minutes ago." She inhaled again, looked at me. "If you mean them, they're *gone,* girlie." She emphasized *gone.*

"What do you mean, gone?"

"They don't live here no more. They're gone. Moved away."

"Moved away?"

I was trying to take it in. I felt sick to my stomach, and the smell of the stopped-up toilet emanating from her bathroom didn't help. "When did they move?"

"I don't know. I don't keep track of nobody's business that ain't my own. Last week? Maybe last week. Left a mess in the whole apartment. Left half their stuff: furniture, everything. It was all garbage, though. George had to spend two days cleaning it up. Took it all to the dump. Maybe that's why he don't want to come fix my toilet. But I'm a good tenant," she said, raising her voice. "Soon as my SSI comes, I pay my rent."

"Did they get evicted?" I asked her.

"How should I know, girlie? They ain't none of my business." Margie took a sip from her coffee cup. "That man, he was strung out on meth all the time. Tried to get off, and I'd hear him screaming. The kid stuck with him, though," she went on. "She didn't seem like a bad kid. He's probably all she has. There was no mother. She helped him carry down whatever he was going to take with him and she drove off with him in his truck. I saw it from my window," she said. "Don't know how that man pays for gas. Don't know how he pays for anything. Maybe he deals. He was always hollering at guys who came by. Day and night. I don't know."

I felt desolate. "Do you have any idea where they went?"

"How should I know? Maybe George knows. You can sit here and wait for George."

Margie rinsed out another pink ashtray and put some water in it for Lizzy. She poured me a Diet Coke. She was being kind to me. I think she could sense how shocked and bereft I was.

I felt so terrible I wasn't even able to make much conversation; but Margie seemed grateful for my company. She told me she had a son who lived in Texas and another son who was in prison. She had a granddaughter in Texas who she thought must be about my age; it had been years since Margie had seen her, but she sent her a card on Christmas and on her birthday every year. "That's what a grandma does," she said. Margie was proud of being a good tenant and a good grandmother. I looked around at her apartment, one small living room and a smaller bedroom. She kept it very neat and clean. I wondered if Gina's apartment had looked like this one.

Margie's television was on the whole time we were talking. In the background to our conversation—which was really Margie's monologue—were the daytime soaps, tragedies packaged for stay-at-homes, just enough to keep them hooked on the fact that some people's lives were worse than their own. I started to worry about getting home, but it was only three-thirty in the afternoon and Dad and Kate were supposed to be home before Jannie's van got there anyway.

Toward four o'clock there was a buzz. Then heavy footsteps coming up the stairs. George, a short, stocky man with a gray buzz cut, was standing in Margie's open doorway. "Toilet still stopped?" he asked.

"What do you think, it fixed itself?" Margie shot back at him. "This is a friend of the junkie's kid. She wants to know where they went when you kicked them out."

"Wasn't me," George said. "It was the landlord."

He looked at me and Lizzy. "The dog yours?" he asked.

I nodded.

"Nice dog," he said.

"Do you know where they went?" I asked.

"George never answers you the first time," Margie commented.

"You got a plunger?" George asked.

"Are you kidding? You're the one supposed to be the manager. You don't have a plunger?" Margie snapped at him.

George looked unflapped. "No need to get worked up. I got one down in the car. Just thought I'd ask if you had one up here. Save me the trip."

"Save you the trip! What do you get paid for? Here I am, been waiting since eleven a.m." Margie shouted at him.

"Well, I'm here now. Got tied up."

George turned to go outside and get his plunger.

"Excuse me. George!" I called after him, afraid to let him out the door.

"What, young lady?" he asked.

"Do you have any idea where Gina Powell and her father went?"

George thought for a moment. "They didn't leave no forwarding address, that's for sure. But the kid did say something about how they had relatives in San Diego. San Diego." George thought for a moment. "Yeah, maybe that's where they went. San Diego. But *where* in San Diego I couldn't tell you."

I felt suddenly dizzy, steadied myself against Margie's table.

George was taking pity on me. "Hey, kid," he repeated, "It wasn't me who kicked them out. The owner did it. I'm just the manager. But that guy—he hadn't paid his rent in at least six months. Maybe more. Kept saying he was going to pay it next week, next week, the week after that. He was here a long time, and the owner tried to cut him some slack; but he ran out of extensions. Wife died in that apartment—eight, nine years ago. Both of them junkies. Finally there was some kind of brawl and the owner had it with him."

I nodded.

"You were friends with the girl?"

I nodded. My eyes stung with tears.

"She wasn't a bad kid. She was good to her dad, better than he deserved. She was real smart, did good in school, always reading and writing. She used to help me around the building sometimes. I taught her to fix things. She could fix a leaky faucet as good as me. Took her to the dump with me in my truck—she liked that." He paused for a moment. "I think that's why the owner let them stay so long. The kid. Because of the kid."

I was trying hard to keep from bursting into tears.

"Well," George said, "Maybe she'll call you from San Diego." And he went downstairs for the plunger.

Margie looked at me. "I'm sorry, honey," she said. She had switched from "girlie" to "honey." I put my head down on her pink formica table and started to sob. She got up, walked around the table—hobbled, really; her arthritis was clearly very bad—and she put a large hand on my back and rubbed it. "You must have been really good friends with that girl, to cry over her so hard. I'm sure you'll hear from her, honey. I'm sure you will."

I couldn't stop crying. Margie wet a dishtowel and brought it to me, to wash my face. She poured some more Diet Coke into my glass. She was so kind it made me start crying all over again.

I took some sips of the Diet Coke and stood up when I heard George coming back up the stairs. "Thanks, Margie," I told her. "I need to go now. I'm sorry to bother you."

"It ain't no bother, honey," she said. "Excuse me for not getting up again and walking you to the door."

Lizzy and I stood in Margie's doorway. "Thanks again." I didn't know what to say to her; she seemed so alone, and so generous. "I hope you get your toilet fixed, Margie."

"Honey, I forgot your name already. But you come back up here and see me whenever you want, okay?"

I nodded.

"And just you wait. Your friend will find you. I know she will, honey."

I turned before I started to cry again. "Bye, Margie," I called to her, and ran downstairs, Lizzy following.

*　*　*

I walked out onto the street feeling dizzy. Why hadn't Gina told me she was moving away? She had my number. Didn't she know it would matter to me that she was gone?

I felt for the ring in the pocket of my jeans. What was I going to do with it now, I wondered. I imagined the scene that would unfold if I were to go home and plant the ring someplace where it could be found. Everyone would be glad: Kate would put it immediately back on her finger and Dad would admire it and understand that she really did love him. Jannie would maybe even be granted an early reprieve and get her conures back. A whole terrible episode would have come to an end and no one would ever have known that I was to blame for it.

But I couldn't do it.

Something in me, something very strong, did not want to take the ring back home and let it be found. I didn't want to see it back on Kate's finger. The ring was for Gina, for Gina's escape. And now she was gone but not in the way she had wanted to go, and I would never be able to give her the ring.

I walked aimlessly with Lizzy down the streets, and found myself heading toward the Marina. It was windy and chilly but the sun was bright. Sailboats rocked back and forth on the bay, happy people enjoying a summer afternoon. I walked all the way out on the pier, past people monitoring fish lines and people cleaning fish they had caught, past kids on skateboards and kids on bicycles and older adults pushing their even more elderly parents in wheelchairs. Overhead, gulls were squawking. Jannie would know which species they were.

I stood looking out at the bay and, beyond it, to the Pacific. Then I took the ring out of the pocket of my jeans, studied it one last time, and threw it far over the railing of the pier into the choppy waters.

CHAPTER 41

2002

Now everything was over.

There was no Martin. There was no Gina. Jannie's birds had been exiled for nothing. The ring would serve no purpose anymore for anyone. There was no redeeming it.

When I got home I went upstairs to my room, calling to Kate that I had another migraine and was going to bed. I slept from the minute I lay down until the next morning, and I stayed in bed then too. When Kate came in to check on me I told her my headache wasn't any better and all I wanted to do was lie in bed with the shades down; and I did that all day, not even reading, not even listening to music. Lizzy lay with me the whole time except when Kate took her outside; and Lizzy was the only one I wanted to be with.

The next morning I came down to breakfast, but went right back upstairs to bed. Dad asked if I wanted to go to the doctor but he backed off the minute I told him no.

Later, when all three of them were gone, I went into the kitchen, lit the stove, leaned over the sink and burned the last poem Gina had given me, the one she'd copied out by hand from her notebook.

It burned so quickly it surprised me, and when it was nothing but charred black ash, I ran the cold faucet and washed the ashes away. I went back upstairs for another hour or two and fell asleep. When I woke, Dad was standing at the foot of my bed.

"Hey, Gracie," he said. "Something came in the mail for you."

He handed me a small envelope. It had Martin's return address on it, in his mother's hand.

Dearest Gracie, it said, *Thank you so much for your card and for your friendship with Martin. I know it meant a lot to him. With love, Dorothea Bachmann.*

That was all.

I felt nothing but the emptiness I'd felt for days. *Maybe that's the last I'll ever hear from her,* I thought.

Dad was still standing there. He asked nothing about the note. Instead, he said, "I have something else for you too."

He handed me a booklet. I didn't even bother looking at it. "What's this?" I asked.

"It's from the DMV," he said. "I thought if you didn't have anything else to do until school starts, you could learn how to drive."

I barely looked up at him. "What the fuck do I need to learn how to drive for?"

"Because it's one of the things people do at your age," was all Dad could find to say. "Even younger than you. You could have done it a year ago. It will give you more freedom."

"I don't want more freedom," I said. *I bet anything Kate put him up to this,* I thought.

Dad ignored what I'd said. "If you study the booklet I'll take you down to the DMV and you can take the permit test. Then I'll take you out driving."

"But school's going to start," I protested.

"There's nothing to keep you from practicing driving once school starts. Anyway, you've still got some time. The booklet has everything you need to know for the test."

I wasn't the least bit interested; but I could see that Dad was trying. I looked at the front page of the booklet and put it on my night table. "Okay, sure," I said to him.

"It's not complicated stuff, Gracie," Dad said. "You could learn it in a few days."

"Sure," I said listlessly.

"So we can plan on you taking the permit test maybe next week?" This was the most insistent he'd been with me in as long as I could remember.

I nodded. Dad left the room. I read Martin's mother's note again and still felt nothing. I closed my eyes but couldn't get myself to sleep. After a while I opened the booklet.

* * *

It is permitted to make a right-hand turn at a red light as long as the vehicle comes to a full stop before doing so.

At a four-way intersection where each vehicle has a stop sign, the vehicles may proceed through the intersection in the order in which they arrive.

I found it comforting, actually, to read the rules in the driving course. I worked my way through it quickly, glad to have something simple and concrete to do. Late the next week Dad drove me to the DMV. I passed my test and got my permit.

"You get to drive home, Gracie," Dad said.

"Just like that?" I asked him. "On Claremont Avenue? I don't know the first thing about driving, and there's a shitload of traffic on Claremont."

"We can practice for a while in the parking lot," Dad said. "It's not all that different from riding a bike. And I'll be right here in the passenger seat. You can do it."

I drove around the parking lot for twenty minutes or so before Dad told me to head out the driveway onto Claremont Avenue. I waited while a long stream of cars sped by. At last there was a red light holding up traffic to the left of us, and I pulled out onto the road.

I was scared; but it was good having Dad there beside me. *I can see what a good teacher he is,* I thought. He told me what to do calmly, anticipated my moves, pointed out things he thought I should be aware of; but he never criticized. I drove up Claremont to Ashby, made a left and drove toward our part of town. The fog had burned off for the first time in a few days, and everything looked sparkling clear.

"Are you all right, Gracie?" Dad asked.

"Yeah," I said. "A little nervous about the traffic. But it's not so bad."

Dad was silent a moment. "I don't just mean about driving, Gracie. I mean are you all right in your life these days."

I didn't know how to answer him. It was so weird having this question coming from Dad. It was more like a Kate question.

"I'm okay," I said.

"I just worry that you don't seem to be hanging out with other kids. You've spent so much time by yourself this summer. I know it must be very . . . very hard to lose Martin."

"I'm okay, Dad," I repeated. "Yeah, Martin. Am I too far from the intersection to go through it with the yellow light?" I asked.

"Go ahead, Gracie. You've got time."

I didn't know how to continue the conversation. *Actually, Dad,* I thought, *it's incredible to me that you haven't noticed how totally fucked up I've been for a long time.*

"Gracie, I wonder if you've been smoking pot," Dad went on. "I'm concerned because the other morning there was a strong smell of something burning in the kitchen."

Shit, I thought. *I cannot believe he's asking me this right now, the first time I'm driving a car.*

"That wasn't pot," I said. "You've *got* to know what pot smells like!"

"What was it, then?"

"It was just some paper I was burning."

"Paper?"

"Yeah. Just something I wrote," I lied, "that I thought wasn't worth keeping for posterity."

"So you had to burn it? It was that terrible?"

"Yeah. It was that terrible."

"Nick told me you're writing," Dad continued.

"Nick told you?" I was angry. Maybe Dad really was paying Nick off to be friends with me. I felt like I had when Mr. B. told me he'd told Gina to talk to me. "When?" I asked.

"A day or two after he came over for dinner. I ran into him on the street. We just talked for a minute. He was on his way to go see his brother."

"You talked about *me*?"

"About you and other things. Whatever we could talk about in a minute."

"Leave me out of it next time," I said, turning the corner of our block. I knew Dad wouldn't take the conversation any farther once I parked the car.

"Just pull into that space over there, Gracie," he said. "You've got plenty of room behind that green car."

* * *

After that foray into finding out how I was, Dad didn't ask anything more. I was sure Kate had engineered it. I could just hear her telling Dad to try and draw me out.

Dad and I started going out driving a little each day. It was a way to get me out of my bed, and it worked. I liked the feeling of being behind the wheel. We talked about driving techniques, about the Giants' latest game, about something Jannie had said. Dad was excited that Jannie would be mainstreamed half the time in a regular school starting in the fall; the special school she went to for autistic kids didn't have academic work in science and math that was challenging enough for her, so the district had agreed to transport her in the van every afternoon back to a Berkeley public school.

There was something reassuring about Dad coming out driving with me. This was how he had always managed to be my dad, I thought. He knows how to do good things, essential things, and he really cares. He just doesn't see what's beneath the obvious. He knows nothing about the kinds of shadowy places I've shared with Gina, and he's not interested in knowing anything about them. Maybe it scares him.

Jannie is the perfect kid for him, I thought. Her failures and successes are all understandable. She has no idea how to lie.

I wondered how it was for Kate to be with him. Kate was so expressive and perceptive; didn't it frustrate her to be with someone like my dad? Kate told me one afternoon while we were quilting that her father had died of a heart attack when she had been four. Kate and her two older sisters had grown up without a dad. Their mom had done her best to piece things together but their farm had always been on the edge of foreclosure and the girls had grown up in an atmosphere of fear and insecurity. Once Kate had said something about Dad being her "rock;" and I figured that was what was in it for her. He was so steady and immovable that she knew she could count on him.

I wondered as well about Emmi's relationship with Dad. Once, on our travels through Europe, Emmi, drunk, had said to me, "The worst mistake I made in my life was to marry your father. I never loved him."

At the time it had made me really angry.

Do you love me? I had asked her then, but silently. I would never have dared to ask her out loud.

Gina had read me the passages from Emmi's journals where she wrote that she did. But I didn't know if I could believe them.

* * *

Now that driving practice was added to my days, I felt I had some kind of purpose. It took my mind off Martin and Gina for a little while each day, gave me something I had to concentrate on. By the end of the week Dad thought I was ready to try the freeway, and we drove out Highway 80 toward El Sobrante and Pinole. "Emmi and I went to a park here once," he said to me. "I almost never come out this way, and I'm not sure I can find it, but maybe . . ." Dad's voice trailed off. "Oh! I think it's the next exit. There!"

We proceeded along a road that had almost no traffic. The grasses were all golden, the way grasses are in California toward the end of summer, after months without rain. The sun lit them so they seemed to be on fire.

"There's the place, Gracie!" My dad seemed so happy to have found it. I realized how infrequently I saw him light up like this. "Let's park and walk a little way up the trail. It's a really nice place, if it's still the way I remember it."

The smell of heat-soaked leaves and pine needles filled the air. I took off my sweatshirt and started up the trail with Dad.

"I remember this," he said. "Emmi was pregnant with you and it was just this time of year. It had been foggy for weeks in Berkeley and we came here looking for sun. Emmi was always depressed by the fog. . . . We parked in that lot and walked up this trail."

I looked at Dad and looked up at the tops of the trees. Birds I couldn't name were flying from one branch to another. *Jannie would know them all,* I thought.

Like the people I'd seen on the pier reeling in fish, Dad seemed to be reeling in memories, one after the next.

"We were walking along this trail holding hands, talking about the baby that was going to be born three months later. Emmi was telling me she wanted to paint your room some bright color, not pale yellow, which was the color a lot of people we knew were painting their babies' rooms."

"So that's how I got my hideous orange room?"

"It was supposed to be a deeper red, but the paint came out orangey once it was on the walls," Dad said apologetically.

"I hate it," I said. "It feels like living on the inside of a pumpkin. It's all chipping and cracking now anyway. It's totally gross. In some places you can see the old wallpaper under it."

We kept walking. A breeze coming up from the Pacific blew the grasses backward; their undersides shone silver in the sunlight.

"Last year I almost painted it something different, but I thought the orange was so bright it would take a million layers of paint to cover it."

"Probably true," Dad said. "I'm kind of glad you didn't try."

"You mean, since it was Emmi's choice?"

"Yeah. There's not much left anymore in the house that was Emmi's. Some books and photographs. Those boxes in your closet."

"Me and Jannie," I said.

"You and Jannie," Dad answered.

"What else did you and Emmi talk about that day? Do you remember?"

"Not much. It was eighteen years ago. I remember we stopped in a sunny meadow somewhere up the trail and ate the sandwiches we'd brought. We stayed there for a while, and Emmi took a nap. It made her tired to be pregnant, but she said it was a tiredness she liked."

This was the most my dad had talked about my mother since we'd come back from Germany. I wanted to keep him talking; who knew when he might open up like this again? "What was she wearing?" I pressed.

"I don't remember," he said. "No, wait—maybe I do. When she started to get big she usually wore this lavender-and-white striped dress. A long loose cotton dress. She looked pretty in that with her long blond hair. She had hair like yours, Gracie. Long and blond."

"Yes," I said. "I look like the German side and Jannie looks like the Jewish side. Do you remember: one day in eighth grade I chopped off my hair, up to my chin? That's because I looked in the mirror and thought I was Emmi. It freaked me out."

"I'm glad you let it grow again," Dad said. "But it's true. You do look a lot like her."

"Am I like her in other ways?"

"A little. Some ways. We should turn around soon, maybe when we get to that clearing over there."

"How am I like Emmi?" I wasn't going to let this go.

"Apart from your looks? You're kind of quiet and solitary like she was. And you love to read. And you're close to dogs. Emmi adored Ruffi, who came along on that walk—how could I have forgotten Ruffi!"

"Are there other ways?"

"What do you mean?"

We were walking back in the direction we'd come from. "Do you think I could ever go crazy like Emmi did?" The minute I asked it I wished I could take it back. It was like asking Emmi whether she loved me. I didn't want to know the answer.

"Are you really afraid of that, Gracie?" Dad's voice was tender.

I didn't reply.

"I don't know what made Emmi the way she was," he went on. "I never thought of her as crazy, though Jannie's psychiatrist has told me that what Emmi had, or what she was *like*, was typical of something called bipolar disorder."

"I *know* what bipolar disorder is, Dad. She obviously had it. She was a classic case. Her father had it too." How naive did my dad think I was?

"Emmi's father's bipolar wasn't as severe," Dad said. "It is biochemical, and it is hereditary," Dad said.

"I know that," I told him. "I've looked it up, like, five thousand times."

"I didn't know anything about bipolar disorder when I was married to Emmi. I just thought she was very unhappy."

Do you even see how unhappy I am? I asked him silently.

"Jannie was pretty crazy too at the time," I ventured.

"Jannie was a baby. A little girl. She was autistic and Emmi wouldn't accept it."

"I know," I said. "Are you still mad at Emmi?"

"Mad?" Dad asked, as though he had never given that name to his feelings. "We should move a little faster, Gracie. Jannie and Kate will be home soon and wonder where we are."

He hadn't answered my question, and I didn't ask him a second time.

* * *

After dinner that night I went upstairs and wrote down what I remembered about our conversation, and how it had made me feel to hear Dad talk about Emmi. Then I wrote some things I remembered about Gina. I tore the pages out of my spiral notebook and put a paper clip around them and wrote at the top of the first page, *All Flesh Is Like Grass.*

Then I lay staring up at the ceiling, realizing I had no way to picture Gina wherever she was. Were she and her dad staying with relatives? Was it some crowded apartment full of junkies where Gina had to sleep on the floor? Were they traveling around aimlessly and sleeping in their truck? In parks? Under freeways?

Was she sorry already that she had gone with him?

Was she relieved, at least, to be away from Bo?

Did she miss me at all?

I thought about how it would be for me to go looking for Gina. Impossible. Where would I even start?

That's what Dad must have felt, I realized, all those months when Emmi was dragging Jannie and me all over Europe, one day here and the next day there.

Impossible.

CHAPTER 42

2017

Jannie texts me asking if I can take care of Scout and her other birds because she's been invited to go to a conference with some people from the Center for two days in Sacramento. *What's the conference about?* I text her. *Disappearance of songbirds,* she texts me back.

Later that day she texts me a link to an article I read sitting in the faculty lunchroom at school: the number of songbirds in North America is, in fact, diminishing to quite a disturbing extent.

Between 1970 and 2014, the number of field sparrows and chimney swifts went down by 50%.

The population of snowy owls declined during that time by 64%.

I think how I love to walk in the hills in the early morning with Carson and listen to the mourning doves, their plaintive four note call punctuating the fog. How I love to watch the birds who come to the feeder outside my kitchen window, which I first put out there almost despite myself as a sort of homage to Jannie and which is now an essential feature of my life.

Without my sister I would have no idea that our world is losing its songbirds.

CHAPTER 43

2002

Nick called me, as he had promised, about taking a hike.
I had been so upset about Gina and the ring that I'd barely
thought about Nick; but the minute I heard his voice I was surprised
at how glad I was to hear from him.

He asked whether I'd like to drive out to Sunol, a regional park
about an hour east of Berkeley, the following day. I had done nothing
for weeks now except sleep, practice driving with Dad, claim I had
migraines, and fend off questions from Kate about how I was feeling.

Kate was the only one who noticed how troubled I was, and she
was clearly concerned. Once I'd heard her tell Dad that he should
make an appointment for me to see Jannie's psychiatrist, and Dad
had replied that he'd talk to me about it. But he hadn't.

Summer was almost over. Jannie would be leaving on Sunday for
her camping trip in the Sierras. A couple of days earlier she had forgotten to get one of her cockatiels in her room for the first time since
her conures had been exiled; there had been a big scene, but Dad had
relented since Jannie was about to leave, and things were calmer now.

I waited for Nick to pull up in front of the house, half wishing he'd call and say something had come up and he couldn't make it. For the first time in days I felt something other than the alternating heaviness and numbness I'd had in my chest since finding out Gina was gone.

Nick walked into the house carrying a wrapped package. "It's for Jannie, for her camping trip," he said.

I called Jannie. She came down still wearing her reading glasses; she'd been studying the birds she might see in the precise area where her group would be camping.

"I got you a flashlight," Nick said. "Every camper needs a good flashlight."

Jannie smiled at him, holding up the beautiful green-and-silver flashlight she had unwrapped. "Thanks," she said, not looking at Nick.

"Eye contact, Jannie," Dad said. He had just walked into the room.

"She was looking at her fucking flashlight," I snapped, and then felt embarrassed in front of Nick.

"I'm sorry," said Jannie, sounding acutely non-autistic. "It's weird with my reading glasses on. They make everything except writing look really blurry."

"That's why you're only supposed to wear them for reading," I said.

"I hope you get some good use out of it," Nick said.

Jannie smiled at him and switched the flashlight on. "It's broken," she said. "It doesn't light up."

"That's because it needs batteries," Nick said, and dug into his pocket. "I just happen to have some on me."

He put the batteries in Jannie's flashlight and handed it back to her. "Now try it."

She switched it on and smiled at the very bright light than radiated out from it.

"Wow! Super bright!" Nick said. "Great for lighting your way in the dark."

"Well, you wouldn't use it when it wasn't dark," Jannie said, giggling. She pointed her flashlight at the wall, the carpet, me.

"Don't waste the batteries, Jannie," said Dad. It was such a Dad thing to say.

Jannie took her new treasure upstairs. "Good choice, Nick," Dad said. "You know you're invited for dinner here after the hike, if you're free." *Don't bother asking me if I want to spend all that time with him,* I thought.

"Sure thing," Nick said, and we went out of the house.

"So what have you been up to, Gracie?" Nick asked once we were in his car.

I had so little to say, I thought he would be bored with me five minutes into our excursion. I told him I was learning to drive. I told him Dad and I had driven to a park in El Sobrante. *What an exciting life I lead,* I thought. I felt dull and tired and like it was a huge effort to say anything at all.

It took about an hour to get to Sunol. Somehow we'd found things to talk about on the drive: how Jannie was doing, what a good driving teacher Dad was. Political stuff. A poet whose work Nick had been trying to learn from. I deliberately kept the conversation away from anything about myself.

Once we were on the trail, Nick turned to me. "So what about you, Gracie?" he asked.

"What do you mean?"

"I mean, what about Gracie? What about your writing, who you've been hanging out with, what you've been thinking?"

Shit, I thought. *I have nothing to tell him.*

"How is your writing going, Gracie?" Nick asked again.

I found myself telling him about the notes I'd made about Martin. At least that wasn't a lie. Somehow it felt easier to talk about that with Nick than I'd imagined it would be; and talking about it made it seem more real.

Then I took a leap and told him I'd made a friend in Mr. B.'s American Lit class who wrote poetry, and she and I had gotten pretty close, but she'd just moved away with her father and I didn't know where. I told Nick I was making some notes so I could write about her as well.

That's how I said it. As though it were simple and straightforward. As though Gina were just another kid.

Nick listened. Nick had some comments to make about how notes were a good way to get started writing, and how interesting it might be to make something about Martin's story and something about Gina's into a single short piece of fiction.

A short piece of fiction . . . Nick was talking to me as though I were really a writer. What would Nick think of me if he saw my pathetic little sheaf of pages?

If he had any idea what I was hiding?

We hiked. Somehow we got on the subject of Mr. B. Nick told me it was Mr. B. who had inspired him, whose every course he had taken at Berkeley High. "You've got to take his Creative Writing class," he told me. "That was what did it for me."

"I don't think I can get in," I told him. "You had to apply for it by May, submit a whole portfolio or something."

"I bet you could talk to him and he'd let you in," Nick said. I was silent.

We stopped and ate our sandwiches by a small waterfall, thin at the end of summer, called Little Yosemite. Nick started talking to me about his longing to be a poet. He had already put some poems together to submit to magazines and he was planning to apply to MFA programs after he finished his BA. He was talking to me like a real friend, so vulnerably and sincerely that for the first time that day I thought maybe he wasn't just taking me out for a walk to make Dad and Kate happy. Or to find out some dirt on me that he could inform them of.

He started talking to me about his own mother, who had been confined to a wheelchair with multiple sclerosis since Nick and his brother had been little boys. Nick's dad had left the family soon after his mom had been diagnosed, and the two boys had cared for the house—cooking, cleaning, buying groceries—since they'd been five and nine, with the help of an aunt who lived a few blocks away.

I'd known nothing of this in the time he had babysat Jannie, while he'd been in high school. I had just thought of him as a kid who lived a normal life, while my life felt totally un-normal.

How can I let him tell me all this, I thought, *and tell him nothing?* At a break in his story I thought of something to say.

"Nick," I began. "Do you think lies and fiction are very far apart?"

"What do you mean?"

"I mean, sometimes a lie feels like a story. And maybe the story is hiding something real, though the facts are lies."

"Sure," he said. "What are you getting at?"

"Well, I've been thinking about that a lot, and I wonder how you can tell the difference—I mean to yourself—because sometimes . . . Sometimes when I tell a lie I start to believe it myself, and then I weave a whole story around it, and I start to believe that whole story. And then I start feeling like a character in a novel someone else is writing, and I don't know . . ."

"You don't know . . ." he prompted me.

"I don't know who I really am. Whether I'm the character I've created or whether I'm someone else, someone I can't even find."

Nick studied me thoughtfully. After a while he asked, "What do you lie about, Gracie?"

"Some small things, like I think everyone lies about sometimes. Where I've gone, what I've been doing. But bigger things too."

"Like what?" His eyes were penetrating but kind.

I chose to dive in. "Like about Emmi, my mother. I never tell people she's dead. I say she's working in Germany, that she never came back to Berkeley because she got some kind of fancy job there."

"Do you think people believe you?" Nick asked. He sounded curious, impartial. Not judgmental.

"I don't know. No one has ever questioned me," I said.

"I asked your dad when I first started babysitting Jannie, and he told me right away that your mom committed suicide when Jannie was five and you were twelve. I just figured it was common knowledge."

"That's what he told you?" I asked, incredulous. "He just said it like that?"

"Yeah," Nick said. "What do you think he tells people? It's normal for people to ask where a kid's mom is if she isn't around. People certainly asked about my dad after he split."

"What did you say?"

"I told them what happened. I mean—I was only five when he left, so it took me a few years even to understand it. But when anyone asked I told them my dad lived somewhere else, which was true. He moved around a lot, and after a while I didn't even keep track of where he was living. I told them he visited once every couple of years."

"Really?" I asked.

"Yeah. He would come to San Francisco and let us know maybe a day before. Chris and I would take BART into the city and meet him at whatever sleazy hotel he was at. He'd take us out for a meal— usually MacDonald's—and we'd go up to his hotel room and watch football or baseball on the TV there, and then he'd just say good-bye and hand each of us a couple of dollars. He never even walked us back to the BART station."

I was shocked. "That's lousy," I told him.

"It was pretty bad. After a while Chris and I told our mom we didn't want to see him, and eventually he stopped getting in touch with us. Mom kept wanting us to see him."

"What for?"

"She thought it was important for us to know our dad. Some kind of bullshit like that. Finally I told her that those visits had nothing to do with knowing our dad. He had no idea who *we* were, and he didn't seem to care."

"Did you want to know him?"

"At first we did. Or I did. Chris was angry at him from the minute he left. But after a while, no, I didn't want to know him."

"Maybe we never really know other people," I said. I was thinking of Gina. I pictured her wearing my sweatshirt. Kissing me.

"There's a line in a novel by Joseph Conrad like that," Nick said. "*We live, as we dream, alone.*"

I nodded. I looked at the thin trickle of water spilling into a shallow pool that, in turn, flowed into another part of the creek. "My mom left all these journals," I started. "I mean, she didn't *mean* to leave them; she just wrote in them and after she died my dad put them in these boxes in my closet. For years. One day a while ago that friend I told you about—Gina—she and I spent a few hours reading some of them. . . ."

"How was that for you?"

"It was weird. I wanted to know what she wrote and I didn't. I kept looking for clues about what made her so unhappy, and it made me feel kind of sick to read some of the things she wrote . . ."

"Did you find out what made her so unhappy?"

"No. Not really. Maybe some things . . . I don't think I'll ever look at them again," I said resolutely. "Maybe one day I'll open the boxes and they'll have been eaten by rats."

"Would that matter to you?" Nick asked.

"I don't know," I said honestly. "I guess I'd feel bad if they were really ruined. But I don't want to look at them anymore."

Nick sat looking at the waterfall. "I used to play little league," he started, "and I would watch the other boys who were there with their dads. I would see their dads whispering things to them between innings or when they were about to come up at bat, and I would imagine my dad—or someone else who would have been my dad, some Body Snatcher Dad who actually cared about me—I would imagine him telling me, 'Your right foot is a little too far forward, Son; try batting this time with it an inch or two back, you'll get more heft when you swing.' Or 'That was an awesome catch you made when the left fielder was sleeping on the job, Son.' I would even have been grateful if I had a dad who yelled at me when I made mistakes, like I heard some dads do with their kids."

"Yeah," I said, throwing a small stone into the water. "I used to think there was a secret about how to live your life that you found out at some point because someone who loved you told it to you. Like there would be one person who was kind of appointed to teach you what you needed to know. And until that person told you, you would be clueless. And if that person never told you, you would never find out."

We both sat watching the water. Then I ventured, "Nick, can I ask you something?"

"Sure."

"Did my dad—or Kate, maybe—ask you to spend time with me?"

"You mean did they ask me to babysit you?"

I could see Nick had taken offense. "I didn't mean like it was your fault. I was just wondering," I told him.

"You were just wondering whether I wanted to spend time with you or if your dad and Kate put me up to it. What do you think, Gracie—they're paying me to get you out of the house? *Here, Nick, let me slip you a twenty, take my kid out for some fresh air. If you throw in the dog, it's another five.*"

I didn't know what to say. *Why can't I just believe that he wants to be my friend?* I thought. And then, *Nick is three years older than I am. Why would he want to be my friend?*

"No, Gracie. No. They didn't ask me. I really like you, Gracie. I like talking to you. I've always thought we could be friends."

"But I'm just seventeen," I protested. "I won't even turn eighteen 'til October . . ."

"So what?" he said.

I didn't know what to answer. I felt relieved and a little wary.

"Sorry if I hurt your feelings," I said at last.

He nodded. Smiled.

I looked at him. He was squinting a little in the sun, and somehow that made him look even more vulnerable and sincere.

CHAPTER 44

2002

I was awakened the next morning by the sound of Jannie's van coming to pick her up for her camping trip. I threw on my sweatpants and ran downstairs to give her a hug good-bye.

She was standing in the hallway with one leg up like an egret. Kate's arm was around her. Jannie was looking tense and agitated and I could tell she was fighting to keep from crying.

"Hey, Jannie," I said to her, "Have a great time. I hope you get to see some awesome birds."

Jannie nodded, afraid if she opened her mouth a sob might escape. The doorbell rang and her teacher Rob was standing outside.

"Ready for some fun?" he announced himself, giving Jannie a high five. Dad had come downstairs with Jannie's duffel, and was on the stairs behind me. A daypack was slung across Jannie's shoulder and the flashlight Nick had given her was sticking out of its outside pocket.

The three of us and Lizzy walked Jannie to the van. She climbed in alongside Hallie, the first kid Rob had picked up. He was going to make the rounds and get five kids, while Karen, the other teacher, would pick up the other four in her van. Then they would meet and caravan off together up the freeway.

I had tears in my eyes as I watched Rob throw Jannie's things in the back of the van. Jannie sat at the window and gave me a tiny wave. *I wish Emmi could see her,* I thought. And then: *Emmi never did half for Jannie what Kate does. Kate took her shopping, did her laundry, helped her pack. Kate is really a mom to Jannie.*

"See you Friday night!" I called to her as the van pulled away.

Kate picked up the newspaper from the front steps and went into the kitchen. Dad went upstairs to shower, and I went back into my bed. I had lain sleepless a long time, thinking of my day with Nick. It now seemed improbable to me that he really intended his offer of friendship. Why would he want to be my friend, when he lived in that house with all those people who seemed interesting and lively? I was only a high school kid.

The happiness I'd felt for a moment the evening before was engulfed again by the now-familiar wave of dread and loneliness, and even Lizzy lying beside me, even the sounds of Dad's shower and Kate's breakfast dishes, couldn't abate it.

* * *

All that day I couldn't find a place to settle. I kept thinking about Nick. About Gina. What did I want with him? With her? What did either of them want with me?

I kept thinking about writing. About how weird it was not to have Jannie at home.

Dad had gone for an all-day meeting with colleagues from his department. Kate asked if I would help her with her quilt, which was nearly finished. I hand-stitched one end of it while she did the other, but after a while I felt too restless to keep going. "Do you want to take Lizzy up into the hills together?" Kate asked. "You could drive."

We drove up to a trail we both liked and walked into the fog, talking mostly about Jannie. "I'm amazed at her," Kate said. "When I think about what I've heard about the way she was when she was small, I can barely put that together with how she is now. She's so independent and resourceful. I could see it was really hard for her to leave this morning, but she did it."

I nodded. "I think Emmi kind of wrecked traveling for us."

"Oh, I hope that's not always going to be the case," Kate said. "But I understand. Traveling can be great, but not when you're in a constant state of terror."

"That's what it was," I told her. "A constant state of terror. We never knew from one hour to the next what we were going to do. And it never really felt like Emmi was taking care of us."

"Your poor mom," Kate said tenderly. "She needed someone to take care of *her*. And it shouldn't have been a twelve-year-old."

"I tried," I said.

"You did everything you could, Gracie. You kept Jannie from harm. You were only a child. And even your oma couldn't keep your mom from killing herself."

We kept walking.

"Kate?"

"Yeah?"

"Do you think anyone can ever save anyone else?"

"What do you mean?"

"I mean, what if, I don't know, what if I had written to Dad and told him the truth? All those months I just kept writing postcards telling him everything was fine. Do you think Dad would have come to Europe and brought Emmi and us home? Like, if he had some way of tracking us down?"

"Maybe," Kate said. "But that still doesn't mean she wouldn't have done what she did at some other point. She could have killed herself here, at home. She was severely bipolar. What she needed was psychiatrists, therapy, medication, maybe hospitalization . . ." Kate's voice was gentle.

It was scary to let my guard down with Kate, but somehow I couldn't help it. Since the previous day with Nick, I'd felt some wall I'd set up around myself beginning to crumble. Piece by piece, like caked mud, it was falling around me. And I couldn't stop it.

Kate turned to me. "Gracie?"

"What?"

"Your dad was a grownup. He could have gotten on a plane. He could have gone looking for you. People hire detectives, all kinds of things. Even if he couldn't have caught up with you when your mom was dragging you kids around, he certainly could have shown up in Germany once you were at your oma's. He knew she was in bad shape before she took you and Jannie away. He would have seen right away at your oma's that she'd gone over the edge. Why your oma didn't see it . . ."

"Oma tried," I defended her. "She had some kind of herb doctor come to the house. She made Emmi these vile-smelling green concoctions. She tried in the best way she knew how . . ."

"Okay," Kate said. "But your dad could have done more. He knew she hadn't taken you girls on a trip to Disneyland."

"So why didn't he? Why didn't Dad come to Oma's once he knew we were there?"

"I've asked him myself," Kate said. "Gracie, I love your dad very much, but don't think I don't see how he walks away from anything emotional that he finds difficult." She was looking straight into my eyes, and her voice was soft. "Your dad didn't *want* to see how disturbed your mother was. He was devastated by her wanting to leave the marriage, and paralyzed by his fear of confronting her. He was afraid that if he went after her and confronted her, he would lose her for good."

"So he did. He did lose her for good. And so did we."

"I know, Gracie," Kate sighed. "I know."

"You've actually talked to him about all this?" I asked her. I was dumbfounded. All these conversations had been going on around me for years, and I hadn't known.

"Oh, we've talked about it a lot. I still find it hard to believe that a father didn't leap to the rescue of his two little girls. He's made up for it since with Jannie—I think everything he's done for Jannie has come from his sense that he needed to make up for not having gone looking for you." We stopped for a moment while Lizzy greeted a German shepherd.

She continued. "Your dad has changed a lot since then. He's learned a lot. But I'm not sure he knows how to make it up to *you*, Gracie. He's worrying about you now, but up until a few months ago he was convinced you were fine."

"Well, I wasn't. I wasn't fine. I was totally fucked up."

"I know that, Gracie. I could see that when I first started coming by, when you were just starting your sophomore year."

"What could you see?" I asked her, feeling partly grateful and partly invaded.

"A smart, thoughtful girl, serious beyond her age—with no life. A girl who had no friends, who stayed home on weekends, who barely opened her mouth. A girl who just went along with whatever was happening in the household, when inside she was seething with anger and confusion. A girl who never told people what was really going on with her."

"You could see all that? It was that obvious?" *So all the effort I put into hiding and lying was just a farce, a ridiculous waste,* I thought.

Kate waited, then spoke. Lizzy was running up ahead to a stagnant pond she liked to swim in. "It always seems to me that you're hiding something, and I've never understood what it could be. I wonder all the time where you go when you do leave the house. When I talk about it with your dad, he just brushes it off. *She likes to take Lizzy for walks,* he tells me. But I don't believe you're just out exercising, Gracie."

"What do you think I'm doing?"

"I have no idea, Gracie. I've wondered." There was an edge in her voice. "You don't seem to have friends, or even to want friends. So I've wondered who or what you're spending your time with. And recently I've wondered whether you've been going up to Telegraph."

"What makes you think that?" I asked as innocently as I could. I wasn't going to tell her I'd heard her tell Dad about her sister having seen me getting high with Gina. I wondered what else Kate's sister had seen happen between me and Gina.

That seemed so long ago. I hadn't been up to Telegraph at all since that afternoon.

"That's where kids go. I'm not stupid, Gracie. I teach high school. I know something about kids your age."

"What else are you wondering about me?" I asked her. It was kind of a challenge and kind of a longing.

"I have no idea, Gracie." I could tell Kate was somewhat frustrated. "I don't feel like I really know you. That's my best shot—that you're hanging out on Telegraph. I don't think you're spending your time shopping for make-up."

I smiled. Kate went on. "I may as well tell you. My sister Carrie said she'd seen you with Lizzy on Telegraph. It was a few weeks ago, I don't remember exactly when. She knew it was you because of Lizzy. She wasn't sure, but she thought you were with a group of kids who were getting stoned. But what Carrie told me only confirmed what I'd already suspected."

"What? That I'm a stoner? You really think I'm a stoner? How do you know that wasn't the only time I was ever there?"

"I *don't* know, Gracie. That's the thing. I have no idea what you do with your time."

I changed the subject. "Kate, did you know that Dad told Nick that Emmi killed herself?"

Kate seemed willing to switch topics. "I didn't know specifically about Nick; but I do know your dad tells everyone who works with Jannie so they'll know her background. Why do you ask? Does it surprise you?"

"It's just that . . ." I almost told her I had been lying all these years about Emmi. But then I couldn't. I just couldn't.

"Just what?" Kate's voice was gentle again.

"I don't know. I just didn't know Nick knew."

"Do you think he'd feel differently about you if he knew what happened to your mother?"

"I don't know. I have no idea how Nick feels about me. Or how I feel about him."

We walked for a while in silence. Then Kate said, "Gracie, I'm worried about you. Dad and I are both worried about you. I know you've been grieving Martin, and of course that has colored your whole summer. But I keep feeling that something else is going on with you that I just don't get."

"I'm not doing drugs, if that's what you're so freaked out about!" I flashed at her. "And stop talking to me as though you were my mother. *Dad and I are both worried about you . . .* You are not my fucking mother, Kate!"

Kate flashed back at me. "Goddammit, Gracie. God fucking damn it. Do you ever let anyone anywhere near you?"

Tears welled in my eyes. Lizzy came running from the stagnant pond and shook herself, soaking us with smelly water. I was giggling and crying at once. "I don't know. I don't know."

Kate took me in her arms and hugged me. We walked back down the hill to the car without speaking. Kate slipped into the driver's seat.

Heading back to the house, Kate put one hand on my leg. "Hey, Gracie," she said.

"Hey," I answered.

CHAPTER 45

2002

When we got home I went back up to my room. The fog was so thick it made it look like night, though it was only maybe six o'clock. I could hear Kate in the kitchen, making dinner. Did Kate ever go back to her own apartment? I wondered. Was she still even *renting* an apartment? She seemed to be here all the time now. Would Dad and Kate ever get married? Was Kate young enough to have kids of her own? Would she want kids of her own? Would Dad want more kids? What if they turned out to be defective, like me and Jannie?

I heard the front door open, heard Dad say hello to Kate. Dad was excited about the new curriculum he was designing with people from his math department. Kate and he would start teaching the week I started back at school. I listened to their voices, the sound of lids placed carefully on pots.

I felt like a ghost in my own life. Listening to but not participating in what happened around me, like the girl in *Our Town* who looks wistfully at the world she has lost by dying at sixteen. We had read the play in Mr. B.'s class, and I had loved it. I had thought about it when Jannie talked about Emmi that time we took a walk, as though she hadn't really died but could come back and stand outside our window and see what had become of us.

What would Emmi think of Kate? I wondered. Kate, who didn't read what Emmi would have considered literature, who mostly read science magazines and books for her Bio students. Kate, who taught high school kids about chimpanzees and amoebas. Kate, who made quilts and cooked lentil soup. Would Emmi be glad someone was here taking care of us, making dinner, helping Jannie pack for camp, worrying about me? Would Emmi be relieved, or would she be jealous? Would she be annoyed by Kate the way I often was? Would she wish *she* were the one in the kitchen, making soup? Would Emmi be sorry for taking her own life and missing everything that happened to me and Jannie afterward?

The house felt cozy. Fog outside, warmth inside. The smell of lentil soup on the stove. Kate chatting happily in the kitchen with Dad as she cooked. *Kate's a good person,* I suddenly thought, *to take on this clueless man who can't express his feelings or listen to anyone else's feelings without squirming. To take on this man and his two strange daughters.*

At dinner Dad announced that he was going to have to work with his colleagues all the following day and probably into the evening. Kate asked whether I wanted to drive out to the beach with her. "You can try your hand at the twisty roads out to Point Reyes," she said; and since I had nothing better to do and no one to do it with, I told her I would.

I wished Gina would call. I wished Nick would call. I was certain neither of them would.

* * *

We drove out over the San Rafael Bridge and onto 101 to Lucas Valley Road. Lizzy stood in the back seat, looking out. Kate, too, looked out at the golden-brown hills of the end of summer. I liked driving, I thought; it gave me something to concentrate on. Dad had been right. Kate and I didn't talk much. We listened to music on the radio. Unlike Dad, Kate didn't mind listening to the music I liked; she even seemed to appreciate it.

On the beach at Point Reyes, the sun was breaking through the fog and other dogs were running along the tideline. Lizzy darted in and out of the water, grabbing long pieces of kelp and shaking them hard. Dropping them, then racing back in the water. I thought of that day long ago on Muir Beach with Emmi and Dad and our old dog Ruffi, the day when Emmi had rowed me in that little boat and sung me the song.

The water is wide
I cannot cross o'er
And neither have I
Wings to fly

Give me a boat
That can carry two
And both shall cross
My child and I

"You lost in thought, Gracie?"

"Kind of."

"It looked like you and Nick had a good time on Saturday," Kate began.

"It was okay," I said.

"Just okay?"

"It was good. I think we might be friends. He's going to be really busy with school, though . . ."

"You'll be too, soon. Senior year. College applications, all that."

"I guess," I said, watching Lizzy.

We were standing still where the tide broke. A family walked ahead of us with a little girl maybe three years old and another child in a Snugli Pack being carried by her mother. The mother had long blond hair, like Emmi's had been. I saw Kate looking intently at the children, and something in me wanted to hurt her.

"Do you ever wish you could have kids of your own?" I asked her.

Kate didn't answer right away. "Sometimes I do," she said at last. "It's nice being around you and Jannie."

"But we're not yours."

Kate looked at me. "I'm aware of that, Gracie."

I pushed it farther. "Anyway, you didn't know us when we were small like that."

"True," was all she said.

Lizzy had found a yellow lab who was willing to play chase with her. They ran after each other up and down the beach.

"By the time I was your age, Gracie," Kate said after a while, not looking at me or at the mother and children, who were sitting down now and digging in the sand, "I had already been pregnant twice and aborted both times."

I was stunned that she would tell me such a thing. "Really?"

"Really. The first was when I was fourteen. The second, a year and a half later. Two different fathers. Both guys I went to high school with."

"Wow," I said. "I had no idea."

"I know you think of me as some kind of cheerleader, but I had a really hard time for a bunch of years when I was a teenager, and even later. My life wasn't perfect, Gracie."

"I never said it was." I felt angry. I wasn't sure where this was going.

Kate ignored my snide comment and went on. "By the time I

would have been going into my senior year like you, I was waiting tables at a truck stop off the I-5, trying to pay back Carrie for the money she fronted me when I was pregnant the second time and our mom threw me out."

"She threw you out?"

"I lied to her about being pregnant. I totally lied the first time. I had the abortion and she never found out. The second time I lied to her too; but someone told her I was pregnant. I hadn't had the second abortion yet."

"But why did she throw you out?"

"Because we were Catholic and it was a sin. Because I had lied to her about still seeing the boy who was the father. She had forbidden me to see him because she guessed we were having sex."

"Did she want you to have the baby?"

Kate nodded. "She said I should go live somewhere else until I had the baby and then give it up for adoption."

"But you had an abortion instead?"

Kate nodded again. "I actually thought for a while that I'd keep the baby. I found the job at the truck stop. I thought I would have the baby and just live on my own and raise it."

"What happened to the father?"

"Oh, he walked out on me as soon as he knew I was pregnant."

"Wow. That must have been hard."

"It was. I was working twelve-hour shifts, throwing up in the smelly bathroom between customers. Just before it would have been really hard to have an abortion, when I was about fourteen weeks along, I kind of fell apart one night and realized I couldn't handle it. I wasn't even sixteen. I'd used Carrie's ID to get the job; we looked enough alike and I always looked older than I was, and could pass for her age."

"So you dropped out of school?"

"Oh yeah. I dropped out. I was living too far away, for one thing. And I needed to work because I had no money coming from anywhere else. I just stayed in the little room I'd rented in somebody's house and kept waiting tables."

"And you had the abortion?"

"Yeah. I went to Planned Parenthood. Carrie came out and drove me and stayed with me overnight in the little rented room. The next day I had to work, and I couldn't stop cramping."

"Wow," I said, taking it in. "Did you live there a long time?"

"A couple of years," Kate answered.

"Did you see your mom?"

"For a while only Carrie would come to see me. She'd come on her days off and buy me food and clothes and stuff. But Mom and my oldest sister Marie—especially when they found out I'd had the abortion, they didn't want anything to do with me. I was the baby in the family—seven years younger than Carrie, nine years younger than Marie—and I was supposed to be perfect."

I tried to picture Kate at fifteen, sixteen, seventeen. Living alone in a rented room, bringing truckers blue plastic plates of fried eggs and bacon.

"How did they start seeing you again?"

"I'd started drinking," Kate continued. "I was drinking a lot. Whenever I wasn't working, I was using Carrie's ID to buy booze. One day the lady I was renting a room from knocked on the door of my room and told me my mother was in her living room. And she was. She paid the lady my last month's rent and told me to pack my things, quit my job, come home with her and go to AA."

"How did she find out?"

"Carrie was worried about me, and she told her. I was mad at Carrie at first; but she did the right thing."

"Wow," was all I could think to say.

"If she hadn't told Mom, who knows where I'd be today. But I did a year of AA and then got my GED and went to community college and fell in love with Biology. And then I came down here and moved in with Carrie and went to Hayward State."

The mother wearing the Snugli and her little daughter were walking back along the beach in the direction they had come from. The long straps of the Snugli dangled behind the mother, flapping green in the wind that blew off the ocean.

"You remind me of Carrie sometimes," Kate said after a while.

"Me? How?"

"I don't know," Kate said. "The way you take care of Jannie. Like I said, I was the baby, and my mom was always kind of nervous and afraid, and she was working so hard all the time and going to mass every morning—she was born in Ireland, and was—still *is*—super devout. Carrie packed my lunches and picked me up at school and walked me home. She kind of watched out for me like you do for Jannie. Marie was always busy studying or praying; she was even more devout than Mom and all she wanted was to get into the convent where she's been since college. Carrie was only eleven when our dad died, but she was the one who kept the household together. "

"I'm not like that," I protested. *If Kate only knew how I'd hurt Jannie*, I thought.

"The circumstances are different," Kate said. "But still, there's something . . . Carrie still looks at me like her baby sister, though I'm thirty-nine and she has two high school kids of her own. She worries that I'm not married to your dad. She worries that I won't have kids before it's too late. And she worries about you and Jannie . . ."

I just nodded. I felt a shudder of shame pass through me. *If Kate knew what I've done . . .* and I couldn't even finish the thought.

After an hour it started to get chilly. The fog was coming back in. Lizzy and Kate and I started back toward the parking lot. I didn't feel much like talking. Kate's story about her life had really shocked me; it was the last thing I would have imagined about her. I felt bad for all the months I'd thought of her as Miss Rosy Cheeks Farm-Bred.

How little we know other people, I thought.

"I can drive back," Kate offered. "If you like, we can stop at a little restaurant I know in Point Reyes Station."

I nodded and stepped into the car. I wasn't hungry, but—unusually for me—I wanted to make Kate happy.

CHAPTER 46

2017

Jannie calls me when she gets home from the conference in Sacramento.

"Did you remember to give Scout her vitamin drops?" is the first thing she says. Not "Hi Gracie."

"Yeah," I tell her. "Two drops a day."

"Gracie, can you help me fill out an application?"

"What for?"

"The vet tech program."

"Really?"

"Yeah. Some people at the conference said I should do it. They told me it's not too hard. And I can do maybe like one or two classes at a time, and still work at the Center. I figured out how long it would take me."

"How long, Jannie?"

"If I do one or two classes at a time, maybe five years. I can do it in less if I take more classes. But I'll still be at most the same age as you when I finish. I mean thirty-two, the age you are now. So that's not so old."

"That's not so old, Jannie."

CHAPTER 47

2002

"Kate," I said when we were seated at our table in the corner of the restaurant and we had ordered our dinner. "I have something I need to tell you."

"Sure, Gracie," said Kate, drinking her water.

"Kate," I began again. "When you said that thing about Jannie . . . About me reminding you of your sister, taking care of Jannie . . ."

"Yeah?"

"What I . . . Kate, I don't deserve . . . I did something horrible to Jannie." I took a sip of my water. "And to you too."

"You, Gracie? What did you do?"

The waitress brought our salads at that exact moment. I pushed mine to the side. I looked outside at the street at Lizzy, sitting in the car, looking out at us through the half-open window.

"I was the one who stole the ring. It wasn't Jannie's birds."

Kate pushed her salad aside as well. "You, Gracie?" she repeated.

I looked into my water glass, watching a piece of ice float around at the top. "I still don't know why I took it. It was just lying there on the shelf over the sink, and I was having a crappy day. And I just kind of felt like taking it."

Kate looked at me. "Where did you put it, Gracie?"

I couldn't look at her. "I buried it."

"Buried it? Where?"

"In the backyard." I paused for a moment. "And then, after a while, I threw it away."

"In the garbage?"

I picked at a little hardened bump of shellac on the wooden table. "No. In the bay."

Kate was silent. She ate a bit of her salad. I looked at my salad. I didn't feel like eating it.

"And you just watched while we blamed it on Jannie's birds?"

I nodded.

"And you watched while your dad took her birds away, and she was so miserable about it?"

"Yes. I just watched."

Kate put her fork down. Very softly, almost too softly for me to hear over the noise of the restaurant, she said to me, "I can't believe you did that. I can't believe you did that, Gracie."

"Well, I did." I started to cry.

The waitress arrived with our bowl of minestrone. "Is everything all right?" she asked. Kate nodded quickly so she would go away.

"Jannie's been devastated all summer about those birds, and she's worked so hard to get them back," she said.

"I know," I said, my voice breaking. "I know."

"What are you going to do about this, Gracie?"

"What do you mean?"

"You need to tell Jannie what you did. As soon as she gets back you need to tell her. And you need to tell your dad."

"I know. I will." Now the tears were streaming down my face.

Kate took a spoonful of minestrone. "You know, Gracie," she started, "It did cross my mind at one point that maybe you had taken the ring. You were so upset that your dad had given it to me. When we couldn't find it in any of the places the birds usually left things, I wondered for a minute that day whether you had put it somewhere, just so I wouldn't have it."

She ate more of her soup. I said nothing.

"But when all that came down with your dad and Jannie, when Jannie was so undone about your dad taking her birds away, I dropped it. I couldn't imagine that you would watch your sister suffer in that way and not say a word if you'd been the one to take the ring. *Gracie would never be that cruel,* I said to myself."

"I guess I was. I guess I am," I said. "I guess I am that cruel." I meant it. And I felt awful.

Kate sat there shaking her head. Then, very softly, "Why? Why, Gracie? Why did you let Jannie take the blame?"

"I don't know." I was sobbing. "I don't know."

Kate sighed. "And why did you throw the ring away?"

I took a few deep breaths. "That was weeks after I buried it. It was just . . . buried there, in the backyard, and then . . . I thought I could give it . . . to someone I know. So she . . . could get some money for it." Between sobs. Tears were spilling into my soup. I pushed the soup away.

"Money?" Kate asked. "For drugs?"

"No!" I shouted at her. Heads turned in the restaurant. "No! It had nothing to do with drugs."

The people in the restaurant turned back to their dinners.

"I feel horrible, Kate," I said, and started sobbing all over again.

"I feel horrible for Jannie," Kate said severely.

I had no answer for her. There was nothing more to say.

Kate finished her minestrone and looked over at my uneaten bowl of soup. "You haven't touched your food, Gracie," she said after a while.

"I'm sorry. I don't feel like eating."

"It was really good. We can take yours to go." Kate had softened a little. "Gracie?" she started.

"Yeah?"

"Your dad was kind of—he didn't use good judgment, to give me that ring. That *particular* ring. It was a family ring, *your* family ring. He could have given me something else for my birthday. He could have bought me another ring."

She stopped for a moment, then continued. "I get why you were upset about his having given it to me. But that doesn't justify what you did."

"I know, Kate. It doesn't. I wish I hadn't taken it. I'm sorry. I'm really sorry."

Kate sat across the table, looking at me, taking her hair out of its pony tail and putting it back again, more smoothly. The waitress came and stared at my untouched food. Kate asked her to pack it up.

We walked in silence out to the car. It was dark already, and Kate drove the winding road back to the freeway slowly, silently. From the back seat, Lizzy put her chin on my shoulder and I started crying all over again.

Just as we neared the San Rafael Bridge, I said, "Kate?" I had been thinking all this time about what to say to her.

"Yeah?"

"I'm sorry for what I did to *you* too. I didn't only hurt Jannie. I also hurt you."

"And your dad," Kate said.

"I know. Dad too. But you—I've treated you like shit for such a long time, and the ring was part of it, and I'm really sorry. I feel like such a terrible person."

Kate was silent for a moment; then she spoke to me gently. "Gracie, you're not a terrible person. You're a very confused and sad and over-whelmed person who did a really terrible thing."

She was silent for a while. Then she continued. "I mean, the terrible thing was not taking the ring and getting rid of it. It was only a ring. The terrible thing was what you did to Jannie."

I sat there in the passenger seat, crying. Lizzy whimpered a little herself in sympathy from the back seat. Kate reached one hand across to me and took my hand.

"Hey, Gracie Levine," she said. "Nobody gets through life without making a few mistakes."

"But that wasn't a mistake,' I said. "I don't know what it was."

"A cry for help?" Kate suggested.

"But I didn't tell anyone . . ."

"A lot of cries for help are mute at first. Then something happens, and someone hears."

I sobbed.

"Gracie," Kate said, and her voice was tender. "Jannie's birds are safe and sound with Peggy Hilverson and Jannie will get them back. You'll tell her what you did when she comes home, and you can tell Dad tonight if he's home before you go to bed. Or tomorrow."

"But the ring is gone forever," I sobbed.

"Okay, Gracie. The ring is gone. It's the least important casualty of this whole story and there's nothing you can do about it. But you *can* set the rest of this right. You've already started."

CHAPTER 48

2002

When we got home there was a message on the machine from Dad, telling us he wouldn't be home until after midnight. There was also a message from Nick, just saying hello and telling me he would call again sometime later that week.

I felt drained, exhausted. I gave Kate a hug and went straight to bed.

By the time I woke up the next morning, Dad had already left to go back to work on his curriculum with his math department friends, and Kate had left to go to the dentist for a root canal. She had left me a note on the kitchen table: *I didn't say anything to your dad,* she'd written. *See you this afternoon.* Kate had drawn a little heart after her name.

I felt uneasy, knowing it was up to me to talk to my dad. And then to Jannie.

I wished I could tell Gina I'd spoken to Kate. I wished I could tell her all of it, what Kate had told me about her life, and how that had convinced me I had to come clean with her. I had felt so protective of Gina when Kate had asked whether I wanted to get the ring to my friend so she could buy drugs. *No, I had cried out!* I wished I had told Kate, *My friend was being abused—beaten—by her boyfriend, or ex-boyfriend. And her father is a junkie, and she needed the money so she could get away from here and save her life. But now she's gone and I have no idea where she went and it doesn't even matter anymore . . .*

Would Kate have understood? How could she not have, after what she'd told me about her own life? What if I'd told Kate Gina's whole story, or as much of it as I knew, anyway?

If I'd told her, Kate might have felt bad for Gina and seen why I'd wanted to give her the ring . . . though that still wouldn't have cancelled out my stealing it in the first place and blaming Jannie.

I wondered suddenly whether Gina might have spoken to Mr. B. before she'd left with her father. Maybe Mr. B. knew where she was. Maybe at least he could find out through some official channels— registration at another school?—where Gina and her dad had gone. Mr. B. might be at school setting up his classroom, or working on curriculum like Dad.

I decided to walk to Berkeley High and talk to him.

* * *

I walked up to Mr. B's classroom on the second floor. It was locked. I stood at the door, looking through the little square window into the classroom. Some of the things that had been on the wall in the middle of June were still there; it felt strange to see them. *Martin was still alive then, and Gina was still here, and I hadn't stolen the ring,* I thought. *Now everything has changed.*

I walked down to the school office, where a few people were working, answering phones, Xeroxing. "Excuse me," I said to one of the women behind the desk. "I'm Gracie Levine. I'm going to be a senior. I wonder whether you know if Mr. Bryzinski is around?"

She checked his mailbox. "It doesn't look like he's been in for the last few days," she told me, "and the teachers don't *have* to come in until next week. Some of them are around, though." I figured she could see my disappointment. "He might come in even later today. He's generally around a lot. You're welcome to write him a note and I can put it in his box for you."

I stood at her desk and scribbled a note on the paper she gave me. "*Hi, Mr. B.,*" I wrote. "*It's Gracie Levine. I have something I need to ask you about. It's important. Please call me as soon as you can. Thanks.*" I wrote my phone number, thanked the secretary, and walked back home.

* * *

An hour after I'd gotten home, the phone rang. I was in the backyard with Lizzy, stretched on the grass, reading. I leapt up, hoping it was Mr. B.

"Hello?" I answered.

"Is this Kate?" I didn't recognize the voice.

"No, it's Gracie. Kate's not here."

"Gracie, is your father home?" *It must be some colleague of his,* I thought.

"No, he's at work. Who's calling?"

"This is Sylvie from Jannie's school. I'm one of the assistant teachers with Jannie's group up here."

"Oh," I said."

"Gracie, is there a way I can reach your dad?"

"Actually no. He's at a meeting and I don't know where. Can I take a message?"

There was a moment's hesitation. Then Sylvie spoke. "Gracie," she said, "Jannie has been missing since early this morning. We've got people out looking for her. Rangers, helicopters, volunteers. Search dogs."

I took a breath. "No!"

"Rob is out with them," she said. Her voice was terse.

"Rangers? Helicopters?" I felt sick to my stomach.

"She slipped out of her tent, probably before dawn. We had no idea she was gone until we woke up and it was light."

I looked at the kitchen clock. "It's twelve-thirty! Oh my god! Jannie's been missing all this time?"

"There are a lot of people out looking for her," Sylvie said. She sounded helpless and on the verge of tears.

"Why didn't you call before?"

"I tried," Sylvie said. "There was no answer, and I didn't want to just leave a message on your answering machine. I tried Kate's cell phone, but she didn't pick up."

"Kate's having a root canal," I said.

I didn't know what else to say.

"Gracie," Sylvie started, "Do you know when Kate will be home?"

"Sometime this afternoon," I said. "I think she was coming straight home from the dentist. Why can't they find Jannie?" I started to cry.

"They're doing everything they can. I'm sorry, Gracie. I don't have anything else I can tell you for now, but I'll keep calling. Let me give you a couple of phone numbers, one for the sheriff's department up here—they're coordinating the search—and a number you can reach me on in this little motel I'm calling from in town. They're being really kind, and they said they're happy to take messages. There's no cell reception right here."

She gave me the numbers. I had to repeat them back to her twice because I couldn't write them down correctly. My hand was shaking, and my brain wasn't working.

"Gracie," Sylvie said, "Have your dad or Kate call me the minute they get in. Maybe Kate knows how to reach your dad. You should probably get up here as soon as you can. But I'll call you an hour from now unless there's any news before."

"Okay," I said. I felt numb and cold.

I went upstairs, Lizzy following. I took a post card out of Dad's desk and addressed it to my mother, as I'd done so many times in the months following her death. *Emmi Levine. Nowhere on Earth*, I wrote on the side reserved for the addressee.

Dear Emmi, Jannie is missing. You have to protect her. This is the one last thing you can do for Jannie. For both of us. Please, please, wherever you are, make Jannie be okay. Love, your daughter Gracie.

Just as I put the postcard in the box under my bed with my letters from Martin, I heard Kate's car pull in front of the house and I ran downstairs.

"Kate!" I shouted as I ran, two stairs at a time. "Jannie is missing! She wandered off somewhere in the mountains. Sylvie called a while ago from some town near where they're camping. She said she tried your phone but she didn't just want to leave a voicemail! And Dad doesn't have his phone . . ."

Kate knew where Dad was having his meeting and she phoned his colleague. Then she phoned the sheriff's number that Sylvie had given me. The sheriff told Kate what he knew, which wasn't a lot more than Sylvie had told me: Jannie apparently had left the tent where she was sleeping with two other girls and Sylvie while it was still dark. Expert as she had been as a small child in crafting escapes, she had escaped so quietly that no one had awakened. One of the girls from the tent, Hallie, had gotten up to pee while it was still dark. She had noticed Jannie's empty sleeping bag, but just went back to sleep; that was how they knew that Jannie had left in the dark.

All the kids on the trip were high-functioning autistic and couldn't be counted on to make accurate inferences about others' behavior; had Hallie thought to awaken Sylvie, Jannie might have been found while she was still nearby. Of course there was no way of knowing; but by now, one-thirty in the afternoon, Jannie had been gone at least eight hours. Rangers and volunteers were combing the area. Dredging three nearby lakes. Checking the river.

"We have to get up there," I told Kate as soon as she relayed to me what she'd heard.

"As soon as your dad gets home we'll drive up. I don't know if they'll let us join the search, but I can't imagine sitting here by the phone either. Pack your things and some food for Lizzy."

I went upstairs and threw a few things in my backpack. A sweatshirt. Blank paper. The chrysoprase necklace I'd bought to give Gina, which somehow felt like a way of keeping her with me. And I took a picture from my dresser, one that Dad had taken of me and Emmi and Jannie when Jannie was one day old. She was lying across my lap wrapped in a yellow blanket. Emmi had one arm around me and the other balancing Jannie's tiny head.

Before we drove off I left a message for Nick. "Nick, this is Gracie," I said. "I got your message last night but it was too late to call back. It's about three o'clock Tuesday afternoon and Dad and Kate and I have to drive up to the mountains because Jannie is missing. They have search parties out looking for her but they haven't found her. I don't know when we'll be back, but I'll try to call you from there and let you know what's happening. And . . . oh, thanks for calling."

Kate called her sister Carrie in Oakland and we took off.

* * *

Nobody talked in the car. We didn't even listen to the radio. A couple of times before we went out of range, Kate called the sheriff's office. Still the same news. Nothing.

I sat in the back seat with Lizzy, unable to stop thinking about how I had made Jannie suffer over the conures. I hadn't had a chance to tell Dad what I'd confessed to Kate, but this clearly wasn't the right situation to do that in. I kept thinking, though, that it was important to clear Jannie's name, to let Dad know she and her birds had had no role in the disappearance of the ring. Especially if anything bad had happened to her.

* * *

In a ladies' room at a rest stop I turned to Kate. We were washing our hands at the line of sinks. "I don't feel it would be good to tell Dad about the ring right now," I said. "But I don't want you to think I'm just avoiding it."

Kate's eyes met mine in the mirror. "I think you're right, Gracie. None of us can think of anything but finding Jannie. If you told your dad now it would only upset him more."

"Yeah," I said. Kate reached over and gave me a hug. My eyes teared up. Hers did too. There was nothing left to say.

CHAPTER 49

2002

We reached the motel Sylvie had phoned from by eight o'clock. Still no news. The rangers we met with told us more about where they were searching and said there was nothing for us to do but wait. They suggested a place where we could get some dinner; we half-heartedly picked at our food and then went up to our room to try to sleep.

It was chilly when I woke up. Dad and Kate, if they'd slept at all, had been up and dressed for some time. While I washed my face in the motel bathroom, I heard Dad use the word "hypothermia" to Kate.

Jannie had spent the night in dangerous temperatures. "How cold do you think it gets here at night, Dad?" Kate was on the phone with her sister.

"End of August. Probably low forties. Maybe even high thirties."

"That's pretty bad, isn't it? For someone as small and skinny as Jannie?"

"It's pretty bad," said Dad, and turned to look at the wall.

The phone in the motel room rang again. Kate picked up. It was one of the rangers, who was—from what I could hear of Kate's end of the conversation—clearly concerned about the cold as well. Kate arranged for someone to guide us to the campsite, and fifteen minutes later a volunteer in a bright orange vest was at the motel to pick us up.

He was a bald, fiftyish man with a round face. He extended his hand to Dad. "Frank Harwood," he said. "Lived in these parts all my life, seen plenty of lost kids get home to their families."

Dad nodded. Frank shook Kate's hand, petted Lizzy's head. "This your dog?"

"Yeah."

"We've got folks from Canine Search and Rescue out there looking for the girl. At least seven, eight search dogs."

Frank drove us to the trailhead, then led us the three and a half miles down the trail. He said he had been volunteering on searches like this since he'd been about my age. He asked me some questions about Jannie; I told him how passionate she was about birds.

"She brought her binoculars," I said, "in case she sighted some of the birds she'd been studying all summer." Frank asked whether I remembered any of their names, since knowing where their territories were might help in the search.

I struggled to remember as many of the bird names I'd heard over the past weeks. *Shit, why can't I remember more,* I told myself: Western tanager, northern pygmy owl, Townsend's solitaire, Williamson's sapsucker, Calliope hummingbird." Frank wrote them down in a small notepad he took from the pocket of his vest.

"She might have spotted a few of those," he said. "I know that teacher, the guy—"

"Rob?"

"Yeah, Rob. His guess was that she left the tent early to go looking for some bird."

"That's the only thing I can think of too," I said to him. "She used to just run away all the time, just randomly; but she never really does that anymore. I think she left the tent for some real reason. Birds are her obsession. She knows everything about them."

Frank and Dad talked about hypothermia. They were having a somewhat unusual cold snap in that part of the mountains; night temperatures didn't usually drop so low until mid-October. Frank said the low that night had been 36, and it was likely that Jannie's core temperature would have dropped, given how thin she was.

A body temperature lower than 95 was the danger point; below that, the heart could be affected. At the very least, Frank said when Dad pressed him for details, Jannie could be slowed down, drowsy, confused, apathetic. Sometimes, Frank said, a person with hypothermia stops caring whether they live or die. "We need to find her today," Frank said in his kind of laconic way. "I don't think a sixty-pound kid could make it another night out here."

I appreciated how straightforward he was, how clearly and without embellishment he told the truth. I thought about Jannie's sleeping bag, good for twenty-five degrees Fahrenheit, left behind in her tent. I thought about her red sweatshirt, the one Emmi had bought her on our first day in Europe, whose sleeves stopped midway down the length of her forearms. I was certain that was what she'd been wearing; Jannie almost never took it off, even when she slept.

Frank maintained contact with the sheriff's office on his walkie-talkie. Nothing had turned up in the three lakes. Nothing had turned up in the river. "That's good news," he said in his laconic manner.

At last we saw the blue and red tents of the camp. Lizzy ran wildly ahead of us, probably thinking she'd find Jannie there; instead, Rob and Sylvie and Karen greeted her, and Hallie, the girl who had first seen Jannie's empty sleeping bag, went up to her too.

Hallie was four years older than Jannie and as tall as me. "Jannie is lost," she said, expressionless. "She's lost," Hallie repeated, drawing out the vowel.

"They found her flashlight a while ago," Sylvie said, handing it to Dad. Hallie was clinging to Sylvie like a toddler. "Hallie is holding herself responsible for Jannie leaving the tent, Gracie," she said. "We've told her she's not, but she's been crying all night about it. She woke up to pee yesterday when it was still dark and saw Jannie was missing, but she didn't think it was anything serious and just went back to sleep."

The camp was eerily subdued. All the kids except Hallie were sitting with Rob in a circle, talking about insects. Clearly the teachers had been trying to keep things as normal for the kids as they could.

Lizzy sniffed every tent. Every backpack. She walked around restlessly, sniffing everything.

"That's a good dog you have there," Frank said. "Make a good search dog."

"Could she do it? Could she go looking for Jannie?" I asked.

Frank shook his head. "Them Search and Rescue people, they don't let dogs go out there unless they've been trained. Might get into some trouble out there with coyotes, you never know. Might mess up the scent for the search dogs."

After a while Frank left us and joined with some rangers to go off in one of the less-than-thoroughly-explored directions.

"What are we supposed to do," I asked Kate. "Just hang around here and wait?"

"Just hang around here and wait," she said. "They'll keep checking back with us."

I was seized with a terrible heaviness. I walked into Jannie's tent. Her sleeping bag lay on its mat, still unzipped; I wondered how Jannie had unzipped it so quietly that it hadn't woken anyone up. I wondered whether she'd planned the night before that she'd sneak away, and deliberately hadn't zipped it up. Jannie always woke early, so getting out of the tent before dawn wouldn't have been a problem. She had her digital watch that lit up, so she could see what time it was, however dark.

I lay down in Jannie's sleeping bag. Lizzy, who had been searching for me, came into the tent and lay down beside me.

* * *

I must have fallen asleep.

One of the volunteers came running into the camp; I was awakened by a flurry of noise. I stepped out of the tent and saw he was carrying Jannie's red sweatshirt.

Kate identified it right away. Then she practically collapsed; Rob caught her, kept her from falling, brought her over to a log where she could sit down with her head between her knees.

"It doesn't necessarily mean anything, Gracie," Dad told me. I hadn't asked; I hadn't opened my mouth. Did he mean it didn't necessarily mean she was dead?

Had my sister been mauled by a bear? A coyote? Had she been attacked by some crazy person?

"She may have had it knotted around her waist, like she often does. And it could have fallen off." He stopped for a moment. I pictured Jannie walking, trying to find a path, her old red sweatshirt falling behind her. And she not noticing, not being able to retrace her steps to find it.

"It could be a good thing," Dad said. "It means they know for sure that she went off in that direction."

"But they don't know if she's still there," I said. "And it means she doesn't even have that thin little sweatshirt to stay warm . . ." Dad didn't answer.

* * *

It was four in the afternoon. It would be light for another three and a half hours. The temperature, especially in the shade of all those trees, would gradually keep dropping; then, come dark, it would plummet.

One of the rangers had told Dad, not knowing I could overhear, that after the second night the chances of finding Jannie alive would vastly decrease.

* * *

We waited. I walked with Lizzy along the periphery of the camp, keeping the tents in sight. I listened for birdcalls over the static of the walkie-talkies and the conversations among the kids and teachers.

Dad and Kate were sitting together on the log, not talking. Holding hands.

Helicopters churned overhead.

* * *

I don't know what I did. I don't know what I thought about. It felt like I was walking through a nightmare, like the things that were happening were happening at some distance from me. I didn't talk to Dad and Kate. I didn't talk to anyone. I just sat by myself on another log, held Lizzy, looked up at the trees.

At about six-thirty there was another flurry of noise. A few volunteers had come down to the camp and were drinking coffee. One of them picked up his walkie-talkie. Stood up from the folding chair he was sitting on. Listened, spoke. Listened, spoke.

Then he called to all of us, "They found her!"

I ran over to where he was. Dad and Kate ran from where they were, and Karen and Sylvie. The volunteer was listening to his walkie-talkie; we could hear something, but it was muffled. He smiled, made a thumbs-up.

Jannie was alive.

* * *

When he put down the walkie-talkie, he told us what he'd heard.

Jannie had been found under a makeshift shelter of leaves and branches she had clearly put together herself.

She had been found asleep. Her heartbeat was slow. Her body temperature was 95 and a half.

The rangers who had found her had searched earlier in that area, maybe an hour's walk for a child Jannie's age from where the red sweatshirt had been found. The discovery of the sweatshirt had made them intensify the search in that area.

She had been found by one of the rescue dogs. When she'd opened her eyes, the first thing she'd said was "Lizzy! Where did Gracie go?"

They had plied her with hot sugary tea and warmed her with blankets. They'd gotten her heart rate and body temperature up a little, and now they were carrying her on a kind of stretcher to the camp. She didn't know where she was or what had happened, but she had told them one thing, over and over.

"I made a nest. I made a nest to sleep in. I made a nest."

* * *

They brought Jannie down to camp just as it was growing dark. The teachers had told the other children to stay as quiet as they could. They had allowed them to see Jannie, who was wrapped in blankets and in one of the rangers' arms; then they had taken all of them into the large tent and were singing some quiet songs with them.

One of the songs was *The Water is Wide*. I heard them sing it as the rangers laid Jannie down on her sleeping bag. They were going to have to take her to the nearest hospital so she could be monitored, and we were waiting for one of the ranger vehicles to come and pick us up.

Thanks, Emmi, I said silently. The song felt like a sign from her. *Thanks.*

CHAPTER 50

2002

Jannie had spent the night under leaves and branches without her sweatshirt. She was still not able to speak very clearly, and seemed confused about where we were.

I lay down next to her.

"Are we going for a hike, Gracie?" she asked.

"No. Not now. Not anymore."

"I wanted to see a Townsend's solitaire," she said.

"Mmmm," I answered.

"It gets so cold here at night. Soon they'll just eat nothing but juniper berries." Her words were slurred; it took me a while to understand what she was saying.

She fell asleep. I looked at her face. My sister seemed so small and fragile. Yet she had survived the night. Kept herself warm by building a nest.

The ranger vehicle arrived and they loaded Jannie in. Dad and Kate rode up front with the ranger, and I rode beside my sister.

Jannie lifted her head. "I wanted to see a Townsend's solitaire," she said again. I knew she was explaining why she had left the tent.

"I know, Jannie. I know."

She was more alert now. The ranger vehicle had cleared the rocky terrain and we were out on the road now, headed toward the hospital.

"I did see one the day before. I went in the direction I saw it. I had the flashlight. The flashlight Nick gave me. But I put it down and I turned it off to not waste the batteries. Don't waste the batteries— that's what Dad said."

"Mmmm . . ."

"But then it rolled down a hill somewhere and I couldn't find it anymore. And I didn't know where I was. And it was really dark. Was that this morning, Gracie?"

"That was yesterday," I said. "You were missing a whole day and a night and almost another whole day."

"Missing?"

"Nobody knew where you were, Jannie. So many people were looking for you. And dogs."

"I was missing?" she repeated.

"Sylvie called to tell us."

"Sylvie called you? Am I in trouble?"

"No, Jannie. Everyone's just glad you're safe."

* * *

At the hospital Dad checked Jannie in while Kate and I sat in the lobby and made some phone calls. Kate called Carrie and their mother, and I left a message for Nick. Frank, the volunteer, kept Lizzy with him; he had followed us in his car. After a while Jannie was checked in, and we sat in her hospital room while a doctor examined her.

The doctor told us they wanted to keep Jannie there overnight so they could monitor her blood pressure, her temperature, her heart. Jannie asked whether I could stay with her and I told her I'd stay until they kicked me out, since I was still a minor and staying with a patient overnight was against the rules. Frank drove Kate and Lizzy back to the motel and then he drove back again, followed by another volunteer, and dropped Dad's car off so we'd have it to drive back in later. I was amazed at how kind he was. It made me think for a minute about Margie, and how kind she had been to me too: strangers who knew nothing about our lives, but simply and generously stepped in when they were needed.

Dad said he would take a nap in the little chapel room until the nurses told me I needed to go.

Jannie and I lay next to each other in the narrow bed in the darkness of her hospital room. We could hear the activity of the ward outside the open door, but we put our arms around each other and felt warm and close.

"Jannie," I started. "I need to tell you something."

"What, Gracie?"

"Your conures didn't take Kate's ring. I did."

"You did?" Her voice was tired and slow.

"I did. And I just let everyone think it was your birds."

"Oh," was all she said.

"I didn't want Kate to have it."

"Oh."

"But the good thing is I told Kate, and you're going to get your birds back."

"Oh."

"Jannie?"

"What?"

"Are you awake? Did you hear what I said?"

"I'm getting my birds back."

"Yes."

"Really?"

"Really."

It seemed like she was drifting in and out of sleep.

"I'm sorry, Jannie," I said. "I'm sorry your birds got sent away. It was all my fault."

"When can they come home?"

"I don't know. When we get back to Berkeley. Soon."

"But two months aren't up yet."

"You don't have to wait anymore. You can get them back right away. Maybe even Friday."

"But Friday I'll still be on my camping trip."

"No, Jannie. If they let you out of the hospital, we'll go home tomorrow."

"Is tomorrow Friday?"

"It's Thursday. But after all this, it's better to go home."

"Oh."

"Jannie? What made you get out of the tent before anyone was awake?"

"I wanted to find the Townsend's solitaire. I saw one the day before, and I thought I remembered where it was. And when it's just dawn, that's the best time to see birds, and I wanted to be there. Where the solitaire was. Before it woke up."

I thought she was drifting off again, but she kept speaking.

"It's better to watch birds when you're not with any other people, because birds get scared when there are too many people."

"Yeah." *Jannie really is like a bird,* I thought.

"I didn't want to wake them up and tell them because I knew they would say I couldn't go. I decided the night before that I'd look for it in the morning."

"Did you know you were lost right away?" I asked her.

"No. I thought I could find my way back. But then I lost the flashlight and I kept walking around. And then, even when it got light, I couldn't find the camp."

"Did you ever see the Townsend's solitaire?"

"Yes," Jannie said, and I could hear the satisfaction in her voice. "I did. I saw it. Just before dawn."

I pulled Jannie closer to me. We lay together quietly for what felt like a long time. Just when I thought she was really asleep, she said, "Remember, Gracie? This is kind of like when we were still with Emmi and sometimes she left us alone in a little hotel room and we slept all twisted around each other in a bed like this."

I was shocked that Jannie remembered this. She had been so young and totally unable to speak during all that time, and I hadn't imagined that she recalled anything from those months.

All this time I had felt that no one had shared that with me, those horrible months of traveling; Jannie didn't count, I thought, because she had been too locked into her autism to take it in. Now I saw that she *had* taken it in, and I hadn't been as alone as I'd thought.

"You remember that, Jannie?"

"I have little pictures of it in my mind," she said drowsily.

Then she sighed, and was asleep.

I didn't want to leave her until the nurse came in and told me I had to. I watched her breathing beside me. Her face, which was usually tense and vigilant, relaxed. I was overcome with an immense tenderness for her. *My sister,* I said to myself. *My little sister.*

She must have been so afraid out there in the wooded mountains by herself, walking around and around all alone and never finding anything that could show her the way home.

At last the nurse came in and I walked out squinting into the brightly lit corridor to find my father.

We got into the car to drive back to the motel. The roads were mountain roads, unlit at night once we got out of the neighborhood the hospital was in. There was a crescent moon and thousands of stars.

I sat in the passenger seat watching Dad drive. It was very late. I could see the tiredness, the strain, in his face. His dark hair, like Jannie's dark hair, hadn't been brushed in a couple of days. Its roughness, its messy curliness, made him look even more weary.

I felt a wave of love for him that I hadn't known I could feel.

"Dad," I started.

"Yeah?"

"Is this an okay time for me to tell you something?"

"Go for it, Gracie."

"I've already told it to Kate, and I just told Jannie."

"What is it?"

"Dad," I began again. "Jannie's birds had nothing to do with stealing the ring you gave Kate."

"Yeah?"

"I stole it myself."

Dad took a deep breath.

"What do you mean, Gracie?"

"I mean just that. I stole Kate's ring."

"You stole it? How come?"

"I didn't know at first, but it had to do with my not wanting Kate to have it. I kind of thought Emmi should have had it. That it should have been buried with her, or something like that. I know that's weird, because maybe it wasn't even a ring that Emmi would have wanted. And I knew *I* didn't want it. But I thought it wasn't right for Kate to have it, and it made me mad."

Dad listened without answering.

I went on. "And I was so messed up all summer anyway from Martin's death and other stuff."

Dad nodded. He had to look so carefully at the road.

"But I didn't know I was feeling all that when I stole it. I just all of a sudden felt like taking it. I just took it off the bathroom shelf because it was there. And I buried it in the backyard."

"And you let us believe it was Jannie's birds . . ." Dad didn't sound angry; it was just like he was trying to put it together.

"Yes. I did. And that's the thing I feel worst about."

I could tell Dad and I weren't going to have a big fight like I did with Kate. We were both too drained.

"Jannie was so upset about those birds," Dad said thoughtfully. "And I was too hard on her."

"I thought you wished Kate was more upset than she was about losing the ring. So we both took out stuff on Jannie. But I started everything," I said.

Dad was still taking it in.

"So you told Kate about it? And Jannie?"

"Yeah," I said.

He took a turn off the main road onto a smaller road.

"Let's put it behind us, then," he said after a while. "The only important thing right now is that Jannie's all right."

CHAPTER 51

2002

I lay in my bed in the motel room, but I couldn't sleep. Dad and Kate and Lizzy were sleeping soundly. Their breathing was reassuring to me, but I was wide awake. At last I pulled the sheets of paper out of my backpack. I turned on Jannie's flashlight and wrote down a few images from the day before: Jannie's face asleep; the song my mother had sung being sung by the children in the big tent; Jannie making use of her knowledge of birds to build a nest for herself, which was possibly what saved her.

At last I slept, and awakened to early sunlight. As soon as Lizzy realized I'd opened my eyes she nuzzled my neck. I held her for a moment, put on my shoes, and went into the bathroom to wash my face.

Then I remembered the necklace with the chrysoprase pendant, still in the pocket of my jeans. I took it out and looked at it, the dark green translucent oval pendant that reminded me of Gina's eyes. That looked as though you were seeing all the way down into the bottomless depths of the ocean.

I placed the necklace very carefully on the edge of the sink.

I stepped back into the room and took one of my sheets of paper and my pen. Lizzy lay on my bed, alert, watching me.

Kate, I want you to have this, I wrote. *Love, Gracie.*

I thought about whether I wanted to add something like "to make up for the ring;" but it had grown clear to me that nothing can ever replace what's lost. It's just something else, with its own significance.

I put the note on the sink next to the necklace and went out into the bright, chilly morning air with Lizzy. We walked, looking up at the mountains where my sister had been lost.

When we came back into the motel room, Kate was wearing the chrysoprase necklace.

* * *

Jannie was discharged from the hospital around four the afternoon. It was very late Thursday night when we arrived home, and everyone wanted to go to bed. Jannie asked to sleep with me, and she and Lizzy and I all climbed into my bed together.

I thought we'd both be asleep within minutes, but Jannie was restless and wanted to talk.

"Gracie," she said, "What did Emmi used to wear to bed?"

"You mean like a nightgown or pajamas?" I asked.

"Which was it?"

I thought for a minute. "Nightgowns. She liked white nightgowns. Kind of lacy."

"Did she sleep lying on her back or on her side? Or her stomach?"

I thought again, tried to conjure an image of Emmi asleep. "Her side," I told Jannie. "Her left side."

Jannie took it in. "Do you think, if she really came back, like in that story I told you once where she wasn't really dead—Do you think I would recognize her? Sometimes I can't even picture what she looked like."

"Oh Jannie," I said, and I held her close. "That's something I think about all the time. Sometimes I try to remember Emmi's face, or what her hands looked like, and I can't."

I wasn't sure she heard me. I think she drifted off to sleep.

I lay there, looking at my sister. Thinking about the nest she had made, and about how she hated her birds to be in cages.

Jannie's birds flying free
Out of the cage of their loneliness

Jannie—cages—our mother—

I wrote that on the back of one of my sheets of paper, without turning on the light. Then I, too, closed my eyes.

CHAPTER 52

2017

Jannie texts me that she has bought a hard plastic kiddie pool for Scout, so that Scout can have someplace to swim. She has also gotten permission from her landlord, who lives in the downstairs flat, to build an enclosure for Scout in the backyard, a large sort of pen with a roof on it to keep the gull safe from predators. "I think she's happier," Jannie tells me when I call after getting the text, "even though it's sad that she can't go back to her flock. She has kind of made friends with me, though, even if she bites me once in a while and her beak is pretty sharp."

"I don't mind it," she says, after some silence. "I know she bites because she's afraid. She's just letting me know I've come a little too close to her at a moment when she's not up for it."

I take that in. I know how well Jannie understands that. I wonder if she knows how deeply I understand it too.

"Oh, and Gracie?" she says off-handedly.

"Yeah?"

"They took me."

"They?"

"The vet tech program. I can start in the fall."

CHAPTER 53

2002

I hadn't thought about Gina in all the time Jannie was missing, or after we'd found her.

Yet when I woke Friday morning she was the first thing on my mind. None of us had even bothered to check the answering machine when we'd gotten home, but now I remembered I'd left that note for Mr. B. asking him to call me.

I left Jannie asleep in my bed and went down the check the machine. Lizzy accompanied me into the kitchen. I let her into the backyard and listened to the messages that were there.

The first was from Kate's mother, who must have called right after we'd left for the mountains, having heard from Carrie about Jannie being missing.

Then there was one from Nick which he must have left as soon as he'd listened to the message I'd left from the hospital. "Gracie, it's Nick. Thanks for letting me know about Jannie. I'm so glad and so relieved. It must have been terrible for all of you while she was missing. I'll call you sometime Friday."

The voice on the third message started a moment after the beep, and at first I thought someone had called and not left a message at all. Gina?

But then I heard, "Oh, sorry, I guess that was the beep..." I recognized Mr. B.'s voice and his tendency to be a little spacy, which we kids teased him about all the time. "Hello, this is Paul Bryzinski from Berkeley High School, calling for Gracie Levine. I got your note. I'm planning to be at school this Friday after ten in the morning, probably 'til about four. If you can stop by my classroom during that time, we can have a talk."

I went upstairs, showered, and dressed. By the time I went back down to the kitchen, Kate was there making coffee. I told her about the messages and she told me Dad was about to call Peggy Hilverson to see whether he and Jannie could drive out to her place and pick up her conures. When I came back from taking Lizzy for a longish walk, Jannie was jumping up and down at the door. "Dad's taking me to get my conures!"

I hugged her and put Lizzy's leash on its hook. "I'm really sorry they had to go there, Jannie. It was all my fault, and I'm sorry."

Jannie totally ignored what I'd said. "She said Annie and Isabella never fight anymore. They just groom each other's feathers."

I told Dad and Kate I was going to walk to Berkeley High to talk to a teacher of mine, and I left the house.

CHAPTER 54

2002

I walked up the staircase to Mr. B.'s room. The lights were on, and most of the poems and photographs that had been on the walls a few days before were now piled on his large, already cluttered desk. There was a tall stack of books alongside the desk, each one with multiple Post-Its sticking out between various pages.

"Hey, Gracie," he called to me, handing me one of the books. It was Theodore Roethke's poetry. "Tell me which two of these three poems you'd have wanted to see in a reader for American Lit."

I read the poems. "'To My Student, Jane, Thrown By a Horse,'" I said. "And 'My Papa's Waltz.'"

"Thanks," he said. "Have a seat. If you can find one." The chairs around his desk, too, were piled with books.

"Can I move these?" I asked.

"Sure," he said. "Just don't get them out of order."

I cleared a seat and sat down. Mr. B. sat down, too, his long legs stretched out straight before him. He was wearing jeans and a faded T-shirt with John Lennon's face on it, and the word *Imagine.*

He turned to look at me. "I saw you're signed up for my Senior Honors World Lit class. I was happy to see your name, Gracie."

I nodded. I suddenly couldn't remember why I was there.

"You have a good summer?" he asked.

"Not that good," I said.

His eyes narrowed. "Oh, I'm sorry, Gracie." His voice was gentle.

"I can tell you more about it sometime," I said. "I just came to ask you whether you'd heard from Gina."

"Gina?" Mr. B. thought for a moment. "Not since the end of school. Why?"

"Well," I began, "I saw her, like, a few times over the summer, and she didn't really seem okay. She had some . . . drama going on with her boyfriend, or ex-boyfriend . . . and her dad was . . . things just didn't seem that good."

"I'm not surprised."

"She was kind of living on the street."

Mr. B. nodded.

"And then one afternoon I went to her house, where she lived with her dad, and her neighbor said they had moved away and she—the neighbor—and the manager of the building—they had no idea where. The manager said maybe San Diego."

"Wow," Mr. B. said. He looked very concerned.

"I just wondered . . . I thought maybe she would have come and talked to you? Because I told her you said she could."

"No, Gracie. She never came after school ended."

I took a deep breath. "Mr. B.?"

"Yeah?"

"Is there any official way to find out where Gina is? Like school records or something? Would the office know anything?"

"I could ask, Gracie. I could go down there later when Mrs. Frier comes in. She's the one who deals with that kind of thing. If Gina enrolled in a school in San Diego, they would send for her transcript from here."

"Could you do that? Would you be able to tell me? Or could I at least give the office a note for her to send to Gina's school?"

"Sure, Gracie. I don't know how much I'd be allowed to tell you, but for sure you could send her a note through the office. But if she didn't enroll anywhere, I don't know how we could find out anything else about her."

I nodded.

"That must be a loss for you," he said. "I'm sorry, Gracie."

I nodded again.

Mr. B. shuffled through some papers on his desk. He put on his reading glasses. I sat there looking at the empty walls, wondering what he'd replace the old posters and pictures with.

"Gracie?" Mr. B. asked.

"Yeah?"

"I see Gina signed up for Creative Writing. If she's not here, that leaves one place open in the class. It's otherwise closed. Do you think you'd like to take Gina's place there? It's zero period, 7:45 in the morning, so if you have nothing else . . ."

"I have nothing else then," I said. The idea scared me; but it also excited me "But what if Gina comes back? What if she, like, just shows up in class on the first day?"

Mr. B. smiled at me. "Then I could make an exception," he said. "I could open the class to one extra student. Gracie Levine. By invitation."

I hesitated. "Do you really think I could do it?"

"Sure, Gracie," he said. "I think you're a natural writer. Fiction. Poetry. I think you should try it all."

I hesitated again. Then, "Sure, Mr. B.," I told him. "I'd like that. Thanks."

He had begun to arrange some poetry books on a shelf.

"I should probably go," I told him.

"Okay, Gracie," he said. "I'm glad you stopped by."

"Sure," I said. I turned toward the door.

"Gracie?"

"Yeah?"

"Gina's lucky to have you as a friend. I'll call you as soon as I speak to Mrs. Frier."

"Thanks," I said. "See you when school starts."

CHAPTER 55

2017 / 2014

S o this is one of the pieces I wrote for that weekend writing workshop I was telling Kate about that night at the Mexican restaurant.
It's about something that happened three years ago. I can see now
how it got me started writing about those years in high school; and
then Jannie's question to me about our mother catalyzed the rest.

We were asked to write for forty-five minutes about something
that had really happened and that had an element of the unknown. It
took me only a moment to figure out what I'd write about. I wrote it
in the second person, I understand now, as though I were speaking
out loud to myself, trying to shake myself awake.

*You're working one evening behind the counter of a bookstore
you've known since you were a child. It's been several years since you
graduated from college with a degree in English, and all you've thought
you would do since senior year in high school was to be a writer; but
the truth is you've written a handful of decent poems but little else.*

*It's winter, 2014. You've started working on a teaching credential
so you can teach writing and literature to middle school kids, and the
man you consider your closest friend—a poet himself who teaches in*

a local community college—keeps encouraging you to write, as he's done for years. But you feel a certain ambivalence about it, as you've felt—for years now—a certain ambivalence (or maybe it's rather a hesitancy?) about your relationship with him. You call it a friendship; yet at times you've been lovers, and once, for more than a year, you actually lived together. You call it a friendship and he says it could be more. He's clear that that's what he wants; you say over and over that you don't know what you want. You say you're not really a writer and he insists you are.

All this is on your mind as you charge books people are bringing to the counter, as you answer questions, look at the clock to see when you need to start to close out. It's been raining for hours; you think about what the best route will be to walk to your car, you think about what you have in the refrigerator that will be simple to cook at ten-thirty at night. All this is on your mind when you catch sight of a woman walking between the tall rows of poetry shelves, between F and L.

Her hair is dark, falls in jagged layers halfway down her back. She's holding a wide-brimmed burgundy hat that has gotten soaked. She wears a thin cotton sweater over black leggings. She is walking among the shelves, pulling out one book after the next, sitting down on the floor to read a few pages, putting the book back and taking another.

You watch her out of the corner of your eye as people come to the counter. The rain beats hard against the roof of the bookstore. You keep turning toward her to see if she's still there. She has moved to the first set of shelves now, sat back down on the floor. Completely absorbed.

Fifteen minutes before closing time you raise your voice and make an announcement that can be heard throughout the store. People line up to make their purchases. You notice she doesn't stir, immersed in whatever book she has been reading.

At last, just before you call out that the register is closed, she comes up to the counter holding a slim volume of poems. The moment she speaks you recognize her voice.

"Is this all you have of June Jordan?" she asks.

You hesitate. "Wait," you start.

It's been twelve years since you've seen her. "Gina?"

She looks at you. For a moment it's clear she doesn't recognize you. You've dyed your hair black for about a year, in your continual effort not to become your mother. Then, shaking her head, "Gracie?" Incredulous.

"Oh my god!" You reach across the counter and take her hand. It's cold, the way you always remember it.

There are still two people in line behind her waiting to buy their books.

"Gina, could you hang around for a couple of minutes, just til I charge these customers out?"

"Sure, Gracie," she says.

You close up the store together. You offer Gina, or Maria, as she tells you she's known by now—"It's my real name, the name my mother gave me. I started using it when I turned twenty-five, as kind of a gift to her. Gina, or Regina, is my middle name"—a ride home. She has moved back up here in the last couple of months from Southern California, she's living in a house in Oakland with a group of people who are all activists, she's a barista at a café but spends hours every day writing poetry.

Gina—Maria—tells you all this sitting in the front seat of your car. It's raining hard now, sheets of rain, rivulets of rain running down the hill. You're parked in front of the house she lives in; you've got the engine on so you can use the windshield wiper and the heater.

You tell her about your life, your on-and-off relationship with Nick. about Jannie and her bird work. You tell her about Justin—"Oh my god, Gracie, you have a brother who's eight already and I never even knew he existed!"—and about wanting to teach middle school.

Maria takes your hand and holds it the whole time you're talking. At one point she says, "Gracie, turn toward me a little more. Like, undo your fucking seatbelt! I want to take you in. I want to really look at you."

You sit looking at each other. "I hoped every day for months after you left that you'd show up in Mr. B's class . . ." you say.

"Mr. B . . ." Maria says pensively. Then, "Gracie?"

"Yeah?"

"I still have your sweatshirt. The one you gave me that day in the park. It was only a couple of days before my dad and I ended up leaving."

She tells you about a friend of hers who was killed by police in LA one night, just walking home, hands in his pockets, and how that changed her life. She doesn't tell you right then what her life was like before that night; but after that night she started working with a group of people against police violence, and eventually she came back up here.

You sit watching the rain for a moment, holding her hand, taking in what she's told you. Then, "Gina Maria," you start. "Maria Regina."

She looks at you hard. A look you remember.

"I have to get home. I have an eight o'clock class in the morning. But I want to see you again. Soon."

"How about tomorrow?" she says. "I can make you dinner if you're not working at the bookstore. I owe you for all those cheese sandwiches on the steps."

CHAPTER 56

2002

I walked around Berkeley for a long time after talking with Mr. B. I walked on Telegraph, stopping at some of the street vendor stands. I saw a few of the people I'd seen when I'd been there with Gina, but I didn't stop to talk to them. The college students were back and the Avenue was more crowded than it had been all summer.

I walked up to the park where I'd last been with Gina. Where Carrie had seen me, and where Gina and I had kissed. I went into the café where Gina and I had sat drinking Italian sodas the day after Martin died, and I ordered a soda like the one I'd had that day. It *did* taste like cough medicine, like Gina had said; and I smiled to myself, remembering.

When I finally got home, Jannie and Dad were sitting on the living room floor playing Monopoly. Kate had gone for a swim. "Did it go okay with the conures?" I asked.

Jannie made the thumbs-up sign. "I just landed on Park Place!" she shouted. "And I already have Boardwalk!"

"Nick called," said Dad, taking three hundred and fifty of Jannie's

Monopoly dollars for the Bank. "He said to let you know he'd call you later. Something about going to see a movie."

I ran up the stairs, Lizzy bounding after me. I opened the door to Jannie's room as quietly as I could so none of her birds could escape.

I walked inside and found the three conures sitting happily together in a single cage. They looked well and content. "I'm really sorry, guys," I told them. "I hope you had an okay time at the Hilversons'. I know I owe you an apology along with everyone else in this family."

In my own room, I took some paper out of my drawer and sat down at my desk. I wrote some notes for a poem about Jannie.

> *Her small hands*
> *Her birds*
> *Their claws*
> *wrapped trustingly around her fingers*

Then Gina came into the poem as well: her hair the color of the parakeet's feathers that day when she stood in Jannie's room with the green parakeet on her head.

> *She was a bird that day*
> *in my house of lies*
> *and my sister was a bird*
> *in the dark of the mountains*

> *Find me, find me*
> *my sister cried*
> *without words*

Find me, my friend cried

I want to be found
I am hard to find

Find me in the mountain night
The street of ruins
Find me in my cage of lies

My cage of silence

Lizzy lay at my feet. I heard the front door open, heard Kate walk into the house. Heard Dad and Jannie greet her, then turn back to their game.

I sat chewing my pencil. Then it occurred to me that I wanted to write a letter to Jannie.

I wanted to say something to her about cages, like I'd thought of the night before, watching her fall asleep. And I remembered the story Kate had told me about the chimpanzee.

Dear Jannie, I wrote. *There's a story I want to tell you: A chimpanzee named Bibi was taught sign language as part of an experiment to see whether animals could communicate with humans and with each other, using words. Bibi was the best signer of all the chimpanzees in the experiment; she grew very attached to the trainers and was always begging them to speak to her, sign to her, teach her the names of things.*

Then the researchers ran out of money and they couldn't take care of the chimps. They were all sent to different facilities and locked in cages. People fed them, but nobody signed to them, nobody even bothered to talk to them. Bibi wound up in a terrible place like that, where there were no other chimps from her experiment, and she had no one to sign to.

For a little while, maybe a year, she signed to herself. The people who fed her and cleaned the cages would see Bibi sitting in a corner of her cage, moving her fingers. But since they didn't know sign language, they had no idea what she was saying. After a while she stopped signing altogether and the keepers assumed she had finally forgotten how. She sat at the back of her cage, barely responding to anything.

Then many years later a man from the original experiment came to some meeting at the facility where Bibi was kept, and he just happened to walk down the corridor where her cage was. The minute she caught sight of him she ran to the bars of her cage and started rattling them. She was jumping up and down wildly to attract his attention. As soon as he looked at her, she began signing, "Me Bibi! Me Bibi! Me Bibi!"

That was all I heard of her story; but ever since, I've been wondering what happened next.

I want to imagine that the man recognized Bibi too, and he was so moved to see her that he started to cry, and they held hands through the bars of Bibi's cage.

I want to imagine that he went to the people who ran that facility and told them, "I know that chimpanzee. She lived at the place I worked at for many years, and we spent a lot of time together."

I want to imagine that he told them he would personally pay any cost they demanded in order to free her, and as soon as he walked back to Bibi's cage she began jumping wildly at the bars again and signing, "Hello, friend! Hello, friend!"

And the man signed to her, "Come on now, Bibi. You're coming with me in my car and we'll drive to my house, where you will live with me and my family for the rest of your life."

And that's just what they did.

Jannie, the story of Bibi makes me think about how you lived alone in the cage of your autism for such a long time, and Emmi lived in a cage of unhappiness, and I lived in a cage of lies; and none of us knew how to get anyone else to understand what we were feeling. And maybe everyone in the world is walking around in some kind of cage, just waiting to be recognized.

I thought I'd tell you also that I'm glad your birds are back.

Love,

Gracie

Afternoon sunlight poured in through the window, flooded my desk, the paper I was writing on.

ACKNOWLEDGMENTS

The Language of Birds was written for my granddaughter Ciel, who was a young child when I first began thinking about writing it, and is now a young woman. She and I discussed the characters and the narrative; she consulted with me through various drafts about Gracie and Jannie and Gina and how real they felt to her, and she wrote Gina's poems when I knew that I could not authentically write poetry in the voice of a teenage girl. This book is in gratitude for Ciel's presence in my life and for the many ways she has inspired me.

Gratitude also to my daughters, Nora and Viva, and to my son-in-law Zach Wyner, each of whom discussed the book with me at dinners and on walks in the East Bay, the Sierra, and in Portland, Oregon. Kathy Wyner, Zach's mom, talked with me about the book with great depth and understanding for a long weekend several years ago in ways that informed successive versions, and she has kept cheering for it ever since. Gratitude to my grandson Dashiell, who delights me infinitely with his humor and imagination. Gratitude as always to my dear friend and co-translator of Rilke, Joanna Macy, who read various drafts of this book and gave me her profound support and perceptive suggestions; to my friend since second grade, Phyllis Osterman, whom I think of as a sister and who happily read draft after draft and agreed to keep them on her computer in case anything happened to mine.

Gratitude to Richard Morris, who first recognized the worth of this book and encouraged me to continue. Gratitude to close friends who read drafts or listened to me talk about the book and generously offered their literary and psychological insight and their love: Amanda Bean Hannigan, Barclay Stone, Mary Elliott, Monika Schrag, Anita Price, David Shaddock, Jai Jai Noire, Ellen Balis, Susan Griffin, Donna Brookman, Jack Schiemann, and Mari Haight. Gratitude to Allen Kanner, Mary Gomes, and Cassidy Kanner-Gomes, with whom I have discussed this book for years at our cherished weekly Friday dinners.

Gratitude to Ann Parker, with whom I have shared patients over the years and contemplated the lives of many children like Jannie; gratitude to Herb Schreier, who was my earliest supervisor in my work with children on the autism spectrum and encouraged me over and over to write something about them. And deep gratitude to the children, adolescents and adults I have had as patients in my psychotherapy practice since the 1980s, who have taught me more than they will ever know. None of them is exactly like any of the characters in this book; but all of them have colored my way of looking at the world.

Gratitude to Drew Lehman, without whose technical assistance and kindness I couldn't have managed to do the work I've done on this book and others; and gratitude to Andy Ross, my agent, who coached me through several versions of this book and brought it eventually to She Writes. Without Andy's belief in it, his dedication to it, his enthusiasm for it, and his patience with me, *The Language of*

Birds would not be published. My affection for Andy and my admiration for his skill and knowledge are boundless.

Gratitude to my non-human family—the dogs, cats and birds with whom I share my household and my life. I like to think that something of what I glean from their companionship has gone into Jannie.

As I was preparing this book for publication my beloved friend Mariolina Freeth died in London, England, where I first met her in 1973. Mariolina was a poet and translator whose work, values, and way of being shaped my writing and my life. She did not live to read this book, but her spirit infuses it, and I hope, as well, some of her wisdom and sensitivity.

ABOUT THE AUTHOR

© Nora Barrows-Friedman

Among Anita Barrows' awards in poetry have been grants from the National Endowment for the Arts, The Ragdale Foundation, The Dorland Mountain Arts Colony, The Quarterly Review of Literature, and The Riverstone Press. She's published three poetry chapbooks with Quelquefois Press, and Kelsay Books recently published three volumes of her poetry. She has also appeared on radio programs on NPR and the BBC. Born in Brooklyn in 1947, Barrows has lived in the Bay Area since 1966 (except for three years in London) and is a clinical psychologist with a private practice in Berkeley, where she specializes in the treatment of children with autism spectrum disorder and other developmental disabilities. Barrows is also a tenured professor of psychology at the Wright Institute, Berkeley, and is a mother, a grandmother, and companion to a menagerie of dogs, cats, and birds.

SELECTED TITLES FROM SHE WRITES PRESS

She Writes Press is an independent publishing company founded to serve women writers everywhere. Visit us at www.shewritespress.com.

The River by Starlight by Ellen Notbohm $16.95, 978-1-63152-335-9
Annie and Adam Fielding's simple dreams of home and family on the Montana frontier shatter in the face of malevolent post-partum illness whose only treatment is involuntarily commitment to the state hospital for the insane.

The Way You Sleep by Christine Mead $16.95, 978-1-63152-691-6
When David's determined search for meaning and independence drives him to decide to live in an isolated New Hampshire cabin inherited from his recently deceased grandfather, his girlfriend's dark past and his family's long-buried secrets prove to be the greatest tests of his resilience.

What is Found, What is Lost by Anne Leigh Parrish
$16.95, 978-1-93831-495-7
After her husband passes away, a series of family crises forces Freddie, a woman raised on religion, to confront long-held questions about her faith.

Don't Put the Boats Away by Ames Sheldon $16.95, 978-1-63152-602-2
In the aftermath of World War II, the members of the Sutton family are reeling from the death of their "golden boy," Eddie. Over the next twenty-five years, they all struggle with loss, grief, and mourning—and pay high prices, including divorce and alcoholism.

Fire & Water by Betsy Graziani Fasbinder $16.95, 978-1-93831-414-8
Kate Murphy has always played by the rules—but when she meets charismatic artist Jake Bloom, she's forced to navigate the treacherous territory of passionate love, friendship, and family devotion.

Hard Cider: A Novel by Barbara Stark-Nemon $16.95, 978-1-63152-475-2
Abbie Rose Stone believes she has navigated the shoals of her long marriage and complicated family and is eager to realize her dream of producing hard apple cider—but when a lovely young stranger exposes a long-held secret, Abbie's plans, loyalties, and definition of family are severely tested.